TO PARADISE
AND BACK

D. H. Master

First published in Great Britain in 1992 by
Nexus
338 Ladbroke Grove
London W10 5AH

Copyright © D. H. Master 1992

ISBN 0 352 32828 2

A catalogue record for this title is available from
the British Library

Typeset by TW Typesetting, Plymouth, Devon
Printed and bound in Great Britain by
Cox & Wyman Ltd, Reading, Berks.

Chapter 1

His Exalted Excellence, Credo III, Master of the World, Royal Duke of the Hinterlands, Baron of the Waterways and numerous other lesser titles too numerous to mention, lay in his bath and contemplated his erection.

Some five minutes earlier, the screens on the opposite wall had warned him of the approach of his wife. He had thoughtfully raised a royal finger and carefully pushed one of the buttons on the console built into the side of the bath. Immediately a measured amount of aphro-gel was added to the swirling, bubbling water.

Almost immediately, Credo began to feel the effects. A gentle tingle started to spread over the entire surface area of his skin. Soon, all the tingles seemed to be heading for his groin. Within three minutes of pressing the button, Credo's genitals felt as though they were on fire.

When the doorchimes sounded, Credo pressed another button and the door shimmered into nothingness, allowing his wife to step through. Once she had entered, another button was pressed and the door molecules rearranged themselves to form a solid barrier once more.

Her Exalted Excellency was not looking her regal best. Her formal, one-piece evening suit was rumpled and creased; her normally immaculately coiffured hair was hanging loose and tangled about her shoulders and her face showed definite signs of tiredness. Nevertheless, Credo thought he detected a gleam of triumph and satisfaction in her large, blue eyes.

He tutted in sympathy.

'A busy evening, my darling?'

She shot him a telling look as she twisted the diamond brooch at her throat.

'You could say that.'

The brooch, as well as being decorative, doubled as the switch that kept her suit on. With a gentle swish the expensive material slipped to the floor. She kicked it half-heartedly towards the autovalet and stepped into the bath.

Even now, seventeen years after her beauty had enslaved him, she was still the most desirable woman he knew. At thirty-four she had taken on the bloom of a mature woman – sexy, self-assured and experienced – yet she had kept the face, figure and skin tone that had half the men on the planet trying to get into her pants from the moment she passed Defloration.

Credo smiled as he remembered his surprise and delight when he discovered that, in those days, she had never bothered to wear any. Nowadays, of course, as Her Exalted Excellency, she was obliged to wear something and settled for the absolute minimum, in pure Tangoran silk, naturally.

Her legs were long and slim, her bottom still pert. She had not allowed the birth of their two children to thicken her waist and her belly remained as flat as ever. Even her breasts were as he remembered them all those years ago. Perhaps the nipples were bigger now, but for Credo, that was a plus.

He noted with interest the bruises on the inside of her thighs as she sank gratefully into the foaming water.

2

'Mmmn, that feels good,' she murmured, ducking under the surface to rinse her hair.

Credo gave her a few minutes to sponge herself clean before mentioning the bruises.

'I think only about half of them came from His Almighty Highness,' she said, 'Tari gave me the others.'

'Poor baby,' Credo sympathised. 'I take it that she wouldn't allow Marlo to have you to himself?'

'That's right,' she had finished washing and was now luxuriating in the creamy water, 'more than once he had to shove her out of the way.'

Credo allowed his hand to rest on his wife's thigh.

'Start from the beginning then,' he urged, his fingers gently brushing against her still swollen lips. 'They were expecting you of course?'

'Of course,' she parted her thighs a little to allow his fingers better access, while her own did a little exploring on their own account. 'My, you are glad to see me aren't you?'

He shrugged nonchalantly and helped her to turn away from him, on to her side. The soft upholstery of the bath quickly adjusted itself to their new positions.

'Anyway, they pretended to be surprised to see me. Marlo was just in his bath shift, he said he'd only just come out, and Tari was just about to take her suit off on the way for one herself.'

She paused while he lifted her upper leg and reached down to help guide him into her.

'Mmn, that's nice. It's a good job this bath is fitted with gel. The way I was feeling when I came in, you'd have had to wait a week for this.'

She pushed her bottom back and began to wriggle it against him.

'They apologised for the informality of their dress and I said they weren't to worry, I was just checking that everything was all right for them. Tari said Marlo was to offer me a drink while she had a quick sluice and that I wasn't to go until she had had a chance to have a quick word with me.

'So naturally I let Marlo give me a drink.'

'Naturally,' agreed Credo, reaching over her side to fondle a breast.

'And of course he admired my suit, especially my brooch. He had a pretty good hard-on by this time, his shift was sticking out a mile, but we both pretended to ignore it as he bent to look at the brooch. "May I?" he said and gave it a twist without waiting for my answer.

'That left me standing, stark naked, with my suit round my ankles. Somehow, I must have forgotten to put any panties on!'

'You do surprise me,' remarked Credo, nuzzling her neck.

'Don't be sarcastic, dear,' she replied, moving his hand to her other breast, 'and don't forget I have two of these.'

'As if I could,' he sighed happily. 'So then what happened?'

'I looked him straight in the eye and said something like, "You have me at a disadvantage, my lord," and he said, "My apologies, my lady, allow me to rectify the situation," and promptly removed his shift.

'I have to say he had quite an impressive tool, not as long as yours, but perhaps a little fatter. He let me look at it for a moment and then went to refill our glasses. While he was doing that I stretched out on the chaise longue, carefully arranging my legs so that he could see everything.'

'I'm surprised he didn't just drop the drinks and jump you. That's what I would have done!'

'And I would be disappointed if you didn't, my dear,'

4

she replied, her breathing beginning to shorten slightly as he maintained his low, steady thrusts. She reached between her legs to play with his balls while he slid his hand down over her belly and into the soft folds of flesh.

'However, Marlo was obviously able to control himself better than you because he allowed me to have a drink before he began to stroke my breasts. He was sitting next to me, the end of his prick about three inches from my face, so I dipped it in my drink and started to suck it.'

She was forced to stop talking at this point as Credo's rhythm had become more urgent. His fingers alone were doing enough to push her over the edge and he was using much more than just them.

She cried out as the sensations blotted out rational thought and Credo shuddered in release a few seconds later. Gently, they separated. Credo gave the gel button another crafty stab as she turned to face him. By the time they had refreshed themselves with some iced champagne he was hard again.

He sat up a little, the bath cushions readjusting to support him in the new position. Ami quickly straddled him and as she lent forwards for a kiss, expertly wriggled herself back on to his cock.

'Then what happened?' Credo prompted, content just to sit still and enjoy the hot tightness that was wrapped round his most sensitive part.

'Well, he let me lick and suck him while he fingered me a little and then he announced I was driving him mad and he just had to stick it up me!'

'He used those words?' Credo was faintly shocked.

'Actually I don't think he was that subtle. If I remember rightly, his exact words were, "Listen, you gorgeous bitch, if I don't fuck you right now I'll come all over your tits!"'

'What a delicate command of language and grammar the man has.'

'My thoughts entirely. I figured though, that if I was responsible for getting him in such a state I owed it to him to help put matters right.'

'You always were a noble creature.' Credo began to stroke her sides and bottom. Ami reciprocated by leaning forward, teasing his lips with her nipples as she gently swung her breasts against him.

'Just so.' She gave a little gasp as he caught a nipple and began to roll it between his lips.

'In the event, he must have been pretty steamed up because he was only in me for a few minutes before he came.'

'Shame on the man!' Credo knew well how his wife delighted in prolonging any penetration of her body for as long as possible.

'All was not lost however, for Tari chose that moment to reappear.'

'Ah ha! Do we detect a little stage management here?'

'I believe we do.' Ami began to raise and lower herself slowly, still tantalising him with her breasts, 'for no sooner had he climbed off than she took over. I do believe she was trying to climb in, head first.'

'But you managed to restrain any objections you might have felt.'

'Of course. After all, they are honoured guests and I their humble hostess.'

'Quite. So after you and she had enjoyed yourself for a while, I presume she managed to make you come?'

'I've yet to meet someone who can't,' she reminded him. 'Anyway, while we were tonguing each other, I was vaguely aware of Marlo trying to join in. Unfortunately we were both having too good a time to let him so he took matters into his own hands. I was on top at the time

6

and I suppose my ass must have looked sufficiently inviting because the next thing I knew, Tari was trying to suck my clit off and shove her hand up me at the same time and Marlo was up to his balls in my bum!'

'Like this you mean?'

She lifted herself off him so he could reposition himself, before sinking back down.

'Just like that,' she moaned.

'And the result?'

'I came and I came and I came . . .' she broke off as a wave of violent shuddering took control of her. She cried out and ground her breasts into his face, pushing her hips down as hard as she could while he arched himself into her as his own release came.

'Rather like that?' he asked, once he was able to speak again.

'Rather like that,' she agreed, relaxing against him.

Eventually they disengaged and spent a few minutes cleaning up. Then Credo hit the appropriate buttons and the water drained away as the blowers came on. The hot, perfumed air, mixed with oil vapour to condition the skin as it dried, did its work in minutes. As they were drying the bath cushions levelled out until they formed the royal bed. Finally, the spray jets all round the bed were activated. As the spray met the air it coagulated to form the lightweight thermal sleep sheet most people slept under and dropped gently over the already dozing couple.

The next morning, Credo and Ami were having a leisurely breakfast. The bed had rearranged itself to form a comfortable backrest against which they leant while eating.

Credo bit hungrily into his Octarian schooner fish, specially imported at enormous expense for his royal breakfast. Specifically bred to contain no bones, they were

7

a luxury only the very rich could afford. Credo was convinced they helped him recover from the sort of evening he had just had.

He looked with pleasure at his wife's breasts as he ate and wondered if it would be wise to suggest a little romp to start the day.

Ami sipped her fruit juice and nibbled delicately on a sliver of toast. She had slept well and felt fit and rested. She noticed Credo's glances at her breasts and guessed he was deciding whether or not to start making love again. She hoped he would; she liked nothing better than to start the day with a good tumble. She felt it set the tone for the day and gave her something to think about during the more boring aspects of her royal duties.

She decided to set things going.

'I told you about my evening,' she reminded him, 'but I cannot believe you simply watched a film or something until I returned.'

He grinned at her.

'As a matter of fact I did watch a film, for some of the time at least. After a while however, my companion became a little restless and we never did manage to see the climax.'

'You were too busy having some of your own, I gather?'

'Exactly.'

Carelessly tossing the remains of her breakfast to one side, she snuggled up to him.

'Come on then, tell me all about it. Who was she?'

'You'll never guess. Olga Gresheck.'

Ami sat up with a start.

'Well, she's certainly a good-looking bitch, I'll grant you that, but I'd never have thought that the Duchess of Krantz would behave like that. Old Krantz must really be in as bad a way as they say. What did she want?'

'You mean apart from the best fuck of her life?'

'Darling,' Ami snuggled down again, 'that goes without saying, but we both know what he thinks of you and the thought of his wife begging for favours must really rankle.'

'I rather gathered that he didn't know,' Credo smirked.

'Don't you believe it! They may want us to think she was acting on her own but I can assure you he would have been well aware of what she was up to. If not,' she added thoughtfully, 'won't be long before he does find out and he will not be pleased at the thought of his young wife screwing for favours – especially if she's screwing you! By the way, you never have told me why he hates you so much.'

'Haven't I, darling? Some other time perhaps. Anyway, what she wanted was for me to ask the Treasury to give them some more time to raise the interest payments on their debt.'

'And you agreed?'

'Of course! Why not? Maybe they will need more time the next time and he'll send her round again. Maybe you won't be otherwise engaged yourself and you'll be able to join us.'

'Mmmn! So what happened?'

'Oh, she pretended for a while that she had always been attracted to me and that she finally summoned up the nerve to do something about it. So, I suggested we watch a film, to set the mood so to speak.'

'Which one did you choose?'

'*The Schooling of Sophie.*'

'I always liked that one.'

'I think Olga liked it too.'

'What makes you say that?'

'Well, you know the bit where Sophie sees a naked man for the first time and he tells her to take hold of it?'

'Like this?' Ami decided to seize the initiative.

'Mmn! That's more or less what she did too.'

'And when Sophie becomes more adventurous?' she began to nuzzle her way down to where her hand was already busy.

'You guessed it. Uh, don't stop.'

Ami looked up.

'Did Olga stop?'

'Not until she made me a happy man. Unlike you,' he added.

'Sorry.'

She returned to her task for a few minutes, not looking up until, she too, had made Credo a happy man.

'Mmmn,' Credo grinned down at her. 'She took a little longer but the result was about the same.'

'Yes, but we haven't time for a full rerun. Then what did she do?'

'By the time I'd turned the tape off she was naked. She pretended she was dismayed at my condition because she was hot for me so she put on a little show to try to awaken my interest.'

'Show?'

'Yes, you know, prancing around, playing with herself, that sort of thing.'

She gave his rapidly softening flesh a squeeze.

'Come on Credo, be specific. You know how I like the details.'

'Very well then. I was reclining on the sofa by now and she stood in front of me. I have to say she has a very good body, you know?'

'I know. Never mind what her figure is like, what did she do?'

'At first she just stood there, making sure I was appreciating her. By the way, did you know she has a gap at the top of her legs too? Even with her thighs together you could stick a couple of fingers through.'

'You like that in a woman don't you?'

'I do. I've always found that those with a gap are better in bed. You're living proof of that.'

She gave him another squeeze, but this time it was more affectionate.

'Go on.'

'She spread her legs slightly and began to sway a little, running her hands over her breasts, cupping and squeezing them. Every now and then she would pinch one of her nipples. Soon they were standing out almost as much as yours do.'

'I bet she practises for hours in front of old Krantz. It's probably the only way she can get him hard.'

'Then she began to rub herself between her legs. She used a couple of fingers of one hand to open herself and began fingering herself with the other.'

'Did you like it?'

'I thought it was pretty good, yes.'

'Had she made you hard yet?'

'No, but I was starting to harden.'

Again the squeeze.

'I bet you were rock hard! You're getting hard again just telling me about it.'

'Trust you to notice!'

'Anyway, go on.'

'She turned round at this point, spread her legs wider and bent down to look at me through them. Then she reached through, halfway up her back, and ran a finger all the way down her crack, turning round so I could see it coming up at the front. She must have been enjoying herself because I could see she was pretty wet by then.

'She slipped a finger into her cunt and showed me the juice on it. Then she very suggestively licked it off. She did it again but this time offered it to me.'

'And of course you accepted?'

11

'Of course.'

'What did she taste like?'

'Not unlike yourself – almost tasteless, just enough to make you want more. I think she had used some sort of scent or something; there was just a hint of strawberries. Anyway, she was standing really close by now and she suggested I had another taste, this time at first hand rather than second hand.'

'It would have been churlish to refuse.'

'Exactly. She had virtually pushed her cunt into my face by this time. All I had to do was stick my tongue out. She put her hands on the back of my head and pulled me into her, rubbing herself up and down and round and round. After she came a couple of times she climbed on to my lap and did all the work until I came again.

'Then she asked what the time was, gasped that Krantz would start to miss her if she didn't return soon, put on her clothes and left.'

'But not before reminding you to have a word with the Treasury.'

'Quite so. I, of course, invited her to come again any time she had any little problems.'

'Mmmn. It feels to me as though you're the one with a problem, and it's not so little!'

Credo slipped his hand between her thighs. She was soaking wet.

'Listen who's talking! You're so turned on you'd do it with Krantz if he was the only man available.'

She slithered expertly on to his rampant weapon.

'I might anyway. If you're going to make a habit of screwing his wife, it's only fair that I can fuck him.'

They stopped talking for a while, saving their breath and concentrating on what they were doing to each other. Soon, because they had talked themselves into a state of high arousal, they spent themselves and, as the bed turned

12

into a bath, contented themselves with basking in the frothing, scented water.

'Seriously though,' Ami said as she waited for the robot manicure to finish with her hands, 'if she liked what you gave her, and I bet she did, you could find yourself with a mistress on your hands.'

'We could, darling. Share and share alike, remember?'

'Could be interesting . . .'

'I doubt anything will come of it. We can decide what to do if and when the time comes. More to the point, what are we going to do about Pooki?'

The Princess of Pulkrington – Pooki to her family and friends – was their seventeen-year-old daughter.

'I did learn last night that Marlo and Tari are, as we thought, looking for a wife for Janus. I mentioned Pooki might be considered a suitable choice and they relaxed visibly. I left them with the understanding that we would discuss the matter further in a few months time.'

'She's your daughter. Do you think she could cope with the demands of such a position?' Credo asked thoughtfully.

'You mean all the "entertaining"?'

'Yes.'

'I was expected to cope at her age.'

'And cope you did, extremely competently as I recall.' Ami smiled fondly at him.

'Things were a bit hectic at the beginning though, weren't they? But then I never expected to inherit quite so soon.'

'There aren't many girls of seventeen who could host a symposium,' she agreed.

'That's more or less what the Council said when we discussed the marriage yesterday. They approved the union but wondered whether Pooki was ready for the responsibilities that go with it. Do you think she's ready?'

13

'Definitely not! In fact, if she hadn't gone through her Defloration so easily I'd think there was something wrong with her.'

'She doesn't prefer girls or anything like that, does she?' Credo asked anxiously.

Ami gave him an old-fashioned look.

'What if she does? As long as it doesn't interfere with her official duties, she can have all the girls she wishes. No, I think she's just a late developer. I mean to say, with parents like ourselves how can she fail to be a good hostess? She's not really done anything over the past year and time is running out. I think we're going to have to arrange something a little more drastic,' Ami said thoughtfully.

'You mean Paradise?'

'Exactly.'

'I agree. I'll set it up. Will you tell her or shall I?' said Credo, relieved to find his wife in full agreement with him over what could become something of an embarrassment. Imagine, the first lady of the planet having an aversion to sex! Unthinkable.

Ami smiled at him.

'We both will, of course. If we're agreed, we'll tell her tonight.'

Breakfast in the mansion belonging to the Duke of Krantz was not so cosy. When a servant had innocently enquired of his lordship whether or not her ladyship would be coming down to breakfast he nearly had his head bitten off. He gathered that her ladyship, unlike himself, was avoiding his lordship's foul temper.

In fact, her ladyship was in no mood to face anyone at all that day.

She had parked her little skimmer feeling extremely pleased with herself. Not only had she gained her husband

14

more time with which to raise some money, but she had also had an extremely satisfying romp with Credo.

When she met Krantz at the top of the stairs she was not unduly concerned. True, she had not expected him to be there – he had left the house some time before she had and had suggested she not wait up for him – but when he heard her news she felt sure he would be pleased.

Krantz, at the age of sixty-three, was nobody's fool. Although it was true that he, like many of his ancestors, had wasted several fortunes, not all of them their own, on gambling and various other excesses, he was a shrewd judge of character.

The slightly dishevelled look of lazy self-satisfaction was one with which he was familiar. As she came closer to him he could even smell what she had been doing. She was so confident about avoiding discovery that she hadn't bothered to shower before returning. The knowledge was like a red rag to a bull, further fuelled by the realisation that if his skimmer hadn't developed engine trouble, causing him to return without being able to visit his mistress, she might very well have escaped detection.

'And where have you been?' he greeted her.

She decided this was not the right time to tell him her news.

'I just popped out to see Juno. You don't mind, do you?'

'Of course not, my dear Olga,' he smiled, 'but it's late. I think we ought to call Juno and let her know you've returned safely.'

'There's no need for that,' she said quickly. 'As you say, it's late. Juno will probably be in bed by now.'

'Oh surely not! It's only ten minutes from her place. Anyway, she won't mind if she knows you're home safe and sound.'

He watched her hesitate, knowing she was trying to

decide whether Juno would catch on quickly enough to give her an alibi. He saw her realise she probably wouldn't and pushed home his advantage.

'You haven't been to see Juno, have you?' he demanded, catching hold of her hair and forcing her to look at him.

He was pleased to see her self-confidence begin to ebb away.

'You've been with another man! Who was it?'

The fact that, if things had gone as planned, he should have been with another woman at this very moment never entered his mind. The thought that his wife, forty-one years his junior, could contemplate (let alone actually consummate) an affair filled him with an icy rage.

Olga hesitated. She knew well of his hatred for Credo and his family which stemmed from an incident that had occurred some three hundred years ago when the Krantzes felt they should be the ruling family and the rest of Rontar's nobility decided they should not.

If he were to learn that Credo himself had just been ploughing in the field where Krantz was the only farmer allowed, who knows what might happen? Better to play dumb and take the consequences, she decided.

'Answer me, damn you! Who was it?' he screamed, incensed at her refusal to talk.

When she still remained silent he began to drag her down the corridor.

'So you won't talk, eh? We'll see about that!'

They arrived at a door at the end of the corridor. Olga had seen the door many times, but this was the first occasion she had been through it. Krantz fumbled in his pocket for the key. Thumbing the button, he barely had the patience to wait for the molecules to rearrange themselves before striding through, pulling her after him.

The main object in the room, taking up most of the

floor space, was a gleaming, metallic frame. Pausing only to close and lock the door behind him, Krantz dragged his now terrified wife towards it.

Ignoring her cries, he forced her down upon it and before she was fully aware of what was happening she was secured at wrist and ankle.

'Now my dear,' he gloated, 'let me introduce you to the Rack.'

He turned to pick up a small control box from a shelf.

'My family invented, developed and refined this machine for just such an occasion as this. The victim is secured and then, with the touch of a few buttons, he or she can be raised, lowered, twisted, turned to virtually any position.'

Krantz's fingers were flying over the keys as he spoke, making the Rack move in a variety of directions to match his words.

'The victim can be stretched . . .'

Olga felt the strain building up in her joints as the machine hummed quietly, effortlessly overcoming her futile resistance.

'. . . Or compressed.'

Suddenly she felt her legs threatening to push themselves out of their sockets and tear themselves up into her ribcage.

Abruptly the pressure stopped.

'Another convenience is that the victim can be positioned, immovably, at the ideal position for the inquisitor to work.'

The Rack pulled her legs apart and then bent them backwards under her. At the same time her arms were pulled back as something pushed hard in the small of her back. Already, her muscles were beginning to protest at the position they were in.

Krantz stepped back to study the effect. Only her head

was free to move; otherwise she was anchored as firmly as though her body was carved out of stone. Nodding with satisfaction he stepped closer again and carelessly stroked her, trailing his hand down over her breasts, her stomach and down to her mound, all of which were being offered up to him in the position she was being held.

'Then, of course, there are the hidden extras.'

He pressed the buttons again and an arm dropped from its recess in the ceiling. At the end of the arm was a long, thin blade.

She watched in terror as the knife approached her throat. Slowly it traced the same path his fingers had covered a few moments earlier. As the blade moved down, her suit, stretched tight over her torso, peeled open behind it.

'No knickers, my dear?' he remarked as the blade reached her mound before pulling back. 'Did you go out without them or couldn't you be bothered to put them back on after he had finished with you?'

Despite her fear Olga was sufficiently aware of what was happening to notice his erection. The thought that he was actually excited by what he was doing to her gave her the strength to resist for a little longer.

'Still not talking?' he asked needlessly.

He fiddled with the control box. The Rack spun her round and bent her forwards. Now she was being held face down at an angle to the floor. She felt a sudden draught on her back and didn't need to feel the remains of her suit falling off to know that the knife had repeated its slit down the length of her spine.

'Do you know what this is?' he asked as the Rack rotated and she found herself looking at another arm. From the end of this one hung a number of leather thongs, each one tipped with what looked like a piece of lead.

'It's called a cat-o'-nine-tails. It's an extremely efficient tool and has been in use for centuries. Some people say it was even used on Old Earth to punish, among other things, crimes committed by sailors on wind-powered ships. Would you believe it? Such a simple thing. But then that is so often the case. The simple things are the best. In the hands of an expert, a dozen strokes with one of these can strip a person's entire back down to the bone. And I, my dear, am such an expert. Now, who were you with tonight?'

Still she couldn't bring herself to confess.

'It's a mistake you know, to be more frightened of him than of me. After all,' he continued reasonably, 'I am here and he is not.'

'I'm not frightened of him,' she blurted out, unable to take her eyes off the thin strips of leather.

'Then why won't you tell me his name?'

'I'm frightened of what you will do if I tell you.'

'If I were you, I'd be more frightened of what I would do if you don't tell me.'

When she said no more he sighed and the Rack rotated once more. He made a few adjustments to her position. She was now held at an angle of about forty-five degrees from the floor. Her arms were outstretched, as were her legs.

Suddenly, her back exploded with pain. Her head snapped up, but she could see nothing through the red mist of pain that enveloped her. She realised she was screaming.

Slowly, the mist cleared and the pain settled down to the point where it felt only as though her back were on fire. She managed to stop screaming.

'Much as it pains me to do this to you,' he lied, 'I really must insist you tell me who you were with. You don't want me to beat you again, do you? Believe me, I will be able to keep going longer than you.'

'Credo. It was Credo,' she whispered and tensed herself for the onslaught she was sure would follow.

19

To her surprise there were no more lashes. She was spun round to face him. His face was white with anger but there was also curiosity. 'Yes, that would explain your reluctance to tell me. But why?'

'I asked him to give you more time to repay your debt,' she whispered.

'And of course, the way things are done on this planet, you had to give something in return. You did this for me,' he mused, half to himself, 'and had to suffer his advances. How you must have suffered, enduring him when this was what you wanted.'

He pulled open his suit, revealing his erection.

'Well, here it is!'

The Rack pulled her into a suitable position, legs apart, pelvis uplifted, waist high off the floor. Krantz stepped between her legs and thrust himself into her. The pain from her back overruled any other sensation, not that she was in any position to object to his brutal assault.

He finished almost immediately and took a step back.

'Credo, eh? It's time I dealt with that man. And his cursed family.'

He seemed to notice her as though for the first time.

'Your suit is ruined,' he remarked as the Rack sighed back to the position it was in when they first entered the room.

She felt the restraints fall from her ankles and wrists.

He tossed the controller back on to the shelf. 'When you're feeling better, why don't you go and buy yourself some new ones?'

He turned on his heel, unlocked the door and walked away, leaving the door open and his wife sobbing where she had fallen.

Somehow, she managed to drag herself to her room. Summoning her maid, she collapsed, face down on her bed as the maid, clicking her tongue in sympathy, but having the sense to make no comment, gently applied a soothing cream.

'Is it a mess?' Olga asked, fearful of what she might learn.

'No, m'lady. It's very red and there'll be some bruising, but the skin is unbroken.'

'Are you sure?' Olga found it hard to believe the servant. At the very least she had expected several deep gashes. Certainly it had felt as though her flesh was being removed.

'In a week's time you won't be able to tell it happened,' the maid promised.

Olga was unconvinced, but the cream was dulling the pain and what she wanted to do most of all was to sleep. Maybe when she woke up things would be different.

The maid finished and, seeing her mistress was asleep, gently covered her with a light sheet before returning to her own bed. Soon the entire household was asleep except for Krantz.

Pacing his study, he brooded on how best to have his revenge. He had already decided what he was going to do. That part was easy. The tricky bit was getting away with it. He had no doubts what his fate would be if he failed and Credo discovered his guilt.

He took a long pull on his drink. Kidnapping was definitely the answer. The ransom he would demand would more than settle his debts, and the anguish that Credo and his family would suffer would go a long way towards repaying the slights his family had suffered over the years.

If the victim were to be that beautiful, arrogant bitch of a daughter, then maybe he could arrange a little session for her on the Rack. He felt a tightness in his groin at the thought.

'If Credo had had his way with my wife,' he thought,

'then it is only fair that I should be allowed my fun with the daughter.'

But how? Although she was free to do as she chose and often stayed with friends, including that aristocratic slut calling herself Gala, her disappearance would cause the biggest manhunt the planet had ever seen. Patience was called for. He had waited all these years for his chance. He would not spoil it by acting hastily. He would have the girl watched. When the time was right he would strike.

Much cheered by these thoughts, the Duke of Krantz finally went to bed.

Chapter 2

It was late afternoon when Pooki returned to her apartments in the west wing of the royal palace. Her skimpy half-suit was soaked in sweat and she wasted no time in wriggling out of it. She dropped it in the auto-valet and punched in the shower setting she wanted.

Working out in free-fall was exhilarating and exhausting at the same time, and Pooki tried to put in at least an hour a day in the dome.

From force of habit she checked her console. Her parents had called, it informed her. Knowing that they expected prompt replies to their messages, she ran the call.

Her mother's face, calm and beautiful as always, filled the screen.

'Pooki, my dear, come and have dinner with us tonight. I'll ask chef to do some of your favourites. There's something your father and I wish to discuss with you.'

As the image faded Pooki quickly sent a prerecorded message accepting the invitation. Her computer had a number of prerecordeds that would answer most calls. It saved time having to record one specially. Strictly speaking, the polite thing to do was to record an original but Pooki was beginning to feel cold as her body cooled down from its workout.

She stepped into the shower and sighed with pleasure as the jets of perfumed, soapy water blasted her skin clean. After three minutes they changed to a hot, light spray, coating her in a light film of body oil. Finally, the water was replaced with gentle draughts of warm air.

Eight minutes later she was looking at herself critically in the mirror.

Try as she might, she couldn't reconcile herself to the fleshy bulge of her pubis. Despite having been told, by both men and women, that they found its prominence attractive, she had always been a little self-conscious of its bulge, clearly obvious whenever she wore anything tight – something she tried not to do.

Below the bulge, with its wispy covering of soft, blonde down, she could clearly see the lips of her labia, gleaming a soft pink as the oil slowly dried. They seemed vaguely obscene to her, spoiling the otherwise neat little gap between her thighs.

Her legs, by contrast, never failed to cheer her up. Long, slim and shapely, they allowed her to look good in virtually any type of clothing and devastating when left bare. Similarly, the sight of her breasts was pleasing to her. Without being overlarge they were nevertheless full and firm. Her nipples, looking like tiny little pink buds, would point upwards and outwards when aroused.

She smiled ironically at herself. How many times had she been aroused since Defloration? Twice? Three times? Whatever the number, it had been a pointless exercise. There had been no one with whom she had wanted to do anything about her arousal.

Was there something wrong with her, she wondered? Since her Defloration there had been plenty of offers. Somehow the idea just hadn't appealed to her, although it seemed that she appealed to others. Perhaps if her Defloration hadn't turned out the way it had? But then again, Gala hadn't had any trouble with it, or since for that matter.

Her Defloration party had started well enough. Her mother had been sympathetic but firm.

'In our position my dear, we do not wait around until we feel ready. We are deflowered on our sixteenth birthday. It must not be said that members of the royal family are not attractive enough to find a suitor. I can understand your reservations,' she had said, seeing the look on Pooki's face, although privately she found it hard to understand what those reservations might be.

When Ami herself had celebrated her sixteenth birthday, she was more than ready to be deflowered, eagerly looking forward to the moment when, amid much cheering and laughter, she led a slightly self-conscious but definitely eager boy upstairs to the ceremonial bed.

An hour later, just when those downstairs were beginning to become impatient, she had emerged from the room brandishing the blood-stained sheet as proof of her Defloration. The couple were supposed to reappear within half an hour or so, but Ami had enjoyed herself so much she had insisted on a more leisurely rerun.

Shortly more than a year later she had married Credo. Although the marriage had been an arranged one, she had never regretted their union and the experience she had managed to gain before their marriage had been both valuable and enjoyable.

And now here was her own daughter, if anything even more attractive than she herself had been, positively dreading the coming occasion. The youth of today, she sighed to herself.

'Don't you like young Rolo?' she asked.

Rolo was the young man chosen to be Pooki's swain. He was a friend of Pooki's older brother and, privately, Ami wouldn't have minded vetting him personally. He was a cheerful, handsome lad of nineteen, due to marry in a few months' time.

It had been known for some girls (and boys, for that matter) to develop a crush on their first partner and so it was usually arranged that their partner would become unavailable shortly after the Defloration. Staying with one partner was no way to gain the valuable experience necessary to become a successful host or hostess.

'He's all right I suppose,' Pooki replied listlessly.

Ami had changed the subject at this point, as it was obvious Pooki had no interest in the matter.

At the party itself, everything had gone smoothly. Dressed in the loose, scarlet-coloured gown that was the traditional garb at such functions – the scarlet signified the blood that was shortly to be spilled, whilst the looseness symbolised the wearer's willingness to allow access to her body – Pooki, having enjoyed the food, was even relaxing a little. Certainly Rolo was going out of his way to put her at ease. Quaffing heartily of his wine, he proceeded to tell her a slightly risqué joke, but so charmingly that she couldn't help laughing.

The wine had continued to flow during the speeches that followed the meal. Old friends of the family, teachers and relations all had their turn to extol Pooki's virtues as a child and predict equal success as an adult.

Finally, as the speeches ended and the pile of presents, for Pooki to open once officially an adult, was complete, the couple headed for the lift that would take them to their room.

Tradition dictated that Pooki had to stand, arms out-stretched sideways, whilst her consort removed her clothes. The gown was held together by two joints, one on each shoulder. When Credo finished his speech, the last, he had ceremoniously handed Rolo the molecular disrupter that would cause the joints to part.

Rolo, his hand shaking slightly as he was finally alone with Pooki, thumbed the button.

With only the merest whisper, the scarlet, Tangoran silk slid down Pooki's body to end in a soft heap around her feet.

Rolo's breath caught in his throat as he saw her naked perfection for the first time.

Pooki watched him anxiously.

'Do you find me pleasing?' she almost whispered.

'Pleasing?' Rolo was still trying to absorb her beauty. Maybe her breasts still had a little filling-out to do, but apart from that . . . 'You're magnificent!'

Unable to restrain himself any longer, spurred on by the alcohol, Rolo swept Pooki into his arms and almost ran with her to the bed.

To Pooki, it suddenly seemed as though Rolo had turned into a multihanded animal. At the same time as he was feverishly kissing her, trying to push his tongue into her mouth, his hands seemed to be everywhere. One moment they were kneading her breasts and pinching her nipples, the next they were sliding down to grope her thighs.

At the same time as he was trying to push his knee between hers in order to allow his hand better access to the pink-lipped join at the top of her legs, he was frantically trying to tear off his own clothes.

Pooki lay there, struggling half-heartedly, her mind in turmoil. She had not been absolutely sure what to expect, but certainly, she hadn't expected this. Part of her was affronted by the way she was being treated. She somehow felt that if Rolo would just lie quietly next to her, perhaps stroking her gently, and talk to her calmly she might have been able to enjoy the experience.

Deep down, a part of her seemed to be, if not actually enjoying what was happening, accepting it. Most of all

27

however, she was frightened at the change in Rolo and the speed at which things were happening.

He had managed to achieve two of his objectives already, he was now naked and his thigh was jammed between hers. She felt something hot and hard pressing into her thigh and looked down to see her first erect penis. It seemed huge!

Rolo was almost beside himself with lust now. He hadn't noticed her lack of cooperation, so eager was he to gorge himself in her. He did remember to take a smear of cream from the jar discreetly placed beside the bed, but even that was more for his benefit than hers.

Pooki gasped as his fingers almost slapped the cream onto her and then gasped again as the head of his prick began to push its way into her.

Instinctively she spread her thighs as wide as possible, raising her knees at the same time. Taking this as a sign of encouragement, Rolo pushed again, harder this time. Pooki felt a sharp tear of pain and then suddenly he slid deep into her.

Hardly daring to move in case the pain came again, Pooki lay still, conscious of the warm trickle of blood running down her thighs as Rolo commenced his thrusts. Rolo continued for three or four minutes before he gasped and shuddered as he fountained his appreciation into her.

As his breathing slowed he remembered his lack of finesse. Too late he tried to make amends, but Pooki, as soon as she felt his final jerks, suddenly felt a calmness descend over her. It was over. Now all she had to do was to make herself presentable and return to the party.

Once he had disentangled himself he tried to stroke her and say the endearments he had meant to say before his lust got the better of him. Unfortunately, Pooki rolled off the bed and disappeared into the bathroom.

When she emerged a few moments later it was just to put on the spare clothing that had been left for her.

'Pooki,' he cried, 'don't go just yet!'

She looked at him lying on the bed. His thing seemed harmless now but she remembered vividly the power and urgency it seemed to possess when it was pushing between her legs.

'I must,' she replied. 'The guests are waiting.'

She looked pointedly at the sheet he was lying on. With a sigh he climbed off the bed and began to dress as Pooki stripped off the stained sheet.

Pushing aside her reminiscences, Pooki pulled on some underwear before donning a comfortable one-piece. At least there was no need for formal dress this night. As long as there were no other guests dining, her parents allowed informality.

Why wasn't she more like her friend Gala, she wondered. Gala hadn't been prepared to wait for her Defloration. Her guardians had tried their best to cover up the scandal of Gala being discovered under a table at a fashionable party with another of the guests.

Apparently believing her to be older than she was, the guest had been flirting with her all evening. Gala had decided that actions spoke louder than words and suggested that they find somewhere secluded for him to put his money where his mouth was, so to speak.

When the table, whose cloth had reached almost to the floor, had been moved to make way for dancing, they were discovered. Gala had been more annoyed than embarrassed – as far as she was concerned, things were just becoming interesting. However, to everyone else, it was obvious that defloration had occurred, regardless of whether or not the interested parties had gained full satisfaction.

Her guardians had despaired of her, but Gala, having tasted the forbidden fruit, would not rest until she had gorged herself. Her official Defloration had been something of a standing joke. Certainly no one believed that the scarlet stains on the duly brandished sheet had just come from between her legs.

Gala of course, couldn't care less what people thought and now that she was officially an adult she threw herself into her sex life with a total lack of restraint, beginning with her party. Her long-suffering guardians, having done their best to raise her as a daughter of an earl should be raised, discreetly withdrew as soon as possible, leaving Gala to finish her party in such a way as to make it the most talked-about Defloration party the planet had ever known.

Having dispensed with the formalities (and the oldies), Gala invited anyone who felt so inclined to help finalise her Defloration. This meant that over the following thirty-six hours she made herself fully available to just about all of her guests, male or female, singly, in pairs or in groups. By the end of it all there was not a bed, a bath or a room that had not been used. Everyone who was there agreed it was a most memorable bash.

Pooki, some three months Gala's junior, had not been eligible to attend, but they had been firm friends for many years and the friendship continued unabated, despite their totally different attitudes to sex.

Their attitudes to sex, in fact, were the only things the girls did not have in common. They discussed and confided in each other about everything else. Apart from having the appetite of a rabbit and the morals of an alley cat Gala was a generous, open-hearted and sympathetic friend. Everyone liked her and even her innumerable discarded lovers remained her friends. She was much sought-after at parties. Her bed companions knew they were just being used to satisfy, however briefly, her need for sex. But Gala gave as good as she got and everyone who had been with her vowed she was the best they had had.

Yes, Pooki thought ruefully, if she herself was more like Gala her life would be simpler in many ways.

Her computer startled her with its announcement that it was time she went to join her parents.

The meal went smoothly enough. The food was excellent, the wine chosen with care. She had always enjoyed the company of her parents and this night was no exception. The reason for the invitation did not emerge until they were sitting comfortably around a cheerful log-effect fire in Ami's den. When the reason was broached, however, there was no beating about the bush.

'Pooki, my dear, we would like you to marry Janus, heir to the throne of Morex,' began her father quietly.

Pooki said nothing. The announcement was not altogether unexpected. The children of the planet's rulers were considered to be one of the planet's assets, to be used by the planet to its best advantage. Pooki had been brought up, virtually from the cradle, knowing that her adult life would not be hers to spend as she wished.

'Unfortunately,' put in Ami, 'the position of First Lady of Morex can be – how should I describe it? – somewhat demanding, and your father and I are not totally convinced that you are ready for such responsibilities.'

'You mean I'm not experienced enough for all the screwing that's involved?'

There were a lot of things that Pooki might be, but stupid was not one of them. Credo, caught between surprise and delight at his daughter's remark, choked on his brandy. Maybe there's hope for her yet, he thought as he struggled for breath.

'I wouldn't have put it quite that way, but yes, you

'cannot deny you have led a very sheltered life compared to that friend of yours, er, Gala,' her mother remarked.

'I think I've led a sheltered life compared to that little hussy,' remarked Credo. 'You wouldn't believe the things she's been up to ...'

'Quite,' interrupted Ami, 'and whilst we wouldn't exactly have been overjoyed if you had led the same kind of life over the last year or so, one cannot deny that she has all the qualifications for the position we hope you will achieve. All that is beside the point however. We have discussed this marriage in Council, as well as with Marlo and Tari, and all are agreed it should proceed. I think we can safely predict, therefore, that within the year you and Janus will be married.

'Now I don't know much about the boy, I haven't seen him in years, but by all accounts he's as shy as you are, so you should do well together. Be that as it may, your royal duties demand that you entertain, so, like it or not, you must learn to be a good hostess. You owe it to yourself, to us, to your planet and, most of all, to your husband and his planet, to be as good a hostess as you possibly can. To that end, we have arranged for you to work on Paradise for six months. To round off your education, so to speak.'

'To learn to become a whore, you mean,' said Pooki.

'In its most basic terms, yes. But that is the way things are done on our worlds. It is a system that has been evolved to suit our needs and no one has yet come up with a better one. Your father and I have come to quite enjoy our duties, although I must admit they came as a bit of a shock to me at first,' said Ami.

'You could, of course, refuse to marry the boy,' said Credo, 'and whilst as your king and queen we would be most annoyed, as your parents we would understand.'

Pooki ran to her father and gave him a hug.

'You mean you won't force me to marry Janus?'

'Not if you really didn't want to,' he smiled.

'What about you, Mother?' Pooki turned to face Ami.

Ami frowned at her daughter for a few seconds and then relented.

'If the thought of what you will have to do is so unbearable then of course we won't force you,' she agreed.

'Then I'll do it!' announced Pooki. 'I'll become the best First Lady that planet has ever had.'

Credo and Ami exchanged looks of relief and pride.

'Good girl!' cried Credo.

'I'm sure you'll find it will not be as bad as you may fear,' said Ami.

Conversation moved on after that and an hour or so later Pooki returned to her apartments. The subject came up once more, just as she was leaving, when Ami told her that, having agreed to the marriage, Pooki was to leave for Paradise on the next flight – in six days' time.

Pooki tried to contact Gala the next day to tell her the news. Unfortunately, all that came back in reply to her calls was a message saying Gala was unavailable at the moment but would call back as soon as possible. Pooki knew the signs. Gala was out on a binge somewhere with goodness only knew whom. Pooki hoped she would be in touch before she had to leave and delayed leaving a message telling Gala about her trip to Paradise until the last moment.

The only thing she had to look forward to was a party two days before she was due to leave. Normally Pooki went to such affairs only for something to do, but she was looking forward to this one as her last chance to say goodbye to her friends.

She dressed with her usual lack of care, choosing an old one-piece that was comfortable, baggy and several months out of date. As usual, she avoided any sort of make-up and let her hair hang where it dried after her shower.

The party was the usual raucous affair. It had all the signs of ending the way all the others did: that was, Pooki chatted to her friends until they found a partner for the night and slipped away.

The first sight that caught her eye and had the effect of cheering her up was that of Gala standing by the bar. As she made her way towards her friend she was struck by her outfit.

Gala was wearing a long coat made, judging by the way it swirled about her as she moved, of some very light material. The coat was open down the front and revealed a very short tunic underneath, so short in fact that anyone watching would quickly realise that Gala was not wearing anything under it.

Pooki said hello and refrained from asking her friend where she had been. Gala would tell her if and when she felt like it: otherwise, no amount of asking would produce an answer.

'Hi Pooki!' Gala greeted her. 'Still dressed in the height of fashion, I see.'

Pooki grinned and nodded pointedly at Gala's outfit.

'Aren't you cold, undressed like that?'

'Maybe, but I bet I'll find something to warm me up before long.'

'I had a long chat with my folks the other night,' Pooki began.

'Oh yes? How are the old royals these days?' Gala had never been noted for her respect to her elders and betters.

'Fine. In fact, you were mentioned.'

'Really?' Gala was interested but her eyes never stopped sweeping the room for likely partners.

'Yes, my mother said she wished I was more like you.'

'You're kidding!'

'Not me. It seems they want me to marry Janus of Morex and become First Lady there. You know what that means.'

'I'll say. Talk about mixing business with pleasure! But what did you say?'

'I said OK.' Pooki shrugged.

'But what about your well-known reticence regarding the pleasures of the flesh?' enquired Gala. 'Won't that be something of a handicap to you?'

'Ah, well, that's what I've been leading up to. They're going to send me to Paradise for a crash course in whoring.'

Gala's eyes focused on Pooki for the first time. 'Honestly?'

'No shit, as we're not supposed to say.'

'When does your exile begin?'

'The day after tomorrow. I have a farewell dinner with the family and then off to the spaceport.'

Gala's eyes lit up with the light of devilry.

'I'll come with you,' she said at once.

'What? But you can't!'

'Why not? It sounds like it could be fun. More fun than this planet's turning out to be, that's for sure.'

Pooki was amazed that anyone could make such a decision on the spur of the moment. 'But things need to be arranged. Paradise won't know anything about you!'

Gala gave Pooki an old-fashioned look. 'Are you trying to tell me that if someone as cute as me turned up and asked to be given work, they'd turn her down?'

'Well . . . no, I guess not.'

'There you are, then. Anyway, you'll need someone to look after you. Dump the flight details into my box tomorrow and I'll see you in Departure. This is great! Life was beginning to become a little dull. Now I can spend the next two days making sure no one will forget me.'

Pooki was about to say more when a boy they both knew came to stand next to them.

After greeting Pooki, whose reputation was well known, he turned his attention to Gala.

Gala favoured him with a brilliant smile and lifted her glass in mock salute. The action raised her tunic and allowed the boy a quick glimpse of dark red fur. He moved closer in response.

Gala hoisted herself on to a barstool, her coat falling away on each side of her as she did so. The hem of her tunic was up around her hips by the time she had finished wriggling herself into a comfortable position. The boy's hands were halfway up her thighs before she had stopped.

Pooki, finding herself completely ignored by this time, retreated to a convenient corner to watch developments.

'Surely she's not going to let him do it to her there?' a voice said beside her.

'You obviously don't know Gala,' Pooki replied without turning her head.

Gala's hands were busy between herself and the boy. He had stepped so close to her that it was impossible to see, though easy to guess, what she was doing.

'Any moment now,' Pooki said, still not sure who it was that had spoken.

Sure enough, as the boy seemed to bend his legs a little and then move closer still, Gala wrapped her own legs around him and used her arms to pull him closer still. A casual observer just might not realise what was going on, but anyone who knew Gala would know instantly.

Pooki turned to see who she had been talking to. She found herself facing a boy of about her own age, but who she didn't recognise.

'Remarkable,' he muttered, 'does everyone around here behave like that?'

'They're not all as blatant as Gala,' Pooki conceded,

'but before the party ends, there'll be a few more semipublic fornications, I'm sure. Everyone else will probably wait until they can be a little more private.'

'Yes, it's pretty much the same back on Morex,' he admitted sadly.

'Morex?' prompted Pooki.

'Yes. My name is Sonus. My parents think it is a good idea for me to travel a little before settling down. I wouldn't be surprised if they don't have a wife waiting for me when I return.'

Pooki was delighted to find a kindred spirit to talk to, especially as Gala, having finished with the boy at the bar, was now heading for the stairs along with a girl they both knew as well as the girl's boyfriend.

Pooki led Sonus to a couple of chairs at the edge of the room and for the next hour or so they chattered about their parents' expectations of them and their own, almost total, lack of ambition.

When she finally left to return home, Pooki found to her surprise that she had finally found someone she wanted to know better. Not only that, she discovered, but if he had suggested they find somewhere quiet, in order that they could do more than just talk, she would have been quite willing to go along with him. In fact, she realised she was just a little disappointed that things hadn't progressed any further.

She consoled herself with the thought that nothing would have come of it. Sonus was from a different planet. He had admitted he had only a few more days on Rontar before resuming his travels and, of course, Pooki was due to leave for Paradise herself very soon.

Still, she thought, it might have been interesting to compare him with the only other person with whom she had shared her body.

The following day was spent packing, saying farewells

to her friends and trying not to worry too much about what the next few months were going to be like.

Typically, she was unable to reach Gala to see if she intended to keep her promise about going with her. In the end, Pooki decided it was just one of those spur-of-the-moment things Gala was so likely to say and then forget about the moment something else turned up.

As such, Pooki was feeling rather sorry for herself as she waited, her last farewells long since said, in the departure lounge of the spaceport. The flight to Paradise had been announced and there was a general movement towards the seats that would whisk them onto the shuttle.

Just as she was taking her place on one of them, there was a commotion behind her and Gala, looking decidedly weary but still ravishing behind her huge, dark wraparounds, burst into the lounge, spotted Pooki and collapsed with a cheeky grin into the seat next to her.

'Phew,' she gasped, 'nearly didn't make it! I meant to be here an hour ago but Iggi just couldn't bear to tear himself away from my sultry body. Said he might never have the opportunity to do it to me again and so he just had to do it one last time.' She grinned again. 'That made it the third "last time" we did it! Do I need a bath!'

Pooki had to giggle at her irrepressible friend and for the few minutes it took them to reach the shuttle, Gala quickly explained how, once word had gone round of her impending absence, there had been a virtual queue of friends wanting to say goodbye to her ever-willing body.

'I'm plumb worn out,' she sighed smugly. 'All I'm going to do on the flight is sleep.'

Of course, once they had been shuttled to the ship, shown to their cabins, had a bath and a meal, Gala was feeling herself once more and studying each passing passenger with more than just a casual interest.

They had watched the ship break orbit from one of the

many bars and, as two stunningly attractive girls, were receiving more than their fair share of appraising looks themselves.

'Hmmn,' cooed Gala, as a handsome, chocolate-coloured man sauntered slowly past, 'there's nothing like a little shipboard romance to pass the time on a long voyage.'

'It's only a thirty-four-hour flight,' protested Pooki. She was feeling insecure enough as it was, without her friend disappearing for hours at a time. Something about her tone of voice registered with Gala and she reluctantly stopped encouraging the man from approaching.

'Feeling homesick?' she enquired sympathetically.

'Not really. I'm more worried about what's going to happen when we arrive. It's all right for you. You love sex. But it's all going to be terribly new for me and I don't know if I'm going to be able to cope.'

Seeing her friend was close to tears, Gala finished her drink, casually scribbled her cabin number on a scrap of paper and, with a meaningful look at the man who had by this time taken a stool near to them, she dropped it on the bar top and led Pooki back to her own cabin.

Pooki flung herself down on her bunk and sobbed for a few minutes while Gala sat in a chair and watched. Presently, Pooki hauled herself up to the top of the bed and drew her knees up to her chest. Hugging them tightly she looked at her friend.

'What am I going to do, Gala?' she sniffed. 'I'm going to make a fool of myself on Paradise and let my family down. I did so want to make a success of this trip.'

'You're going to stop feeling sorry for yourself, that's what.' Gala approached the bed, plumped up the pillows and sat next to her friend. 'You're going to have to go through with it, so you may as well make the best of it.'

'That's easy for you to say, but I just don't know what I'm supposed to do.'

'Tell me honestly,' Gala asked, 'have you really never had a climax?'

'Never. I've only ever been with one man.'

'Pooh!' Gala snorted dismissively. 'You don't have to be with a man to have a climax, or a woman either. Are you telling me you've never even touched yourself between your legs?'

'Of course not. Why should I?'

'Because you can find out a lot about yourself that way. Also, it can be a lot of fun.'

'What do you mean?'

Gala sighed. 'If you are serious about wanting to make the best of the next six months, I'm going to have to give you a few quick lessons. Although you're not going to be able to learn much in the time it takes us to reach Paradise.'

Pooki sat up a bit straighter and gave a long sigh.

'You're right. I have to make the best of it.'

'That's my girl.' Gala stood up and peeled off her suit. 'Now, take off your clothes and copy what I do.' She kicked off her panties and sat back on the bed.

Hesitantly, Pooki removed her own clothes and sat back again.

Gala gave her a quick once-over. 'You've a sensational body you know. Once you learn how to use it, you'll be a wow!'

Pooki risked a glance at Gala's nakedness. 'Yours seems pretty good as far as I can tell.'

Gala looked down at herself critically. 'It's OK,' she conceded, 'but I'll have to start watching what I eat before too long, whereas you'll never have that problem. Anyway, stretch out and close your eyes.'

Once they were lying comfortably Gala told Pooki to

start stroking her breasts. After a few minutes she glanced at her friend.

'Not like that! Don't be afraid of them. Try to make your nipples stand out. Look, like this.'

She fondled her own breasts, gently squeezing them and pushing them together. Under her expert touch, her nipples soon hardened. She watched as Pooki tried to copy her actions without success.

'Not like that, like this. Just close your eyes and relax. Forget who we are and where we are. Concentrate on the sensations you're having.'

She reached over and began toying with Pooki's breasts. At first Pooki lay as stiff as a plank, but as Gala murmured her admiration of the body she was caressing and did not limit her attentions to Pooki's breasts but stroked her shoulders, arms and neck as well, she began to relax.

Soon she began to sigh a little. 'Mmn, that does feel good,' she said, opening her eyes to watch her friend's hands gliding over her skin.

'Your nipples seem to think so anyway,' agreed Gala as she felt them stiffening under her palms. 'Now, I'm going to start kissing you. This adds to the effect.'

Gala began to kiss and nuzzle Pooki's neck and shoulders, all the while continuing her stroking. Pooki closed her eyes again and relaxed further. When she judged the time was right, Gala began to tease Pooki's nipples with her tongue, flicking them lightly and then sucking on them gently.

Her hands, meanwhile, began to stroke Pooki's sides, belly and thighs. Soon they became more adventurous, sliding slowly up and down the soft inner skin above the knees. Without realising she was doing so, Pooki opened her thighs slightly to allow easier access.

Ever so gently, Gala brushed across the lips she found there with a fingertip. She smiled to herself. The dampness

41

was indicative of Pooki's increasing arousal. Slowly, she began to kiss her way towards the enticing mound her fingers had discovered. Pooki's breathing was shallower now and becoming faster.

Gala paused as her lips arrived at the soft blonde fur, savouring the subtle aroma that was beginning to strengthen as her fingers began stroking the tender flesh at the top of Pooki's thighs.

Pooki moaned with pleasure. 'What are you doing to me?' she whispered.

'Something that should have been done long ago,' Gala replied, her breath stirring the dampening curls. 'Do you like it?'

'Oh yes, don't stop. I can't believe anything could feel this good.'

Thus encouraged Gala buried her face between her friend's legs. As her hands continued kneading the flesh of Pooki's thighs, her tongue probed the folds of flesh, one moment pushing into the tight little hole, the next sliding upwards to titillate the little button a centimetre or two away.

As Pooki began to arch her back, rubbing herself against Gala's face, Gala slipped her thumb into Pooki's hot wetness. She used her remaining fingers to stroke between the cheeks of Pooki's bottom.

Never having experienced anything like the current three-pronged assault on her virtually virginal and previously private parts Pooki was unable to withstand the sensations for very long. With a howl that almost hid the whine of the ship's motors, she had her first, shattering climax.

An hour or so later she had her fifth, after which she was so emotionally drained she simply fell asleep. Gala slipped off the bed and covered her friend's exhausted body with the thermo-sheet that had long ago fallen to the floor.

Quickly, she used Pooki's bathroom for a quick shower. She had encouraged her friend to return the caresses she was receiving and the result had been quite satisfying. She had no doubt that Pooki would be able to both give and receive pleasure, providing she was not treated too roughly to begin with.

However, Pooki might be exhausted as well as satisfied with the events that had just taken place, but for Gala, they had merely served as an appetiser. Fingers and tongues were all very well, but Gala was now firmly in the mood for something a lot more substantial between her legs.

She would return to her cabin. She would give the man from the bar half an hour in which to pay his respects. If he didn't show up then she would find somebody else.

Stepping into her suit, she gave Pooki one last glance before closing the cabin door quietly behind her.

Chapter 3

When Pooki awoke the next morning, it was with such a feeling of wellbeing that she found it hard to believe she was on a space-cruiser heading for Paradise.

She lay contentedly in the bed, reliving the incredible events of the previous evening. Had they really happened, she wondered, or was it just wishful thinking?

Cautiously, nervously, she slid a finger down through her fur to the soft little slit whose reactions had so surprised her. Trying to remember the things Gala had shown her, she began to massage herself.

Sure enough, she could feel the sensations beginning anew. Not so vividly as when Gala was doing it, but still fresh and exciting. With a feeling of great daring, as well as accomplishment, she managed to make herself shudder with release.

Suddenly she wished Gala were here so that they could do it to each other again. She decided to have a quick shower and then see if Gala was still in bed. If she was, Pooki thought, she would just snuggle in with her and see what happened.

Ten minutes later she eased open Gala's door and peered round its edge.

Gala was certainly still in bed, but most definitely not

asleep. Judging from the look on her face as the man pumped away between her legs, there was little Pooki would have been able to do to increase her pleasure. Feeling slightly foolish, Pooki gently closed the door and, suddenly feeling depressed, wandered disconsolately away to have a lonely breakfast.

'Where have you been?' Pooki demanded of her friend when Gala finally tapped on her cabin door some time in the afternoon.

'I have been having one of the best fucks of my life,' Gala announced proudly.

'I thought at the least you might have come to see me,' replied Pooki, 'especially after what happened last night.'

'I have come to see you,' Gala pointed out. 'And as for last night – well, it was fun, but we don't own each other, you know. What you should have done was to find someone else to keep you warm.'

Seeing the doubtful look on her friend's face she hurried on.

'Look, Pooki. You proved last night that there's nothing wrong with you. You reacted absolutely normally to what we did – you enjoyed it, didn't you?' When Pooki nodded, Gala continued, 'There you are then. The only difference between us is that I've had more experience. You should be able to have just as much fun with someone else, more so if he's got a big donger and knows how to use it.' She grinned. 'Why don't you give it a try? N'suma was asking where you were last night. I rather gained the impression he fancied you more than me, until we hit the sheets, that is. I left him trying to crawl back to his cabin.'

Pooki had to laugh at Gala's earthiness. Nevertheless, she decided there would be enough men on Paradise to keep her busy without looking for some in advance.

'I was hoping you would show me some more, you know, things,' she confessed.

45

'Well, let me catch up on my sleep and I will,' replied Gala. 'First thing after dinner, we'll practise a few moves, but don't be upset if I leave you afterwards. You're my best friend and I enjoyed what we did last night, but I enjoy what men have to offer as well.'

Gala returned to her cabin to catch up on some sleep leaving Pooki at a loose end. She decided to find out more about her destination. Thumbing the remote control for the cabin's video, she asked for the promo-tape on Paradise.

Paradise, it transpired, was created from a desolate, mined-out shell of a planet. Someone at IGX had had the bright idea of creating a rest and recreation resort for their personnel. As most of them spent their working lives on far-flung outposts of distant galaxies, clawing minerals from inhospitable worlds incapable of supporting human life, their need for a safe, comfortable environment in which to relax was high on their list of priorities.

At a cost of untold millions of credits, the spaceport was reactivated and linked by some of the thousands of abandoned mining tunnels to a huge dome in which the San Francisco of Earth in the late 1800s was lovingly recreated.

The vast underground caverns and mineshafts were packed with machinery to maintain an Earth-like environment above ground. Space tankers by the score brought in water, sand and stone to help build the illusion.

It was decided to build a replica of San Francisco as IGX felt it would capture the flavour of a rough, tough mining town in which their own miners would feel at home.

Discreet advertisements were placed throughout the known worlds for young, attractive men and women to work in the dome and cater for the various needs of the IGX personnel.

The idea was an instant success. Vacation time on Paradise became a commodity that rivalled the value of the legendary gold that was so sought after on Earth. Murders were rumoured to have been committed in order to gain VT, as vacation time became known.

VT was about the only thing the hard-bitten miners would refuse to gamble with. Credits, ground cars, houses, even wives, yes, but not VT.

It didn't take the executives of IGX long to realise they were on to a good thing. Too good to restrict just to their few million employees.

The whole concept was rethought and expanded. The entire planet would be rebuilt. Since all mankind originated from Earth, the themes behind each zone would be modelled on a time taken from Earth's pre-space-travel history. Anyone with sufficient credits could buy themselves time on the planet.

True, IGX workers were given substantial discounts, but now they would have to book their VT like anyone else. The original dome containing San Francisco was now long gone, replaced by California of the late sixties.

Fifty years ago the conversion of the planet was complete. Paradise boasted some twenty zones and could cope with a hundred million visitors at any one time. There were over five million permanent staff based on the planet simply maintaining the systems and handling essential imports like food and drink.

As well as these faceless workers, however, there were the highly visible men and women who mingled with the visitors and provided the services for which the planet was renowned. Each zone boasted countless attractive 'natives' who were not only highly approachable but infinitely accommodating. These skilled workers represented the cream of the galaxies in their looks and talents. It was to be one of these that Pooki and Gala were heading.

Because the twin planets of Morex and Rontar provided much of Paradise's agricultural requirements, the two governments had been able to add a clause to their contracts with IGX allowing them to send certain of their sons and daughters to Paradise to finish their education and polish up their entertaining skills.

Pooki shut down the video and wondered which zones she would be sent to. Her reverie was interrupted by the return of Gala.

'Hi, P.! What've you been up to?'

'Just boning up on the history of Paradise.'

'It's the present that interests me,' Gala grinned. 'Why, it's even possible that I might finally have to cry, "Enough!"'

'Yeah, and I'm a Tangoran silkworm,' said Pooki.

'Speaking of which,' said Gala, 'did you know there's a species of silkworm that can be trained to wriggle up your, er, fanny, and brush your insides with its fur? It's supposed to be the ultimate in self-stimulation. Not that it's really self-stimulation,' she added as an afterthought.

'I don't believe it!' gasped Pooki. 'Letting a worm crawl inside you . . .' Words failed her.

'It's true, I swear it. They're supposed to be fantastically expensive, but you can pop them in before you go out somewhere and spend the whole time having one orgasm after another. Of course, everyone would want to know why you were grinning like an idiot and moaning every five minutes or so, but that would be a small price to pay.'

'No, thank you!' declared Pooki emphatically.

'Are you kidding? It sounds great!' Gala grinned wickedly.

'Not for me,' Pooki said firmly.

'That's a shame then, 'cos I've managed to borrow one until we reach Paradise.'

'Gala!' Pooki was shocked. 'You haven't!'

'Well, no,' she admitted, 'but I do have something that's almost as good.'

'What's that?' Pooki asked suspiciously.

'My trusty old Wondavibe,' said Gala, 'but there'll be time for that later. How have you been managing on your own? Had yourself a man yet?'

'No, of course not. I did manage to make myself come though,' Pooki admitted shyly.

'Good for you, you're learning. Show me how you did it.'

'What! Now?'

'Why not? On Paradise you're not going to be given the chance to set the scene you know. If your partner is hot to trot, so must you be. In cases like that, a touch of aphro-gel can be a girl's best friend.'

'I've heard of that. Is it any good?'

'Judge for yourself, baby.'

Gala waved a tube under Pooki's nose. Pooki took it uncertainly. 'I just rub some on?' she asked, squeezing a little on to a fingertip.

'That's right. Don't use too much, though, or it'll have you climbing up the walls.'

Hiding her embarrassment as well as she could, Pooki slipped her finger into her panties and dabbed the gel on to her lips. She examined her finger afterwards as though it might have changed into a phallus under the influence of the gel.

'Are you sure this stuff works?' she asked after a few moments.

'It works,' replied Gala, watching her friend's face with interest.

'Perhaps I didn't use enough ... Oh!' she gasped as the cream began to be absorbed.

'Doesn't work, eh?'

'Oh, wow!'

Almost without realising what she was doing, Pooki's hand disappeared back into her panties. Gala watched the movement under the one-piece.

'Don't rub too hard,' she warned, 'or you'll be as sore as hell afterwards.'

'I don't care,' moaned Pooki, eyes closed.

'Why don't I help you?' suggested Gala.

'Oooh yes, but be quick.'

Pooki almost tore her clothes off in her urgency. She sprawled back on the bunk, legs apart, fingers working feverishly between her swollen lips. Gala grinned down at her.

'I'm on fire,' gasped Pooki. 'It's incredible.'

'Yes, I think you put a little too much gel on,' replied Gala. 'This may help, though.'

She gave her vibrator a quick shake to turn it on and then set it to its smallest, thinnest and smoothest setting. It was absolutely silent as it began to work and Pooki had no inkling of what Gala was doing as she began to apply the tip to Pooki's engorged clitoris.

'Oh yes! I love it!' Pooki moaned as Gala began to slide the tip up and down the length of her slippery lips.

When Gala judged Pooki was ready for more she began to push the vibrator gently into her. She was rewarded by Pooki spreading her legs even wider and, thus encouraged, eased it in to its full extent.

For a few moments she left it to do its subtle work. Pooki was beginning to push up against it and, taking her lead from her friend, Gala began a thrusting motion to match. Ever so carefully she began to adjust the settings.

Soon the vibrator had increased in both length and thickness and as Pooki was still apparently wanting more, Gala adjusted the texture as well.

Pooki was now writhing almost uncontrollably as the combination of gel and vibrator brought her to fresh plateaux of pleasure, each one more intense than its predecessor.

Her head was whipping from side to side on the pillow as one hand kneaded her breasts while the other frantically rubbed her button.

'I'm coming,' she moaned. 'It feels so good!'

As she arched her back off the bunk, Gala triggered the pump and Pooki almost screamed as the warm liquid fountained into her. She flopped back down and lay, gasping, as Gala gently pulled the vibrator out.

'What is that thing?' she croaked as the ability to speak slowly returned.

'Just a little something I picked up down town,' Gala replied carelessly. 'Let me show you how it works. You need two hands to begin with. If you twist the end it expands or contracts – depending which way you turn it, obviously.' Gala showed Pooki how it could be made to swell to the thickness of an old-fashioned rolling-pin. 'If you hold it and pull the base it goes longer.' Again she demonstrated and Pooki gulped as the vibrator stretched effortlessly and seamlessly to a full thirty centimetres.

'If you press this button on the base, the texture changes.' The vibrator slowly altered from being perfectly smooth to a ridged and lumpy unevenness. 'Finally, if you press this button, it squirts.'

'So I see,' remarked Pooki, wiping the liquid from her stomach. 'How do you turn it on?'

'Simple. Just give it a shake. When you've finished, shake it again and it turns itself off. Clever, eh?'

'I'll say.' Pooki was still a little shaken from her experience. 'It's fantastic. Why would anyone want a man when they can have one of these?'

'Are you kidding?' Gala was shocked. 'These things may be fully adjustable and state-of-the-art et cetera, but you can't beat the real thing. This is strictly do-it-yourself.

When you have someone else doing it to you for real, it makes no difference how big he is. You have different sounds and smells and tastes . . .' her voice trailed off as she conjured up some of her innumerable memories.

'Which reminds me,' she continued, glancing at her time-ring, 'I promised Whatsisname I'd join him for a drink.' She looked round for her shoes which she'd kicked off earlier. 'You're going to need some more of that before the gel wears off,' she said, nodding at the vibrator in Pooki's hands. 'I'll leave you to it. Bye!'

Before Pooki could say anything Gala was gone. Pooki looked at the vibrator and then down at her little furry mound. Gala was right. She could feel the fire beginning to flare up again. She gave the machine a shake and then placed it tentatively against a nipple.

A few hours later she was awoken by a gentle voice. At first she couldn't place it until she suddenly realised it was the computer console. It was informing her that the ship was now in orbit around Paradise and all passengers should be preparing to shuttle down.

Fourteen minutes later, showered, packed and flustered, Pooki joined Gala at their shuttle bay.

'Hi! How did you and Wondavibe get along?'

Pooki found herself blushing. 'Ssh, Gala! Someone might hear you!'

'So what? They're either coming here to work or coming here to play. Whichever it is, they've probably all tried one at some stage or another.'

'That's right, baby,' a tall, gorgeous black girl agreed with Gala. 'Though from what I've heard they're the last things you need on this planet.'

'Let's hope so,' grinned Gala.

They sat in their allocated bank of seats and certified that the luggage stowed in the lockers underneath belonged to them. Once every seat was occupied and all the luggage checked, the seats slid into the shuttle. The shuttle's body closed itself around them with a sound like a long, loud sigh – a louder version of the one Pooki had just given. As long as she was on the ship, Paradise was just some place she'd seen on a film. Now she was not only going to see it, but experience it for real.

As soon as the airlock was vented they slipped out into their descent to Paradise. At first, there was little to be seen but as they came closer the passengers amused themselves by trying to guess which zones were which. Once the planet had been converted in a big way, IGX found it possible to restore the atmosphere. Now there was no need for the earlier domes. The millions of trees, either imported or grown from seedlings, were capable of maintaining the critical oxygen balance. Enough water had been brought in to start a water cycle and any deficiencies were corrected by the machines deep underground.

Cunningly placed satellites reflected and concentrated sunlight on to those zones that were supposed to have it, whilst the others were left to enjoy the planet's natural, temperate climate.

'It looks as though everyone on this shuttle is going to Paradise to work,' remarked Gala.

Pooki just nodded. They were very nearly there and she was feeling insecure again. Despite finding out a few surprising things about herself, with more than a little help from Gala, she felt she was still not ready for the work she was going to be expected to do.

If the journey had been a little longer, she told herself, she might have followed Gala's suggestion and permitted someone to share her bunk. As it was, it was more than likely that the first person to do so would be a visitor who would be expecting something special.

She had little time to dwell on these matters however, as once the shuttle landed they barely had time to think.

No sooner had the cover lifted off them than the bank of seats sped away to 'Central', as the reception and training area was known. On the way, a disembodied voice instructed them to fill in the questionnaires in front of them. Before the voice had finished speaking, a computer terminal dropped down from its foldaway position in the seat back in front of each passenger.

As it powered up, a screen, also in the back of each chair, came alive with the questions. Pooki barely had time to fill in the answers before they arrived at Central.

Nervously clutching their luggage they assembled in a large hall to be addressed by an elegant, beautifully dressed woman in her early forties.

'Welcome to Paradise,' the woman greeted them. 'Most of you should be feeling a little nervous. This is only natural. However it may help if I tell you that the drop-out rate among your type of worker is currently running at two point five-seven percent.

'At present our main computer is analysing the answers you gave on your way here to determine which zone you will be assigned to first. While we are waiting for its recommendations you will be shown to your rooms. Your computer terminal will then give you all further information. This system is fully interactive so you may ask it any questions you like. If you have a valid reason for questioning your assignment I can assure you that your query will be dealt with sympathetically.

'You will have noticed the terminals around this room. When I have finished speaking to you I suggest you enter your name on one and you will receive a printout of your room allocation and how to find it. Remember, if at any time you feel you have a problem, or you wish to terminate your employment, you have only to use a terminal to gain instant attention. Good luck and try to enjoy yourselves.'

The woman smiled briefly and then turned gracefully and left the hall. After a moment or two of silence there was a sudden movement to the terminals and soon the air was filled with the hum of excited conversation punctuated by the whirr of the printers.

Gradually, the hall began to empty as people headed off towards their rooms. Pooki stood waiting nervously for Gala, who seemed to be having some trouble with her machine. Finally it gave in and issued her with a slip like the one Pooki was clutching.

'That's it then, all fixed,' she announced with satisfaction.

'Just like that?' Pooki was surprised.

'Sure. It started off telling me it had no record of my application. However once it checked out my references it nearly blew its chips accepting me.'

'They don't use chips any more.'

'Just a figure of speech. Anyway, I'm in.'

'Who were these referees anyway?'

Gala looked wickedly at Pooki. 'Your mum and dad.'

'What! You're kidding?'

'Not me. I just told the machine to buzz the royal palace on Rontar if it wanted to check my bona fides. Looks like someone there was prepared to vouch for me. I bet once they realised I was here to hold your hand they gave me a five-star rating.'

Pooki shook her head at her friend's cheek and they set about finding their rooms.

'Someone must have pulled a few strings,' Gala said when it transpired they had adjacent rooms. 'What's the betting we both end up in the same zone?'

'No takers!'

Sure enough, their respective terminals informed them they had been allocated to the Californian zone. Pooki spent a thoughtful hour reading and rereading her instructions before knocking on Gala's door.

'California, hey? Can't wait!' was Gala's reaction.

'What about the drugs?' Pooki wanted to know.

'You've read the blurb. You won't really be smoking cannabis, just some harmless stuff that gives the same sensation. Same with the LSD. Any problems, hit the panic button and you're whipped off to the detox unit. Anyway we haven't time to sit here talking – we're supposed to be under the old UV.'

She almost dragged Pooki with her as they headed for the solarium. Half an hour under the special lamps not only gave them convincing tans but conditioned their skins against the sunlight to which they would actually be exposed.

Many miles away, in one of the luxury transit hotels visitors stayed in before heading for their chosen zone, a man unplugged his equipment from the room's terminal. Hacking into the planet's main database had been ridiculously easy. Security was virtually non-existent, but then why shouldn't it have been? Personnel details and movements were hardly the most classified of information.

So, he thought, she's heading for the Californian zone. We'll have to see what can be arranged.

He entered his choice of zone in the legitimate way and allowed himself a smile of satisfaction as the computer confirmed his choice and began to feed him details of the zone and its attractions.

There may be a slight hold-up while I actually locate her, he thought, but then . . .

He arranged for an auto-page to alert him in good time

for his connection the next day and fell asleep working on the details for the snatch.

When Pooki, Gala and three other girls emerged into the rest room of the diner the next morning it was hard for them not to feel a surge of excitement. They had been whisked by a high-speed underground train to a little platform under the diner. As soon as Pooki and the others had climbed out, the train sped off to the next drop-off point. The elevator quickly brought them up to ground level, a video screen informed them the rest room was currently unoccupied and a few seconds later they walked out into the diner.

They had discussed their plans in the train. The three girls were going to try their luck hitch-hiking along the highway; Pooki and Gala were going to cross the road and head on down to the beach.

'Let's have a drink first,' begged Pooki, trying to delay the inevitable as the others headed for the door.

'OK,' agreed Gala.

They ordered coffee and doughnuts and sat at a table by the window. Next to the diner was a garage. Pooki had read about such things and they had been mentioned in the briefing, but it was still strange to see the odd-looking, four-wheeled vehicles making those funny noises, pulling up to the pumps and 'filling up'.

The vehicles didn't actually use a fossil fuel, of course, but the effect was the same. On the wide, black road there was a steady stream of such vehicles, some huge, noisy trucks, others small two-wheelers that miraculously managed to stay upright, as well as a host of others of varying shape and size.

Pooki watched with interest as a sixteen-wheeler pulled up alongside the girls. She noticed the quick sign they gave the driver to make sure he wasn't another worker whose assignment was to pick up visitors looking to sample life on the road.

He obviously didn't return the sign as one of the girls heaved herself into the cab. This meant he was a visitor opting for a spell as a truck driver, picking up hitchers, hanging out in honky-tonks and doing whatever else it was that truckers did in those days.

'Sure looks hot out there,' Gala said, coming back with refills of coffee.

'At least we're dressed for it,' Pooki replied. She was wearing tight, faded blue jeans and a loose shirt knotted to expose a few inches of smooth, brown midriff. She was very conscious that even a casual observer would be able to tell that they were the only articles of clothing she was wearing. On her feet she wore a scuffed pair of sandals that were kept on only by a strap across the toes and a thong in between two of them. On the floor next to her lay a sort of sack with a shoulder strap that held a pair of shorts, a loose skirt, another shirt and a toothbrush. She hoped there would be somewhere she could keep rinsing them through.

Gala had no such worries. She wore a simple loose dress that came down to her knees. Despite its unflattering appearance it suited her. Whenever she moved, her breasts would joggle in an interesting way under the thin material and if she bent over it would stretch across her buttocks revealing that she, too, was wearing no underclothes.

They watched three boys in their early twenties come along the track that led between the dunes from the beach. The boys waited for some traffic to pass and then crossed the road and entered the diner, pausing to savour the air-conditioned interior before heading for the counter.

They ordered Cokes and several six-packs of beer to go. One of them sauntered over to the jukebox behind Pooki. She heard him drop in a coin and then the sound of the Beach Boys blasted out. His friends had, in the meantime, set up the balls on the pool table.

'Fancy a game, girls?' one of them suggested.

'Sure,' Gala said, getting up.

'But we can't play whatever game that is,' hissed Pooki.

'We can learn, can't we?' Gala headed for the table, her hips swaying suggestively.

She gave the boys their sign but received no acknow-ledgement. This is it, Pooki told herself as she followed more slowly.

Gala confessed to their lack of skill which promptly led the boys to offer to partner each of them. Introductions were made and Pooki found herself playing with Jim. He was good company, frequently giggling at the most trivial things. Gala's partner, who called himself Cosmic, was taller and darker than Jim. The third boy, Jerry, contented himself with feeding coins into the jukebox.

After a couple of games Jerry suggested they head back to the beach.

'The others'll be wondering where we are,' he said.

'Yeah, OK. What about you girls? Why not come down for something to eat? Have a swim or something?'

'Far out!' Gala replied brightly.

Watch it, Gala, you're overdoing things, thought Pooki. But the boys just grinned and, picking up the beer, led the way out.

The heat was incredible after the coolness of the diner. Before they had crossed the road Pooki was looking forward to the chance of taking off her jeans and plunging into the sea. She refused to think about the fact that she had no swimming costume.

She tried kicking off her sandals once they reached the beach but the sand was so hot that she very quickly put them back on. The boys laughed good-naturedly at her discomfort and Jim offered to carry her.

She smiled her thanks at him but declined. After a walk of about half a mile they arrived at a line of beach houses. There were half a dozen of them, each more or less the same. They were built on piles, about four feet high. Around the front and sides was a veranda, with steps leading down to the sand. There were about thirty yards of sand between them and the sea.

'There's no surf at the moment,' Jerry said apologetically. 'The wind's wrong.'

The group was greeted by shouts and jeers from a dozen or so others of roughly the same age. Introductions were quickly and casually made as the beer was handed out. Pooki noted that the numbers matched very neatly. As well as two of the girls, two of the boys were also workers.

Further talk revealed that there were another eight in the group but they had headed for the nearest town to pick up some food.

'They should be back sometime this afternoon,' Jim told Pooki and then shouted to one of the girls, 'Hey Alison, what's happened to the food?'

'Hang on, you glutton, and I'll go see.'

She disappeared into one of the shacks and then stuck her head back out again.

'About fifteen minutes, I'd say.'

'Great! Anyone fancy an appetiser?' Cosmic held up what Pooki recognised as a joint.

This idea seemed to meet with general approval and everyone began to troop indoors.

'Aren't you coming?' Jim asked, seeing Pooki's hesitation.

'I think I'll have a swim first, but you go ahead,' she replied, noticing that Gala had already gone inside.

'I'll join you,' he said, pulling off his T-shirt. 'Last one in's a turkey.'

He kicked off his shorts and ran, naked, for the water, shouting in mock agony at the heat of the sand.

Oh well, it had to happen sometime, Pooki thought as she peeled down her jeans and undid her top. The sand was sufficiently hot to make her forget her nudity and concentrate on reaching the sea as quickly as possible.

The water was fantastic. Pooki suddenly felt free. She swam about enthusiastically, splashing Jim as he surfaced beside her. For ten minutes they messed about and then someone called to them from the veranda. 'Hey, you two! Munchies!'

When Jim grabbed her hand for the dash back to the shack Pooki had forgotten they were naked, but the sight of his shrunken prick bouncing as he ran seemed more funny than threatening. She grabbed her clothes as they arrived at the house and ducked into the shade under the veranda to dress.

Deciding the jeans were too hot for the beach, she stuffed them into her bag and wrapped her skirt round herself instead. She left her shirt untied but did up just a few of the buttons instead. Jim simply stepped into his jeans and slung his T-shirt over his shoulder.

The meal was very informal. Everyone flopped down on big cushions or into battered armchairs, passing around bowls of salad, a plate of steaks and bottles of the local wine. Pooki decided she felt hungry and dug in with gusto.

When joints were passed round after the meal she only hesitated briefly before accepting. Gala, she noticed, was getting on very well with Cosmic, leaning back against his legs while he played with her hair. She noticed Pooki looking at her and, jerking her head slightly at Jim, winked. Pooki shrugged and grinned. She was beginning to feel the effects of the wine and the dope.

'Siesta time,' someone said, heaving himself to his feet. Some of the others followed, some just stayed where they were. The Mamas and the Papas were singing from somewhere and Pooki decided she had never felt so relaxed.

'Fancy another joint?' Jim murmured in her ear.

'Far out,' she replied, pleased with herself for being able to enter into the spirit of things.

'Come on then,' Jim pulled her to her feet.

'Aw, I was really comfy then,' she complained. 'Where are we going?'

'Two huts down. You'll be just as comfy there.'

'Oh, all right.'

It wasn't worth worrying about, she thought. Much easier just to go along with things. It seemed to take forever to reach the hut, and once there she collapsed gratefully on to a pile of cushions in the main room as Jim went to fetch his stash.

Pausing only to slap on a record, Jim began to roll a 'little number', as he put it. Soon Pooki felt the buzz starting again as she really began to appreciate The Doors.

When Jim gently pulled her into his arms and began to kiss her, it took her several seconds before she realised what was happening. By then she was responding and even though the kiss seemed to go on for a long time she had no objection, when, after a pause during which they both took a mouthful of beer from the can he had found somewhere, he kissed her again.

She felt his tongue pushing against her teeth and opened her mouth to let it in. Her own tongue seemed to be able to feel every contour of his and she decided to find out what the inside of his mouth felt like.

They paused for more beer, each feeling quite pleased with themselves and each other. This time it was Pooki who instigated the kiss. She felt his fingers carefully undoing the buttons of her shirt and wondered if he would do the same sort of things that Gala had done.

More or less she concluded a few moments later. His hands were not as soft as Gala's and his caresses had more urgency to them. When he began nuzzling her nipples, however, she was forced to admit that it was more exciting than when Gala had done it.

She ran her hands through his hair and then began stroking his neck and shoulders as he continued to fondle and kiss her breasts.

He returned to kiss her face and then her lips again as his hand began to feel for the fastening of her skirt. Pooki raised her hips a little to allow him to tug it clear and then began to nibble at his neck as he started to stroke her thighs.

When his hand made its way slowly to the join at the top, her legs were already parted to give him access. She sighed deeply and then bit his shoulder as a finger made its cautious entry.

She was puzzled for a while at the long lump she could feel pressing against her hip. When realisation dawned as to what it was she reached down lazily to check the shape. He gasped as her fingers closed round his erection and quickly stopped what he was doing to yank down his jeans.

Holding an erect penis for the first time, Pooki was surprised to find how stiff it felt. She ran her hand up and down the shaft, assessing its texture and rigidity. This led to the interesting discovery of his balls. She hefted them cautiously, curious at their weight and the fact that the skin seemed so loose and wrinkled in comparison to his prick.

She was a little disappointed when he sat up to remove her shirt and his jeans completely, but was somewhat mollified when he gazed at her body in obvious admiration. 'You're fantastic,' he breathed.

'So was what you were doing to me just then,' she murmured. 'Why have you stopped?'

'I just wanted to look at you,' he said.

'Mmn, well, that's OK then, but don't take too long about it.'

She closed her eyes again and reached back down for his hardness. Maybe Gala was right. We'll soon see. But for some reason he seemed to have disappeared. She was just summoning up the effort to open her eyes to see where he had gone when she felt his tongue probing her navel. She relaxed again as his lips moved lower.

He wriggled further round, the better to kiss her, and brought his prick closer to her face. Holding him with both hands she ran her tongue lightly down the stem. This brought such a gratifying reaction from his own tongue, which had somehow managed to locate her own, much smaller stem, that she was encouraged to continue.

There was a warm glow spreading throughout her body emanating from between her legs. It was similar to the effects of aphro-gel, but gentler somehow. It seemed the natural thing to do to tug his face gently back up to hers and wriggle herself under him.

'Your thing tasted all salty,' she told him when they were face to face again.

'I think it's just about to be washed,' he answered, easing the head into her wetness.

'About time too,' she murmured, reaching down to guide it in.

His entrance was effortless, although Pooki was aware of being stretched to accommodate him.

'Stars above, you're tight,' he gasped.

'Now you're in I don't want you slipping out,' she replied, amazed at herself for being able to say such things.

For a few moments they were both content to lie without moving, simply enjoying the feel of each other. Slowly, however, Jim began to rotate his pelvis, grinding himself against Pooki's mound whilst staying deep inside her.

Pooki couldn't believe the sensations she was receiving. All too soon the fireworks went off all round her body and she gasped and moaned as she pushed herself against him, trying to prolong the feeling.

Jim grinned down at her.

'You OK, baby?'

'I'll say,' she sighed and then went cold as she remembered that she was supposed to be satisfying him. 'But how about you?'

'So far so good,' he grinned, starting to ease himself out.

Thank the stars for that, Pooki said to herself, preparing to wriggle out from under him.

'Can you manage?' she enquired as he seemed in no hurry to roll off.

Jim completely misinterpreted Pooki's movement and question.

'Far out,' he said, pulling out of her and helping her to turn over.

To Pooki's amazement, he helped her onto her hands and knees and then positioned himself behind her. She was still wondering what on earth he was doing when he slid smoothly into her again.

Almost immediately he began to thrust steadily. He reached round with one hand to stroke a breast, rolling the nipple between thumb and forefinger from time to time. Pooki found her surprise giving way to desire as the feelings he had aroused in her a few minutes previously began to build again.

'Ooh yes,' she cried in encouragement.

His other hand slipped down over her belly to allow his fingers to massage the folds of flesh and slide up and down her slit. She reached back and began to fondle his balls as they slapped against her at the end of each thrust. As she did so he stopped his caressing and seized hold

65

of her by her hips. She could hear his breathing becoming more ragged as he slammed himself into her.

Pooki found she was no longer able to support herself on one hand and allowed herself to settle face down into the cushions. Jim still held her firmly by the hips and she continued to play with him as he pounded away.

Suddenly he stiffened and thrust himself even harder inside her, jerking a few times before collapsing across her. Pooki allowed herself to settle down fully, doing her best to keep Jim with her.

'Oh, wow,' he muttered, half to himself, as he lay across her.

Pooki decided that that meant he had enjoyed himself. Silently she congratulated herself. It hadn't been so bad after all – in fact, she had quite enjoyed it. Nevertheless, she wished she had been able to share his climax. Having experienced her first, male-originated orgasm, she had been greedily looking forward to her second. What would Gala do in these circumstances, she asked herself? Make darned sure she did not remain unsatisfied for long, Pooki decided. Right then, that's what she would do.

Jim rolled off her and flopped down beside her, a self-satisfied grin on his face. 'Why don't you find us a drink,' he suggested, 'and I'll rustle us up another little number?'

Obediently, Pooki headed for the kitchen. In the fridge she found a carton of orange juice. She filled a glass and padded back to the lounge.

Jim was where she had left him, except that he had pulled himself up into a sitting position. Across his lap was a backgammon board and on it was a little pile of what looked like grass and a packet of cigarette papers.

He took a long pull at the orange juice and then continued with his preparations. Pooki watched with interest as he quickly rolled three long, thin joints. Putting the board to one side he lit one and inhaled the fragrant smoke. He offered the joint to Pooki. She took a long drag and then, as Jim settled down further into the cushions, she leaned over him and gently exhaled over his limp prick.

She watched the smoke swirling through his pubic hair for a moment before bending her head to kiss him. She was rewarded by a gentle groan of approval and he shifted his legs slightly to give her more room. Soon, Pooki could feel him beginning to swell and harden and, pausing only to take a few drags from the joint, she continued.

She was fascinated by the change in his flesh. When she had started it had been like a roll of uncooked pastry, albeit slightly stickier. Now it was a solid column of hot, tight flesh. She paused again as Jim nudged her and passed her the joint. As she took a hit she studied the purplish, round head with its tiny slit.

Where Rolo's, in the few short moments she had glimpsed it, had appeared threatening to her, Jim's prick seemed friendly, now that she knew what it could offer. She passed the joint back and began to suck the straining smoothness.

To start with, Jim had been content to let her work on him without moving. Now however, he began to push upwards, simulating his earlier movements when it had been elsewhere in Pooki's body. Holding him steady with one hand, she began to toy with his balls again, occasionally running a finger along the valley she found behind them.

It was as her fingers were probing gently at the root of his member, just where it merged with the looser skin below, that she felt his surge and suddenly her mouth was being filled with a thick, warm fluid. Instinctively she swallowed as his hands grabbed her head to hold her in position.

Once his tremblings had stopped she could feel the change as the rigid, straining bar that had threatened to choke her began to soften. As he eased his grip on her hair she let him slip out of her mouth and sat up again.

'I said it before and I'll say it again,' he grinned. 'You're fantastic!'

Pooki shrugged nonchalantly and grinned back at him. Jim had obviously had enough for the moment as he gave a contented sigh and closed his eyes. Pooki watched him for a few moments before carefully rising to her feet.

Her initiation had gone quite well, she decided. Jim certainly seemed satisfied. The only trouble was, her efforts had backfired somewhat. She had hoped that, once aroused, he would have sought relief in a more conventional way. Perhaps a swim would cool her down.

Stepping out into the bright afternoon sunshine she found the beach deserted. Sprinting lightly across the sand she plunged gratefully into the gentle surf. After a few minutes and feeling suitably refreshed, she steeled herself for yet another dash across the hot sand.

She was just about to start when a voice shouted to her.

'Hang on, I'll give you a lift.'

One of the other boys loped across the sand towards her. He was wearing only a pair of ragged cut-offs but his feet seemed impervious to the heat.

Scooping Pooki into his arms he began to plod back to the huts. 'It takes a while for your soles to harden,' he explained as she hung on to his muscular shoulders for the short ride.

'Fancy a beer?' he asked once he had put her down in the shade cast by the upturned hull of a small sailing boat.

'Yes, please,' she replied, looking round for somewhere to sit.

'Why don't you wait under the hut? There's some towels spread out there.'

Pooki ducked under the veranda and sat down. The boy joined her a few moments later, carrying a couple of cans that were wet with condensation. They drank in companionable silence for a while, Pooki enjoying the bite of the cold liquid on the back of her throat.

'Just arrived?' he asked.

'Yeah, a couple of hours ago.'

'Alison said there were some new arrivals. We've just come back from town. The others are inside somewhere.' He was staring openly at Pooki's breasts.

'I'll meet them later, I guess,' she said, lying back on the towel and closing her eyes.

She was not in the least surprised to feel a hand begin stroking her breasts, or a pair of lips press themselves firmly on to hers. She opened her eyes long enough to unzip his shorts and help him out of them. She noticed with interest that there was a difference between this new piece of flesh and Jim's. She made a mental note to do a comparison, although this did not seem to be the right time.

Instead she allowed her legs to be parted and reached down to help him make his entry. The sensations were pretty much the same, she decided, although her new lover seemed to be going about things in a much more vigorous way. It was probably because Jim had been smoking, she thought.

Whatever the reason, she began to reciprocate. After much back-raking, neck-biting and hip-thrusting they both exploded against each other with wails of pleasure.

Pooki realised they had moved about six feet under the hut and her back was feeling tender where it had scraped along the sand. This was a minor discomfort when set against the feeling of wellbeing that filled her body.

She marvelled at herself. Within the space of a few

short hours she had not only been had by two different men, but everyone concerned had enjoyed themselves!

Over the next few days Pooki and Gala settled into life on the beach. Their days were spent eating, drinking and getting high, lying around in the huts, or out in the sun, and swimming, sailing and surfing. During these occupations, or at any time in between, they could also be making love.

Pooki became quite used to the gritty feel of sand underneath her bottom and a man on top, or the slightly abrasive feel of salt water mixing with her natural lubricants as someone took her in the sea.

By the end of her first week in California Pooki had been able to make a detailed comparison of ten penises. She was slightly surprised to find that although there were considerable variations in both length and thickness, once they were buried between her legs, there was no noticeable difference. Where there was a difference, she discovered, was in the manner in which the respective owners used their weapons and, although the girls were not supposed to have preferences, she found she preferred the lovemaking of Steve, the boy who had carried her over the sand on her first day.

She mentioned as much to Gala as they were sunbathing one morning.

'Yeah, he's quite good,' she agreed. 'I think Cosmic's better, though.'

'He's OK,' Pooki admitted, 'but he just seems to pump away until he's done.'

Gala grinned at her. 'Then it's up to you to liven him up a bit,' she said.

'How d'you mean?'

'Have you tried biting his shoulder just as he slips it in?' Gala enquired.

Pooki had to admit that she hadn't.

'Try it next time. What's his name, Jerry, likes you to talk dirty to him, that usually gets him going. There's all sorts of things you can try. If they don't work, try something else and remember, what can drive one guy mad can put another right off, so don't expect the same reaction every time. But don't worry, you're doing all right – they keep coming back for more, don't they?'

By the end of the second week Pooki had to agree that, although she tended to spend most time with either Steve or Jim, the other guys did indeed manage to take their turns between her thighs. Perhaps she wasn't in such demand as Gala, who rarely seemed to be able to do anything restful for more than an hour at a time before some boy would amble up and suggest a swim or a sail or a smoke.

Whatever the suggestion, the end result was the same – Gala would return with a big grin on her face while the boy disappeared for a while to regain his strength.

Occasionally, Pooki would go with some of the others into the town a few miles down the coast. There, they would pick up supplies for the group, do a little window shopping and look for one of the numerous seedy characters who always seemed to have sackfuls of grass to sell.

Although the drugs that were available on Paradise were, in fact, supplied by IGX and their contents extremely carefully controlled, it was part of the ethos of the zone that the buying, selling and using of drugs was 'illegal'. As such, the people who sold them avoided doing so openly for fear of being arrested.

On this particular day, Pooki had gone into town with Gala and two boys. Almost immediately they split up. The boys were trying to buy tickets for a rock concert that was taking place that night a few miles up the coast.

Pooki and Gala strolled up the town's main street, pausing to look in various windows.

'Don't look now,' remarked Gala as they stopped to look at a display of shoes, 'but I think we're being followed.'

'By whom?'

'Some funny little guy about three shops away.'

Pooki managed to glance casually up the street. 'I think I know who you mean. He looks a bit old for this zone.'

'He's probably some old pervert who gets his kicks molesting nubile young virgins such as ourselves,' said Gala.

'What's a virgin?' Pooki enquired innocently.

Gala choked with laughter. 'Well, whatever they are, we sure as hell aren't,' she giggled.

'It wasn't so long ago that I was,' replied Pooki.

'Hey, once it's gone, it's gone.'

'I know, and to tell you the truth I'm rather enjoying myself. Maybe I'm destined to become a galaxy-famous courtesan, fêted by rich men who travel millions of light years just to kiss my feet.'

'You can kiss my ass, you silly sod! Come on, let's have some coffee and a doughnut.'

'OK. Just one coffee, but let's make it six doughnuts.'

Laughing, arm in arm, the girls ducked into a coffee shop. When they left some time later, they walked a few hundred yards before Gala discovered she had left her purse behind.

'Hang on, I'll be with you in a minute,' she promised, heading back to the coffee shop.

Pooki carried on strolling. She hadn't gone more than a few steps when the man they had thought was following them approached her.

'Hey babe, wanna score?' he said.

Why not? thought Pooki. If we go to the gig tonight everyone will want some dope.

'Sure,' she replied, 'I'll take some grass off you.'

The man pulled her off the street into an alley.

'How much d'you want?'

'A couple of ounces,' she replied.

Quickly the man pulled some polythene bags from an inside pocket.

'There you go. Now, how about some acid?'

Pooki knew that several of the others took LSD a couple of times a week. She had never tried any herself. Her self-confidence was fragile enough when she was in full control of herself. She didn't dare risk losing it. On the other hand, some of the others might appreciate it if she brought some back.

'Yeah, OK, give me about a dozen tabs. Some of the guys might like them.'

Once again the man delved into his pockets and came up with a screw of paper. He opened it to show her the contents. Pooki paid for the drugs and was about to go when he grabbed her arm.

'Aren't you scoring for yourself, sister?'

'No, I'll stick to grass, thanks.'

'You're missing a treat, you know.' He seemed to consider for a moment. 'Tell you what. Seeing as you've just made a big deal I'll throw in a couple of extra ones just for you. These are only like a quarter of a tab, you'll hardly notice it. You'll just get a nice buzz. Hey, are you going to the gig up the coast tonight?'

'Probably, if we can get tickets.'

'Well then, drop these an hour or so before you go and you'll be amazed at the effect.'

He pressed a tiny screw of paper into Pooki's hand.

'Remember now, about an hour before you go.'

'Er, right. Thanks man.'

Pooki was still not sure she wanted to take the tabs, but it seemed the easiest way to get rid of him. She put the twist of paper into one of the breast pockets of her denim jacket. He seemed satisfied with this and giving her a last grin, scuttled out of the alley and back on to the street.

Pooki carefully buried her purchases at the bottom of the bag she was carrying before following him. Gala caught up to her a few moments later.

'Did you find it?'

'Yeah. I left it on the seat back there.' She jerked her head in the direction of the coffee shop. 'It must be true what they say about dope – I think my mind's going.'

'Speaking of which, that guy you thought was following us turned out to be a dealer. I just scored some grass and a few tabs.'

'Hey, far out! Just what we need for tonight.'

'I thought so too.'

'Do you have any skins with you? We ought to try the stuff first.'

'Good thinking, but no, I haven't.'

'Never mind, I'll buy some.'

As soon as she had bought some Gala disappeared into a boutique. Under the pretext of trying on a dress she quickly rolled a couple of joints. By the time they met up with the boys again they were nicely stoned. The boys didn't notice at first, being jubilant at having picked up enough tickets for everyone. Once they realised, however, they refused to drive anywhere until they had caught up with the girls.

Pooki had different ideas. 'Don't think we're just going to sit and watch,' she declared. 'If you're rolling up then we are too.'

'But that means you'll stay ahead of us,' they complained.

'So what's new?' giggled Gala. 'We're always ahead of you.'

'Speaking of head . . .' Cosmic pulled Gala towards him.

74

Pooki sat next to Steve as he drove back to the beach. Both of them tried to ignore the sounds coming from behind them.

Pooki forgot all about the twist of paper in her top pocket. When they were relaxing after dinner, passing round joints and cans of beer she casually laid the tabs she had bought for the others on the table, she still didn't remember them.

Consequently, Pooki went with all the others to the concert. They piled into the half dozen or so worn out pick-up trucks, Beetles and minibuses for the thirty-mile trip up the coast. Everyone was well stoned and most of the boys had a few joints stashed away for later. Despite laws to the contrary, cans of beer continued to be passed round the interiors of the vehicles. By the time they had reached the venue, parked and trekked into the concert arena, they were barely able to stand. Nobody noticed however, as most of the audience were in exactly the same condition.

Back at the beach, at around the time the concert was due to start, the man who had sold Pooki the drugs was anxiously searching the huts. If Pooki had taken the tabs he had given her she would have quickly lapsed into unconsciousness. Her friends would have assumed she had had either too much beer or too much blow or both.

They would have left her to sleep it off, the man reasoned, which would have left the way clear for her abduction.

Eventually he admitted defeat. Either she had taken them too late or not at all. If she had given them to one of her friends, they would have been left behind.

He cursed. It had taken him all this time to find the opportunity to give her the drugs. It was the first time she had been alone in all the time he had been watching her.

Now the chance had gone. He just knew that he wouldn't be given another chance before the bitch changed zones. And then he'd have to go through it all again.

He sighed heavily and trudged back over the dunes to where he had left his car. The Duke of Krantz would not be pleased. He had been hoping for an early success. The man decided to delay telling His Grace until the morning. He fished out some of the grass he had been selling. Why should they have all the fun? he thought. When in California . . .

At the concert, things were starting to warm up. Fifteen thousand not-quite-with-it people had roared their approval of the supporting bands and were now eagerly awaiting the main event.

Pooki was feeling great. A general feeling of wellbeing caused by the alcohol and drugs was being amplified by the atmosphere and the music. They had managed to elbow their way through the good-natured crowd almost to the edge of the stage. Along with everyone else they had clapped and swayed to the music.

With the start of the main act came the signal for everyone to climb to their feet and let it all hang out. Under the additional influence of rock and roll the only ones who weren't dancing were those who were so stoned as to be incapable.

It was a warm, almost sultry night with more than a hint of thunder to come. Pooki was fascinated by the animal magnetism of the lead singer as he strutted about the stage. When he dramatically ripped off his shirt and threw it away it was the signal for many of the audience to do the same.

Pooki followed Gala's lead, enthusiastically pulling off her own shirt and letting it fall on to her already discarded jacket. She revelled in the feeling of her breasts bouncing free in time to the beat of the music. The thump of the

76

bass drum, combined with the low throb of the bass guitar, seemed to hit her like a blow.

Watching Gala's dancing becoming more suggestive by the minute she found her own doing the same. She began jerking her pelvis in time to the music, shaking her head and watching, as if in a dream, the band moving about through the wildly swaying curtain of her hair.

There was a break in the music while a guitarist changed a string. To fill in, the singer chatted to the audience.

'Are you all having a good time?'

It was corny and far from original but exactly what they all wanted to hear. A vast roar of 'Ye-a-h' rolled back to the stage.

'Do you want to hear some more?'

Again the roar, even louder this time.

'There's some chicks down here dancing up a storm. Do you want to see them?'

'*Yeah!*'

Pooki realised he was referring to Gala and herself only when she found herself being half pushed, half carried on to the stage. She stood there uncertainly, blinded by the spotlights and confused by the roar of approval from the audience.

She heard a count of four from behind her and then the band broke into a fast boogie. Gala was right there with them, holding her arms up, shaking her breasts and twitching her hips. Belatedly, Pooki joined in, suddenly feeling very exposed and self-conscious. However, the singer nodded his approval and she began to lose herself to the music. During the instrumental break he joined them, parodying their movements and inciting more roars of approval from the audience.

When the number ended Pooki had no time to escape from the stage. The band launched straight into a slow blues number. Almost unconsciously she began to grind her hips to the insistent beat. She was over her initial nervousness now and beginning to enjoy herself.

She noticed Gala closing in slowly on the singer and quickly began to do the same. When they were next to him, Gala began to rub herself against him. Again Pooki followed suit. Their movements became more blatant as the singer began to stroke their breasts, first Gala's and then Pooki's.

The situation was not unlike a dream Pooki used to have, where, under the stern direction of her parents, she had to make love to someone in the middle of the planetary council chamber. In the dream Pooki had always woken to find herself covered in sweat and shaking. She was doing both now, but not only was this not a dream, she told herself, but she was actually enjoying it!

She could see rivulets of sweat running down the chests of the three of them and could feel her jeans clinging clammily to her thighs. When she noticed the singer's growing erection she realised that it wasn't just perspiration that was soaking her crotch.

It was fast becoming a sort of competition now between Gala and herself as to who could claim the most of the singer's attention as he tried to continue with the song. Both the girls were stroking him from shoulder to hip as well as raising their knees to rub his thighs with their own.

Pooki watched with a kind of lazy interest as Gala's slim fingers drifted across the front of his jeans, lingering teasingly where they bulged the most. As the band began an instrumental break he turned to Gala and pulled her into a clinch. There were more roars from the audience as they watched him kneading her breasts.

She gave a moue of disappointment as he disengaged and turned to Pooki. Acting on a wild impulse, the memory of which made her blood run cold the next day, she dropped into a crouch and, hardly knowing what she was doing, tugged down the zip of his flies.

She heard the drummer drop a beat as he saw what was happening but the rest of the band simply kept going, grinning all over their faces as they, like the spellbound audience, watched Pooki deftly pull out the singer's impressive cock and begin to suck on it.

By the time the break should have ended it was all he could do to wave frantically at the band to keep it going. There was no way he was going to be able to sing for the moment.

Pooki had to admit to herself she was having fun. Over the past couple of weeks she had discovered that not only did she enjoy the feel of a tongue between her legs, but also that she enjoyed using her tongue between someone else's legs. To do it in full view of several thousand approving and probably envious people simply heightened the pleasure. The only trouble was, it was not a very comfortable position from which to work.

She had very soon discovered, starting with Gala's lessons on the voyage out, confirmed by most of the boys from the beach, that to give and receive maximum pleasure, the parties involved should have somewhere comfortable in which to indulge themselves, preferably with no time limits imposed.

She could sense the singer was torn between his enjoyment of her ministrations and his sense of duty to the band. The loudest roar yet from the audience prompted her to look round as best she could. From the corner of her eye she saw Gala stepping out of her ankle-length peasant skirt. Naturally she was not wearing panties.

As the singer also looked to see what was happening Gala stepped towards him. It was as if she was using a magnet. He turned towards her, pulling himself away from Pooki. Gala simply put her arms round his neck and then lightly jumped up and wrapped her legs around his waist.

Not to be completely left out of things, Pooki reached round his thighs and held his prick in position as Gala lowered herself on to it.

The band were well into the swing of it all by now and immediately started playing very softly. As Gala began to raise and lower herself, partly supported by the singer and partly by Pooki, they increased their volume in time with the speed of her movements.

By the time Gala had lost all control and was writhing up and down in a frenzy, her head thrown back, mouth wide open in a scream of pure gratification, the band were building up to their own, musical, climax.

Privately, the guitarist was praying for them to finish quickly. He only had two notches left on his volume control and was rapidly running out of frets on his guitar.

At last, to the accompaniment of much shouting and cheering from the audience and cymbal-clashing and power-chord crashing from the band, the singer's knees buckled as he stabbed upwards into Gala's hot wetness. Pooki didn't think she noticed, so lost was she in her own, highly public orgasm.

Once the singer had had a quick can of beer and a few tokes provided by one of the roadies, he was able to carry on. Pooki and Gala had, meanwhile, returned to their friends.

Although they all tried their best, it was obvious that the high point of the show had come and gone and it wound up two numbers later. Gala had remembered to pick up her skirt as they left the stage but they were unable to find their shirts or Pooki's jacket. The audience had crowded forward to obtain a better view and any dropped clothing had been kicked and trampled in the surge.

In the event the girls returned to their stretch of beach

without them. Everyone plunged into the sea t̶
down and then, as the rain finally arrived, scamp̶
back to their huts to watch the lightning flickering ove̶
the bay.

Pooki was still on a high from her activities at the
concert and as a result, Jim didn't really know what hit
him. When he finally pushed her away, drained after
virtually being forced into performing four times in less
than an hour, she went looking for satisfaction elsewhere.

She found Cosmic staring dreamily out over the ocean
and shortly afterwards discovered that Gala was right.
With a little bit of encouragement he could be stimulated
into giving a girl just what she needed.

When Pooki at last prepared herself for sleep she was,
for the first time that she could remember, feeling satisfied
with herself both physically and mentally.

Chapter 4

Pooki eyed the small tattoo dubiously. That it had been expertly done there was no doubt. The tiny butterfly had been exquisitely drawn and coloured. Pooki half expected it to fly away at any moment.

The tattooing had been completely painless and it was, she was told, fully waterproof, impervious to soap and guaranteed not to fade. Nevertheless, she was not convinced that it enhanced her appearance.

The medics had reassured her that, if she didn't want to keep it after she finished in the zone, it could be just as neatly and painlessly removed.

She stroked it for the umpteenth time. There was no perceptible difference in skin texture. The butterfly felt as smooth and silky as the rest of her skin. She shrugged mentally. Maybe she would become used to it, maybe not. Either way, it was something all the girls had to endure whilst in this zone.

During their briefing, back at Central after a month in California, they had been offered a choice of designs along with a variety of positions. Pooki had opted for the butterfly, just below her right hip, more or less at the top of her thigh. She remembered Gala bursting in on her after returning from the medi-centre.

'Hi Pooks! Well, what do you think?'

'Hi Gala. About what?'

'Oops, silly me. I meant my tattoo.'

Pooki could tell from Gala's expectant grin that more was expected of her.

'Go on then,' she sighed, 'show me what you had.'

Gala's grin became positively wicked. She turned round and began to ease her one-piece off her shoulders, twitching her hips and humming some stripping music as she did so.

Slowly she began to bare more and more of her back and still no tattoo. Fully expecting to see one on her bottom, Pooki peered in vain as Gala's delectable cheeks were revealed. Even when the one-piece was on the floor and Gala, still with her back to Pooki, stood there naked, there was no sign of a tattoo.

The tune Gala was humming was reaching its end. As she hit the last few notes she spun round and lifted her left foot onto Pooki's bed. There, on the inside of her thigh, almost disappearing into the dark curls was a picture of a snake.

Pooki was impressed.

'Wow! That looks great. You'd almost believe it was trying to crawl into your . . . you know what.'

Gala was gratified by Pooki's reaction.

'That's the idea. It's showing whoever may be interested the way to heaven,' she giggled. 'Although by the time they get to see it they'll just about be there anyway.'

She began to pull her suit on again.

'Where'd you have yours done?'

Reluctantly, Pooki bared her thigh. Gala idly trailed her fingertips over it.

'In the dark you wouldn't know it was there,' she said admiringly.

Pooki shivered at her friend's touch.

83

'I wish it wasn't,' she said.

'Oh come on,' Gala snorted. 'It's only a bit of fun. You can always have it removed afterwards. I don't think I will, though. I rather like it.'

A banging on the wall brought Pooki back to the present. A quick look at her ring showed her that she was late. She had arranged to call for Gala before heading for the shops. They were going to go shopping for new evening gowns.

Giving a quick knock of acknowledgement, she began to dress. What a difference to California, she thought. There you could wear whatever you liked or even go naked if you wished. But here in Monte Carlo you had to be carefully dressed at all times.

Quickly she slipped on a cream silk shirt. It felt deliciously cool and light against her skin and she liked the feel of her breasts bobbing under it as she moved. She stepped into a flimsy pair of panties and covered them with a short white skirt before donning a matching pair of sandals. A glance in the mirror showed that the shortness of her skirt made her legs seem endless, whilst the colour showed off her tan. She gave her hair a few vigorous strokes with a brush, picked up her shoulder bag and left the room.

Gala was waiting for her by the lift, wearing a soft, pink sweater and a pair of white jeans.

'I'd nearly given up on you,' she remarked. 'Mind you, you look good enough to eat.'

'Let's hope someone else thinks so,' replied Pooki, referring to the fact that the girls had been in the zone for three days now and had yet to be picked up.

Their routine was simple. They left the hotel around mid-morning and wandered around the busy, narrow streets, browsing in shops and boutiques, more or less instantly available should they take anyone's fancy.

They would have a light lunch at one of the numerous pavement cafés before returning to their hotel which was set some way back from the exclusive seafront. After a short siesta to avoid the mid-day heat they would head to the beach or swimming pool to show off their figures in skimpy costumes.

Back at the hotel they would shower and have dinner before preparing themselves for the evening. Tonight they were due to be in the casino, offering encouragement or solace to anyone in need of it – hence their decision to find themselves some tasteful yet seductive attire.

They had a pleasant but uneventful shopping trip – uneventful, that is, for Pooki. They were just about to pay for their dresses when an elderly man, impeccably dressed, entered the shop. He stared at Gala for a few moments and then approached.

'Excuse me, my dear,' he began, moving Gala gently but firmly away from the cashier, 'but a beautiful young thing like yourself should not have to buy a dress like that. It should be a gift, from an admirer such as myself. Please allow me to present it to you.'

He turned to the cashier and reached for his wallet. Gala raised her eyebrows at Pooki, grinned and shrugged. She left the shop arm in arm with her benefactor and Pooki found herself alone. Stunned by the speed at which she had been deserted, she paid for her own dress and headed back to her hotel.

She decided to forgo her siesta in favour of some solitude on the beach. Borrowing a moped from another employee who worked in the hotel she rode a mile or so down the coast. A rocky promontory seemed promising, so she bumped off the road along a little path for a short way and then abandoned the machine to walk the fifty yards or so to the sea.

After clambering over the rocks for a while she found

a place that seemed perfect. It was a flat slab about two feet above the water. An overhang meant no one would be able to look down on her, whilst the rocks to the left and right made an almost complete screen from both sides. Pooki wasted no time dropping her bag and stripping off her shorts and T-shirt.

There was just enough depth for her to dive straight into the sea. After cooling down for a few minutes she climbed out, spread her towel, applied a little lotion and lay face down in the sun.

Her all-over tan was already beginning to fade around her hips and now was a good opportunity to top it up. After twenty minutes she felt herself beginning to burn so she dived into the water again.

This time she applied the lotion to her front. Rubbing the oil over her breasts brought memories flooding back. She remembered how she and Steve had smothered each other in oil after staying out sailing a little too long. Just applying the stuff had been a turn-on and she had been almost begging for him by the time he had finished.

She watched with interest as her nipples stiffened under her repeated stroking. Quickly she covered her belly and thighs and then prepared to do her groin area. It wouldn't do to burn herself there, she decided.

She poured a little oil into the hollows where her thighs joined her body. She had to spread her legs a little in order to prevent the oil running away and the heat on her exposed pussy felt good. She lay back, closed her eyes and continued her gentle massage.

Soon the combination of heat and caress began to have their effects. She moved one hand back to her breasts to check that they weren't drying out. She decided they could use some more oil and applied some. As her left hand alternated between breasts and nipples her right was making sure her groin was still protected.

Her fingers slid leisurely up and down the slippery folds of flesh, working the oil over every possible square millimetre. Some of it had run down the tops of her thighs, so she rubbed it in, right round to the tight little aperture further back.

That felt good too, so she spent some time experimenting with a fingertip. She managed to make herself moan a few times before switching her attentions back to more familiar ground.

Feeling totally abandoned, she continued to massage as much of herself as she could before letting out a long shuddering sigh of release.

Her relaxation afterwards was rudely interrupted by the sound of someone clapping gently. Startled, she sat up and looked around. Perched on a nearby rock, about the only position from which it was possible to see into her little solarium, was a man in his early thirties. He was very brown and very muscular and very naked. Even his cock was brown, Pooki noted, gratified to see that it was standing up in a most interesting way.

He had obviously been watching her for some time and she would have been insulted if he had not had an erection of some kind.

'How long have you been watching me?' she demanded.

'Oh, about ten minutes or so,' he grinned.

Pooki thought his teeth looked very white in contrast to the rest of him.

'Well, what are you doing here and where are your clothes?' she asked.

'My clothes are back on my boat.' He pointed to a small sailing boat moored about fifty yards away. 'I was just sailing along, minding my own business, when I saw you on the rocks. You looked so interesting I thought I just had to take a closer look.'

87

'I see,' said Pooki. 'Aren't you worried your boat will drift away?'

'It shouldn't do. I dropped an anchor.'

His erection seemed as firm as ever, Pooki saw. It seemed a shame to let it go to waste.

She moved over to make some room on her towel.

'Either go away or come and sit down,' she commanded. 'Squinting up at you is giving me a headache.'

'Now, that would never do,' he smiled, moving nimbly to her side.

'Would you mind if I borrowed some of your oil?' he asked apologetically. 'I'd hate to burn.'

'Help yourself,' Pooki passed over the bottle and watched with interest as her new friend poured some into his hand.

Slowly, tantalisingly, he began to rub the oil on to his erection, never taking his eyes from Pooki's face as he did so. She found herself licking her lips as his penis seemed to swell even more and began to gleam dully.

'That's better,' he said, passing the bottle back.

'Even so, you'll have to be careful. I wouldn't risk it for more than ten minutes if I were you.'

'I'll have to find somewhere shady for it then, won't I?' He looked challengingly at her.

'That would seem to be the wisest course,' she agreed.

'Now where would be a suitable place?' He looked round as though seeking inspiration.

'Perhaps you could rub a little oil on me while you're thinking?' Pooki suggested innocently. 'Seeing as you have disturbed my solitude.'

'That sounds fair,' he conceded. 'Now, where should I start?'

Pooki left him to figure that one out for himself. She just lay back and waited.

Within three minutes she felt him slide easily into her well-oiled and expectant slit.

'This is a trifle presumptuous of you,' she murmured, locking her legs around his waist.

'It was the only piece of shade I could find,' he explained, beginning an easy rhythm. 'It might be shady,' he remarked a few moments later, 'but it's certainly no cooler!'

'Well, what did you expect?' Pooki protested. 'It's been baking out here for an hour at least.'

'I can tell.' His breath was coming in short gasps now, matching his thrusts. 'In fact I'd say it was almost done!'

'I think you're right,' Pooki gasped in return, the rest of her words dissolving into a series of little cries and moans. She felt him shudder into her and then lie still.

'Well,' he said at last, 'I've done all I can to put out the fire.'

'So I notice,' she remarked drily.

'But maybe I'd better stick around just in case?'

'How thoughtful of you.'

In the event, it was just as well that he did. Three more times that afternoon they agreed that either he needed to find some more shade or she needed her fire quenching.

When he finally swam back to his boat, Pooki waved goodbye, feeling pleased with herself. With no Gala to rely on and no drugs to relax her, she had managed to cope quite well. She never found out who the man was, although he did say that he might see her at the casino later. She returned to her hotel, no longer dreading the coming evening.

After dinner Pooki began to make herself ready. The dress she had bought was a snug-fitting sheath in black silk. It buttoned up to her neck and had long sleeves. She had chosen it for three reasons, the first being that, like her white miniskirt, it showed off her tan. Secondly, it fitted like a glove and accentuated her figure, although she belatedly realised that if she were to wear anything under it, its lines would be spoiled. The last reason for choosing it was the slit up the side. As long as she didn't move there was no hint of it. The moment she took a step however, the seam parted to reveal a long, slim leg topped by a tiny butterfly.

As soon as she saw it Gala had insisted that Pooki buy it. Pooki agreed that it made her look sensational but the idea of appearing at a formal and highly public occasion with only a thin covering of silk between nudity and the world was something she was not sure she was ready for. But swallowing her doubts, Pooki had taken a deep breath and agreed to take it.

When she made her entrance at the casino, heads turned in her direction. She was an arresting sight – tall, blonde, slim, elegant and sheathed in figure-hugging black. Within a few moments, several men had indicated that they would welcome her as their companion. Pooki even imagined one or two of the women had looked questioningly at her.

She spent the first half hour drifting round the various rooms, vainly trying to spot her friend of the afternoon. Deciding at last that he was not there she resigned herself to finding someone else. With this in mind she took a spare place at one of the roulette wheels and waited.

A distinguished-looking gentleman in his late forties was occupying the place on her left. As the wheel spun and they made their bets they struck up a conversation. Soon they were chatting like old friends and after he had allowed his hand to rest on hers a couple of times she reciprocated by putting hers on his arm once or twice.

When he suggested they try a different game she readily agreed and allowed him to take her arm and steer her towards a blackjack table. Pooki stood behind his chair and watched as he played recklessly, winning large amounts now and again but nonetheless steadily losing.

After half an hour he became bored with that and they made their way to another roulette table. Here there was no room to sit, so they played standing up, leaning over to place their bets.

It seemed quite natural for him to slip his arm round her waist and Pooki felt a little shiver go through her as the evening's direction now seemed assured.

For a while he continued to play at the roulette wheel, one hand casually round her waist, the tips of his fingers just managing to find their way through the break in the silk and on to her thigh.

Having lost a further amount he turned to her apologetically. 'That's all for me, I'm afraid, my dear.'

'I'm sorry I couldn't bring you better luck,' Pooki apologised in turn.

'You could allow me to buy you a drink perhaps?' he suggested.

'That sounds like a good idea,' she said. 'But is there somewhere quieter we could go? It's so hot and noisy in here.'

'I know just the place,' he smiled.

The place Roger Forquet had in mind turned out to be one of the gleaming white yachts Pooki had often admired. Their sensual sleekness promised undreamed-of luxury below their polished decks. Roger's was too big to tie up in the harbour and so was forced to anchor just outside.

It fully lived up to her expectations. As they made their way up the companionway from the speedboat that had been waiting for them at the quayside, she felt a quiver of anticipation. They had yachts back on Rontar, it was true, but none so sumptuous as this.

She was ushered into what Roger called the stateroom.

91

If it had been a house she supposed it would have been called the lounge. For all the differences she could see, it might as well have been in a house. There was the deep-pile carpet, the leather furniture, the paintings hanging on the wall – even a fire in a fireplace. Only the slight rocking motion and the small, thickly glazed windows suggested this was not a room in a rich man's house.

After a servant presented them with glasses of champagne, Roger excused himself. He returned a few moments later with a tall, equally elegant woman. Pooki guessed she was about ten years younger than Roger, about thirty-eight. She was beautifully dressed in a simple white blouse and a long, black skirt that fitted snugly round her hips but flared out towards the floor. The only thing that spoiled the effect was that her left leg was in plaster and she needed crutches with which to walk.

'May I introduce you to my wife?' Roger smiled.

Once the introductions were made and everyone was seated, Chantelle explained, rather sheepishly, that she had slipped trying to climb into the speedboat a few days previously and had broken her leg.

'Now they've got me back on this boat,' she confessed, 'I daren't try to leave it again. Poor Roger has to go ashore without me.'

'That's the least of your problems, though, isn't it, my love?'

'Yes, it is,' she agreed ruefully, 'but you've made an excellent choice, my dear, so I dare say things will improve.'

Pooki wondered what they were talking about. She was even more puzzled when Roger excused himself again and bade them both goodnight. She was not left in doubt for long.

After finishing her drink Chantelle pulled her crutches towards herself.

'Would you mind awfully helping me to my cabin?' she asked. 'I feel so helpless with these damn things.'

'Yes, of course.'

Chantelle's cabin was down a short corridor leading forward from the stateroom. Fortunately it was on the same deck so there were no stairs to negotiate. Once in the cabin Chantelle looked at Pooki rather pathetically.

'You'll have to help me undress,' she said.

Once Chantelle had unbuttoned her blouse, Pooki had to support her as she laid down her crutches and shrugged it off. Her breasts subsequently revealed, were small and firm. Pooki found herself admiring their neat curves and the flat belly below them.

Chantelle smiled as she noted Pooki's interest. 'Now my skirt, if you please.'

Chantelle had to hop out of it once Pooki had dropped it to the carpeted deck and then stood, unsteadily, in nothing but the smallest of G-strings. As far as Pooki could see there was not an ounce of fat on her. Her thighs were slim, almost muscular, whilst her buttocks were as firm as those of a sixteen-year-old. She made Pooki feel positively plump.

'Just one more left,' Chantelle announced cheerfully, 'and then you could hold the bathroom door for me.'

Pooki carefully peeled the scrap of silk downwards. It felt slightly damp and exuded a soft, musky scent. She felt her own dampness beginning as she saw Chantelle's soft, pink lips were gleaming with moisture.

The lack of pubic hair caught her by surprise. Chantelle noticed her reaction.

'It's a nuisance having to shave every day,' she explained, 'but it's so much cooler. Besides, Roger likes me this way. I think he must have a thing about young girls.'

Before Pooki could answer Chantelle hobbled towards

a door and paused expectantly. She re-emerged amidst a soft cloud of perfume, slightly musky like her own, natural scent.

She smiled at Pooki.

'Come sit beside me on the bed,' she suggested.

Pooki helped her to lean back against a pile of pillows and sat obediently next to her.

'You have lovely hair, my dear,' Chantelle remarked, stroking it softly. 'Is it natural?'

Pooki smiled and stood up. She raised the hem of her dress until Chantelle was able to confirm for herself the natural colour of her hair.

'Why don't you take that lovely dress off?' she suggested. 'It will only get creased and it's far too hot in here anyway.'

This was not strictly true. Somewhere in the ship, an air conditioner was sending a gentle draught of cool air through a vent near the ceiling. The temperature in the cabin was perfectly comfortable. Pooki decided that it would not be polite to contradict her hostess, however, and gracefully shrugged her way out of her dress.

'You could hang it over that chair,' Chantelle suggested, her eyes gleaming at the sight of Pooki's body.

Pooki returned to her position next to Chantelle, on the bed, and Chantelle started stroking her hair again. Only this time it was not the hair on Pooki's head that was being stroked.

'It's this blasted leg,' Chantelle explained, her voice beginning to thicken as she felt Pooki's body responding to her touch. 'I'm terrified that if I let Roger screw me he's going to hurt me. So I sent him off to find a sympathetic girl. I'm sure we can manage just as well without him for once.'

'I'm sure we can.' Pooki had to break off from nuzzling

one of Chantelle's nipples to reply. 'But won't he feel a little left out of things?' She returned to the nipple.

'Oooh, keep doing that, keep doing that. He'll get by. There just happen to be two very attractive female seamen on board this boat.' Chantelle judged the time was right to slide a finger into Pooki. Pooki's reaction proved she was correct. 'And if I know Roger, I wouldn't be a bit surprised if, even as I speak, he's pumping semen into seamen.'

Pooki chuckled as she began to slither down over Chantelle's flat belly to the hairless little mound below. Soon her inquisitive tongue was darting and probing into the soft flesh it encountered. 'Yummy,' she said, pausing for breath.

'Now don't be selfish dear,' Chantelle chided gently. 'Remember I'm not as mobile as you. You'll have to move round a bit so I can try some of yours.'

Obligingly, Pooki wriggled round until she had a thigh on each side of Chantelle's head. For a while neither of them spoke, although they continued to explore each other.

Pooki found herself hard put to concentrate as Chantelle was rapidly driving her past the point of no return. In desperation she pushed a sodden fingertip into Chantelle's anus, remembering the feeling it had given her. She was rewarded by a muffled groan and a frantic arching of Chantelle's back. Thus encouraged, she worked her finger fully in, still sucking hard on the stiff little bud between her lips.

Chantelle was forced to stop playing with Pooki as she lost control and shuddered helplessly, clinging almost painfully tightly to Pooki's hips as she did so.

Pooki carefully disentangled herself and straightened up alongside Chantelle. After a while she opened her eyes and smiled gratefully at Pooki.

'That was very, very good, my dear. I feel quite worn out. Why don't you send for some more champagne?'

Pooki pressed the bell-push next to the bed. Almost immediately a muscular sailor appeared. He showed absolutely no reaction to the sight of the two naked women sprawled on the bed, hair tousled and legs entwined.

Once he had left with their order Chantelle turned to Pooki.

'If you get the chance you ought to try him. He doesn't talk much, but boy can he fuck! However, the thought of him in my condition is not a pleasant one.'

She sighed sadly and Pooki gave her a kiss to cheer her up. Her lips tasted of Pooki's juices, a taste Pooki was becoming used to, having encountered it on Gala's lips as well as on those of the boys in California. And not just on their lips, she reminded herself.

Chantelle's tongue was probing round inside Pooki's mouth while her hands were busy teasing Pooki's nipples. Neither of them heard the sailor return with the champagne. It was just there by the bedside when they paused for breath.

Pooki began dribbling champagne from her fingertips over Chantelle's still-engorged lips.

'Stars, that's cold,' she gasped and then gave a different sort of gasp as Pooki quickly bent down to lick it all off.

Chantelle tolerated the treatment for a few more minutes before begging her to stop.

'I need something inside me,' she gasped.

'Shall I ring for the steward?' suggested Pooki.

'Of course not! Use my Wondavibe.'

She waved weakly in the general direction of some drawers. Pooki had a quick rummage and found it almost immediately. It was identical to Gala's and began to throb as soon as Pooki gave it a shake.

She began carefully, just as Gala had done to her, playing it over Chantelle's taut little nipples. Soon she had moved it down and was teasing Chantelle by running it round and round her eager hole without quite pushing it in.

'You rotten tease,' Chantelle moaned. 'Stick it in! For Star's sake stick it in!'

'Not just yet,' Pooki grinned, enjoying the sight of Chantelle writhing helplessly on the bed. 'I don't think you're quite ready yet.'

'I'll get even with you for this,' she vowed. 'Now stop messing about. I want it in me.'

'Where?' Pooki asked innocently. 'In here?' she ran the head round to where her finger had been earlier. 'Or here?' she dragged it back along the slippery channel to where she had started.

'In my cunt!' Chantelle almost screamed. 'Shove it in my cunt!'

Her words died away as Pooki obliged. Slowly she began to work it in and out, trying to copy the now familiar movements of a man. As she did so she increased its length and width. Chantelle was trying her best to thrust up against it, her head rolling from side to side on the pillows.

Pooki adjusted the texture, bringing further moans from Chantelle as she felt the Wondavibe change inside her. Her climax was not long in coming and was even more spectacular than her last.

Over the last of the champagne she looked consideringly at Pooki.

'You made me beg,' she said. 'No one has ever made me beg before.'

Pooki shrugged modestly.

'But I'll have my revenge. You wait and see. Now, I want to watch you do it to yourself. You've exhausted me but before I go to sleep I want to see you do it.'

Obediently, Pooki put down her glass and picked up the vibrator.

Pooki awoke with a vague feeling of unease. There was something not quite right. She lay there trying to decide what it was. Gradually the events of the previous night surfaced in her memory and she realised it was the motion of the boat that had disturbed her.

It seemed to be pitching more this morning, but she decided that this was probably due to the breeze. Carefully sliding out from under Chantelle's possessive arm she headed for the bathroom and the shower she noticed it contained.

Afterwards she puzzled over what to wear. Somehow her silk evening dress seemed a little inappropriate for early morning on a yacht. She settled for a large towelling robe she found hanging on the back of the bathroom door. Chantelle was still dead to the world, so Pooki tiptoed out and headed for the stateroom.

She found Roger sitting there, reading a paper and drinking a cup of coffee. He rose to his feet as Pooki entered.

'Good morning, my dear. I trust you slept well?'

'Extremely well, thank you.'

Pooki was distracted by the sight of a table laden with breakfast things just beyond the double doors of the stateroom. Roger followed her gaze.

'Forgive me. What must you think of me? Would you care for some breakfast? Chantelle usually eats in bed.'

'Don't I know,' Pooki grinned. 'But yes, I am feeling a trifle peckish.'

'Would you like it on deck,' he gestured to the table, 'or shall I have it brought in?'

'No, no. On deck will be fine.'

Roger inclined his head graciously and gestured for her to go first. The piece of deck was at the stern of the boat. Immediately outside the stateroom was the table and a few chairs. Behind them were a few mattresses which Pooki presumed were for sunbathing on. A canvas screen protected the deck from the sun but could obviously be rolled back when desired. She looked across the harbour and blinked. All she could see was sea. The boat must have swung on her anchor she decided and turned round to look the other way.

There was still no sign of Monte Carlo, however. What she saw instead was the coastline sliding slowly past about two miles away. Villas, trees and villages could be seen but no Monte Carlo.

Back in Monte Carlo a man was searching in vain for the yacht that had been anchored just beyond the harbour only the night before. When he was at last convinced that the boat was gone he returned to his hotel and prepared a message for the Duke of Krantz. Scratch another plan he thought bitterly.

On the departed yacht Pooki turned full circle to face Roger. He held up his hands in a defensive gesture.

'Not my idea,' he said quickly. 'Chantelle thought you might like to take a little cruise.'

Pooki sat down and began to butter a croissant.

'When did you see her?' she asked.

'I popped in last night. You were asleep.'

'She did say something about getting her own back,' Pooki recalled. 'Being stuck on a strange boat in the middle of the sea with only an evening gown to wear is a fairly neat revenge.'

Roger smiled and sat down to keep her company while she ate. After breakfast he gave her a tour of the yacht and Pooki was impressed by the size and luxury of the craft. She was also impressed by the crew. They were all immaculately dressed in white and were without doubt a fine-looking lot. Most of them were Paradise employees like herself, but there were a few who weren't.

Pooki had asked one of the controllers back at Central how it was that so many visitors to Paradise seemed happy to be workers, or servants, for others. The answer was primarily down to credits. A vacation as a worker was far cheaper than one such as Roger had decided upon.

The 'work' was never really arduous and the Paradise employees were instructed to be as generous with their favours to these 'co-workers' as they were to their 'bosses'. The 'bosses' had first choice, however.

Even so, being able to brag that you had simply been a worker on Paradise was enough to make you the envy of your friends back on whichever planet you lived.

By the time Pooki's tour was over it was time for lunch. Having had such a late breakfast Pooki wasn't really hungry but as both Roger and Chantelle, who had finally put in an appearance, insisted, she nibbled at some cheese and ate a couple of peaches.

Chantelle was wearing what, under normal circumstances, would be a very sexy, yellow bikini. The top half was barely big enough to cover her nipples whilst the lower half was not much more than a G-string. Unfortunately, the effect was once again spoiled by the plaster cast which stretched from foot to mid-thigh.

'When I finally have the damn thing removed,' she complained, 'I'm going to have one brown leg and one white one.'

Roger and Pooki made sympathetic noises and then, lunch finished, they all stretched out on the mattresses to catch a little sun. Roger thumbed a remote and the overhead screen rolled back, flooding the area with sunshine. There was a gentle breeze blowing across the stern which kept them from becoming too hot and after a while Pooki found herself nodding off to sleep.

When she awoke she was alone. The overhead screen had been unfurled again which was probably just as well, she thought, as otherwise she could have been burnt. She tried to sit up to see what had happened to the robe she had been wearing but found that she couldn't.

After a moment's panic she became aware that she was, in fact, tied down. Someone had very carefully and very gently tied her wrists and ankles to some hooks she had noticed before, but put down as being used for lashing down furniture in bad weather.

She was not uncomfortable, she realised. The silk scarves were not even noticeable until she tried to move. They allowed her a few inches of movement in various directions, but basically she was stuck, legs apart and arms outspread, on her back. There was not a lot she could do, she decided, until someone let her go. She resigned herself to waiting.

In fact, she didn't have long to wait. Roger popped his head out from the stateroom and saw she was awake. A few moments later he emerged, helping Chantelle. A crew member positioned a chair for her and she sat down. She caught Pooki's eye and smiled. From where she was sitting she could see every intimate part of Pooki's anatomy. The crew member returned with an ice bucket, a bottle of wine and two glasses.

Once the wine had been opened Chantelle sipped delicately, her eyes devouring Pooki's exposed body.

'I'm ready, dear,' she announced.

Roger put down his own glass and knelt next to Pooki. 'Where should I start?' he asked Chantelle.

She thought for a moment, her head cocked slightly to one side.

'With her feet, I think,' she decided.

Roger knelt down and, taking hold of Pooki's left ankle, began to massage her foot. Pooki, who up until then had been more than a little worried about her situation, relaxed a little as Roger's strong fingers expertly massaged the sole of her foot. When he had finished he repeated the treatment on the other one.

He looked up at Chantelle, who nodded, and then began to massage Pooki's calves. When he had worked his way up to her knees he began to use his lips as well. Pooki had never had the smooth skin of the backs of her knees kissed before and found the experience quite pleasant.

Soon Roger had progressed upwards to her thighs and the combination of his hands kneading and his lips teasing was beginning to have a profound effect on her. She began to wriggle her bottom slightly, willing him to move even higher. She could feel herself starting to lubricate in anticipation of what was surely to follow.

When Roger had finally arrived at the top of her thighs she was already imagining what his lips and fingers would feel like once they began their assault on her helpless slit. She could feel his breath on her lips and strained towards him. When a finger brushed lightly across her clitoris she gasped at the shock, even though she was expecting it.

Suddenly he stopped. Pooki looked down in annoyance to see him sitting back on his heels calmly sipping his drink. Chantelle was smiling down at her with every appearance of nonchalance, but Pooki couldn't help but notice the darker yellow patch slowly spreading between her legs.

Roger put down his drink and peeled off his shirt. He had a well-developed chest without being overmuscular, and the light sheen of sweat which covered his body made it all the more appealing.

He knelt by her side and began stroking her face and hair. Bending over her he began to kiss her gently, on her cheeks, her eyelids, her ears and throat. He ran his tongue the length of her jawbone and nibbled her neck. At first Pooki had turned her face eagerly towards him, expecting him to kiss her on her lips, but he quickly moved away and began somewhere else.

By now Pooki was more than ready for him. She could feel her juices trickling down the tops of her thighs and round to her bottom. She found it incredibly frustrating that he was doing all these heavenly things to her and she couldn't even touch him.

When he moved down on to her breasts she thought she was going to explode. The nipples had been stiff for quite some time and although he played with them expertly enough, his attentions only heightened her frustration. Alternating between breasts he would squeeze and knead one while sucking on the nipple of the other.

Then, at a murmur from Chantelle, he moved lower. His hand slid across her belly and on to her mound. He paused for a moment, his finger gently plucking at the soft blonde fur, before continuing down along a thigh.

Pooki was moaning steadily now, her nerves stretched as tight as guitar strings as Roger maintained his teasing.

A new dimension was added to her frustration as Chantelle passed him her Wondavibe and its vibrating tip began to repeat all Roger's earlier caresses. He was obviously expert in its use as each time she thought she was going to win and he would nudge her over the edge of release, he would change his angle of attack and she would slip back a little from her climax.

In all of this he was being directed by Chantelle. She was watching Pooki's reactions carefully and would swiftly warn Roger if she thought Pooki was nearing release.

'Leave her thigh now,' she would say. 'Work on her left nipple for a while.'

Pooki felt as though she was lying in a puddle – that is, the few times her body was actually on the mattress. Whether it was the sweat which was pouring off her, or her juices which were in full flow, she didn't know or care. Most of the time she was arching herself towards Roger, demanding more. But every so often she was forced to settle back again to give her muscles a rest.

When Roger took another break from his tormenting of her and poured Chantelle and himself another drink, Pooki noticed that the scrap of cloth between her legs was now a completely different shade of yellow than that of her top. Chantelle was almost as aroused as she was herself.

When Roger took off his shorts, revealing a very respectable erection, Pooki forced herself not to look. Surely he was going to put her out of her misery this time. She was sure that he wouldn't even have time to push it more than halfway in her before she exploded.

When she felt his penis nudging her face she had to open her eyes. There it was, right in front of her, a gorgeous deep red. She opened her mouth without even thinking, desperate for him to let her suck it.

He paused and glanced back at Chantelle. She had given up all pretence of nonchalance and was busily fingering herself, the sodden G-string now discarded. Pooki could imagine all too clearly what sensations she would be feeling and tried to whisper to Roger.

Her words came out as a croak, although it was just discernible: 'Let me, Roger, let me suck it, please!'

Roger inched forwards until the head was just within Pooki's reach. She flicked at it with her tongue and just managed to touch it before he pulled it away again. Then he knelt between her thighs and used his cock to massage the other, equally greedy pair of lips it encountered.

'Yes, yes,' she moaned. 'Just a little further, just a little further. Oooh, I want it in me. Put it in me, please just push it in. Just a little bit, please.'

She was startled to hear Chantelle's voice next to her. Somehow she had managed to move herself from the chair to the next mattress.

'No, Roger! Put it in me!'

Roger, too caught up in his game to notice Chantelle's change of position, turned to her in surprise.

'But darling, what about your leg?'

'To hell with my leg! Watching you doing those things to her has got me so worked up I'll worry about my leg afterwards. Now, leave her alone and fuck me!'

Pooki could not believe this was happening. Having been subjected to the most thorough arousal she could imagine it was possible to have, she was now being abandoned. Even worse, she was the unwilling witness to the slaking of Chantelle's lust. Under normal circumstances she might have quite enjoyed watching, but these circumstances were far from normal.

She gritted her teeth and tried to force her consciousness away from what was going on next to her. It proved impossible. She watched Chantelle raising her hips to encourage Roger's entry. She almost wept as she heard their sighs of gratification as he buried himself to the full.

They were oblivious of her as they writhed and twisted. They seemed to go on and on interminably before they shuddered and gasped and moaned and finally lay still.

When Roger helped Chantelle to her feet some time later, they seemed to notice Pooki for the first time.

'You'd better tell someone to untie her,' Chantelle suggested, almost as an afterthought, as they disappeared into the stateroom.

The sailor who had served Pooki with champagne the previous night came to untie her. He had barely loosened the last knot before she was scrabbling at his trousers with frantic fingers. If he had refused her she would have thrown herself overboard.

As it was, he proved every bit as satisfying as Chantelle had said, although, Pooki confessed afterwards to Gala when they met up again at Central, she would have settled for virtually anything that was stiff and reasonably long.

Chapter 5

Pooki collapsed, exhausted, on to her bed. She had an hour's break before returning to the rehearsal room and resuming the intensive practice. Gala and some of the other girls had gone to have some lunch but Pooki didn't feel like any. She was just too tired. Maybe after she had rested for a while.

Since returning from the Mediterranean zone they had been subjected to a full briefing on their new assignment and then told to report for rehearsals. That last assignment seemed an age away.

After Chantelle had exacted her revenge, life on the boat settled into a more conventional routine. Pooki had found herself being shared by Roger and his wife. Often, she would be lying, physically drained by Chantelle's demands, when she would buzz for her husband on the intercom.

Roger would then appear and proceed to make use of her while Chantelle, propped up on one elbow, would watch with interest, offering suggestions and encouragement. The encouragement was usually in the form of words, invariably obscene, which acted as a spur to Roger's actions.

Sometimes she took a more active part in the proceedings, fondling his balls or slapping his buttocks. If she thought Pooki was not responding sufficiently she would slip her hand between them to play with her clitoris.

Once or twice Chantelle drove them both into a frenzy by using a finger in each anus as they heaved about next to where she lay.

After Roger had gone, she often dived straight between Pooki's trembling thighs and proceeded to lick Pooki clean.

'I just adore a man's juices,' she would grin, greedily, licking her lips to make sure she hadn't missed any. 'Especially Roger's and even more especially if they're mixed with someone else's.'

Pooki was usually too shattered to reply and although the surreptitious application of aphro-gel meant she was always able to respond in a satisfactory manner, there were times when she just wanted the healing oblivion of sleep.

Things had been a little easier when they called in at Monte Carlo again. Pooki was left on the boat when the other two went ashore. Roger returned with half a dozen guests, four men and two women, and Chantelle returned without her plaster. She still had to use a stick until her leg regained its strength, but thanks to the drugs she had been given, she was able to dispense with it after three days.

The extra guests were Roger's idea of celebrating the removal of the cast. Pooki was grateful for the lessening demands made upon herself, although she was never able to sleep alone and frequently found herself in two or three different beds at various times during the course of any given day.

She thought that returning to Central would give her a welcome break. Insofar as sex was concerned she was right, but the demands on her body continued unabated.

At present they were learning the routines they would be using when they assumed the role of saloon girls in the Wild West zone. The role itself was fairly straightforward. They would perform two or three times each night and act as waitresses the rest of the time. Naturally, if they caught a cowboy's fancy, they were expected to invite him up to their room in the 'hotel' above the bar.

Some of the girls were assigned the role of squaws for those who wanted to be Red Indians. One or two acted the lonely schoolteacher, often woken in the middle of the night as a cowboy fulfilled his 'rape' fantasy.

But learning the routines was no joke. To start with they had to wear wrist and ankle bands. These were controlled by a microwave link from a computer and virtually forced the girls' arms and legs through the correct movements of their dances. They had been warned not to resist the urging of the bands as they could tear muscles and ligaments that way.

As they became used to being jerked around like puppets and as the steps became more familiar, they were able to move with the bands and suddenly everything became smoother and more realistic. It was from one such session that Pooki was taking a breather.

Two days later they were speeding through the tunnels on their way to the zone. They were all much fitter than they had been a few days earlier. If it hadn't been for the special drugs they took each night, they would have been incapable of walking. As it was, they didn't even feel stiff.

The train left them below an abandoned shack a couple of miles out of town. When they emerged they found a stagecoach waiting for them and they all piled in for the ride into town. They arrived mid-morning and were shown to their rooms in the hotel. As soon as they had freshened up they went downstairs to the saloon.

The layout of the saloon was exactly the same as the

one in which they had spent so many exhausting hours practising. After a short time familiarising themselves with everything, they strolled up and down the main street, letting those who hadn't witnessed their arrival know that there were new girls in town.

The afternoon was spent having a last rehearsal in preparation for their debut that night. The only difference Pooki could notice between the rehearsal room and the actual venue was the stale smell of tobacco smoke and alcohol which lingered in the air.

For once Pooki was ready early and went to talk to Gala as she struggled into her flouncy red dress, black stockings and high heels.

Gala clipped her stockings on to their suspender belt and pointed to her snake before letting the dress fall back down.

'I might even have another done before I leave here,' she said.

'I haven't made my mind up about mine yet,' said Pooki. 'But we may be sent to a zone where such things didn't exist.'

'I never thought of that,' said Gala. 'Ah well, we shall see. Are you ready?'

'Of course I am!' Pooki retorted indignantly. 'I'm waiting for you, remember?'

'So you are,' laughed Gala. 'Well, let's go suck it to them.'

'Er, don't you mean sock it to them?'

'No!'

Business was brisk in the saloon. Many of the townsfolk had dropped in to see the new girls in action and for the first hour Pooki and Gala were busy serving drinks, flirting with the customers and trying to prevent their bottoms from being pinched black and blue.

Their first show was given rapturous applause. Whenever the girls did some high kicks, revealing their previously hidden charms, the atmosphere became decidedly warm. As the girls cartwheeled off the stage they left their audience stamping on the tables, peppering the ceiling with bullets and screaming for more. They had to be consoled by the news that the show would be repeated at the end of the evening.

When the girls returned to serving drinks, the hands that had previously contented themselves with slaps and pinches now developed the tendency of slipping under the dresses and then heading upwards to check that the girls were still wearing no knickers.

Although the customers were allowed to proposition the girls, they were not allowed to go upstairs until after the second show. Judging from the mood of some of the cowboys, this seemed a sensible rule. Otherwise it was more than likely that there would have been no girls available to do another show.

Pooki and Gala had promised a couple of cowboys sitting near the stage that they would indeed be free to have a drink after the show.

'But not down here, boys,' Gala had protested. 'It's far too noisy.'

This appeared to be just what the cowboys had been thinking. During the second show, Pooki and Gala had made a point of flicking up their dresses each time they were in front of the cowboys' table. Since all the other girls were doing similar things for their dates, the temperature in the room was several degrees higher during the second show than it was during the first. The air was now not only thick with smoke and whiskey fumes, but with anticipation and lust also.

At last, to much cheering, whistling and other sundry applause, the girls cartwheeled off for the second time. As they emerged from the wings back onto the floor of the saloon they were quickly claimed. Soon, amid much laughter and mock reluctance, the dozen or so girls were either finishing last drinks or heading for the stairs.

Pooki and Luke followed Gala and Jeff along the wooden corridor to their rooms. Bidding each other goodnight, accompanied by nods and winks, they entered their rooms.

Behind a screen standing in one corner of the room was a large tin bath. While the girls had been approaching the end of their act it had been filled with hot, soapy water. A bucket, still steaming with yet more hot water, stood next to it.

The impression was that a servant had carried countless such buckets up to each room, providing the girls with a chance to freshen up after their exertions. The reality was that there was a hidden tap behind a false panel and the water was piped in, in a matter of seconds, from a tank in the service area underground.

Pooki disentangled herself from Luke's amorous clutches and headed for the screen.

'Why don't you have yourself a drink, honey, while I make myself all pretty for you?'

'OK, but don't be long now.'

Luke unstrapped his gunbelt and put it carefully on a small table. As Pooki disappeared behind the screen he was hopping about on one foot, trying to pull off a boot.

Quickly, she pulled off her dress and threw it carelessly into a corner. Tomorrow it would be spirited away to return, fresh and clean, in time for Pooki's next session in the saloon.

She kicked off her shoes, unclipped and rolled down her stockings, pulled off her suspender belt and stepped into the tub. A few minutes' work with a cloth and she was ready for action. She carefully placed the bar of soap on the floor and then flicked it out of reach.

'Luke honey, are you still there?' she called artlessly.

'I sure am,' his voice came eagerly from the other side of the screen.

'Would you be a saviour and come and pick up the soap for me? I seem to have dropped it.'

'It'd be a pleasure,' he replied.

'It certainly will,' Pooki murmured to herself.

Luke appeared round the screen, barefoot, and wearing only his white flannel long johns. He glanced down and stooped to pick up the soap.

'Now would you be an angel and soap my back for me?' she smiled prettily, leaning forward slowly enough to allow him a good look at her breasts, pink and shining from the water and soap. Her pert little nipples were pointing cheekily upwards and outwards.

As she gracefully wrapped her arms around her knees she turned to watch him. There was already a promising bulge in the front of his underwear. As his hands began to soap her she watched it grow. Soon she could see the outline of his erection reaching up towards his waist.

'Mmn, that feels good,' she said as his hands, surprisingly gently, continued to wash her back and neck.

After a while they became a little more adventurous, stroking her sides and just managing to come into contact with the curves of her breasts. At last Pooki sat back again.

'Now it's your turn,' she declared. 'Take off that ridiculous suit and come and sit down.'

Luke was out of his long johns faster than Pooki would have believed possible. The bath water rose dangerously as he climbed in. Soon he was happily soaping her breasts whilst she lay back with her legs on either side of him.

When he started on her thighs she began to do a little washing of her own. His prick was thick and heavy, its tip just able to reach the surface of the water. Pooki gave

113

it a thorough wash with the cloth as Luke made sure its target was scrupulously clean.

'I think,' Pooki sighed reluctantly, 'we ought to get out now. I'd hate to start wrinkling.'

It was far too late for the objects she had been fondling so carefully for the last few minutes. They had been wrinkled to begin with.

It took far longer than was strictly necessary for them to dry each other and by the time they expressed themselves satisfied with their efforts they were both breathing heavily. Taking him firmly by the gland, Pooki led him to the bed. She didn't bother to get in, merely sat on the edge and then lay back, her feet resting on the floor.

She guided the head of his prick towards her entrance. Luke needed no further encouragement. With a steady push, he thrust himself into her. Soon he was pounding away at her and she had locked her legs around his hips and was urging him on with gasps and moans.

They were both too excited to prolong the encounter for very long and shortly afterwards they were snuggled under the heavy blankets, exploring each other with fingers and lips. This time, they took their time and managed to make their second attempt last a lot longer.

They were just sitting up to have a much-needed drink when there was a light tapping at the door. It opened far enough for Gala to pop her tousled head round the edge.

'Hi, you two! Not interrupting anything, am I?'

'No, why?'

'It's just that we've run out of hooch and wondered if you had any spare.'

'Sure, come on in,' suggested Luke.

Gala appeared, stark naked, pulling an embarrassed and equally naked Jeff after her.

'I told you they wouldn't mind,' she said triumphantly,

114

seating herself crosslegged on the foot of the bed and holding out her hand for the bottle.

Jeff perched himself a little more circumspectly as Pooki shifted her legs to give him room. She noted that Luke's eyes were riveted on the swollen lips that were blatantly obvious through Gala's dampened fur.

As the bottle was passed round and conversation began, Gala managed to inch her way up the bed without seeming to move. Jeff seemed to relax a little and sat more fully on the bed. Pooki found herself looking at his prick and wondering how it would compare to Luke's.

She slid an artful hand under the covers and found her suspicions were confirmed. Luke was hard again from watching Gala's clever little wriggles and shifts of position, all designed to draw attention to her breasts and pussy.

Pooki thought she knew what Gala had in mind and waited with interest to see how she would start things moving. She didn't have to wait long.

'I'm getting cold,' Gala complained, 'and Jeff over there just doesn't care. I bet you do, don't you?' she appealed to Luke.

Before Jeff had a chance to protest, or Luke a chance to answer, she had wriggled under the covers next to him. Her claim to being cold was, of course, nonsense. The rooms were air-conditioned so subtly that it was virtually impossible to detect any air flow. Pooki had set the thermostat so that they would be comfortably warm even if, as indeed it did, nudity prevailed.

'I thought so,' she cried triumphantly, having discovered Luke's condition. 'At least someone's glad to see me.'

The covers moved in an interesting way as she confirmed her findings. Pooki looked at Jeff.

'It's a good job this is a big bed,' she said. 'I think I

need some consolation, seeing as your friend has stolen mine.'

She lifted the covers invitingly and Jeff quickly joined them. Shy he might be, thought Pooki as his hand slid down to cup her mound, but he knows what he wants.

Gala meanwhile, had disappeared under the covers to see for herself what Luke had to offer. The look on his face suggested that he was enjoying the exploration.

Pooki was also enjoying herself. Jeff was gently massaging her mound and nibbling on her breasts. Having both hands free for the moment she put a hand on either side of Luke's face and pulled him towards her. They kissed, deeply. She pushed her tongue into his mouth and began fencing with his.

They stopped when the covers were suddenly pulled away.

'So this is what you get up to when I'm not around!' Gala accused them, still holding Luke's erection in both hands. 'Oh!'

She stopped abruptly as Jeff, still playing with Pooki's clitoris, nosed his way up between her thighs.

'That looks like fun,' Luke remarked, tugging Pooki into a similar position.

Almost before she was aware of what was happening, Pooki found herself making up one side of a square. As everyone else seemed busy between the legs of the next person, she decided it would be churlish not to follow suit.

She quickly established a rapport with Jeff's prick which suggested a more intimate friendship would soon follow. She thought for one moment that it was going to show its appreciation of her actions a little prematurely, but the situation was saved by Gala who, enjoying herself hugely, decided that they all had to change direction.

Obediently, with much giggling and feigned reluctance,

116

they turned round and Pooki found herself renewing her acquaintance with Luke's rampant manhood. Gala had coaxed it to full stiffness and Pooki was careful not to excite it too much. After all, it was only fair that Gala should reap the rewards of her work. Besides which, she was rather looking forward to trying out Jeff.

It was difficult to concentrate properly when someone was doing such delightful things between her own legs, but from the grunts and little jerks that Luke was making, she guessed she wasn't doing too badly. Soon however she found her own feelings beginning to boil over.

She relinquished her position and rolled on to her back. 'Come on Jeff,' she urged, 'do it to me.'

He needed no further encouragement. Quickly wriggling free from Gala he took up station between her thighs and, with one smooth thrust, slid deep into her clinging heat.

Pooki came almost at once, such was her state of readiness. Jeff paused to watch her writhe, impaled helplessly on his shaft and then, as the spasms passed and she opened her eyes to grin up at him, began a slow steady rhythm of thrusts that began to bring her to the boil again.

Gala, meanwhile, had not been content simply to watch. She straddled Luke and sighed with satisfaction as she settled down onto him. Soon she was raising and lowering herself, rotating her hips as she did so.

Pooki thought she looked magnificent, hair tousled, eyes half closed, a grin of pure lust spread across her face as she arched her back and kneaded her own breasts. After a moment or two she would lean forward and drag them across Luke's face, allow him a few moments of nuzzling before sitting upright again, letting them jiggle and sway as her greedy slit worked him ever nearer to the inevitable.

Pooki's attention was forced away from this spectacle as Jeff's poundings in her own slit made a more urgent

117

claim. She raked his back with her nails to urge him on as his thrusting became fiercer. Each time he pulled back prior to stabbing forward again she clenched her muscles to try to prevent him withdrawing.

She could plainly hear, above the breathing and the moans and the grunts that were filling the room, the wet, slurping sounds of rigid flesh sliding into wet, pliant flesh. Whether it was herself or Gala she was hearing she neither knew nor cared. It was probably both of them. Either way, the sounds only served to heighten the pleasure.

Suddenly, and in what order Pooki was never sure, their climaxes arrived. One after another they gasped and shivered and jerked, trying to prolong the intensity of release as long as possible.

They spent the rest of the night in Pooki's bed. She lost count of how many times she opened herself to accommodate one or other of the men. They lay in a confused jumble of arms and legs and it seemed there was always some part of someone within reach that was worth touching or stroking, kissing or sucking.

She remembered Gala and herself doing it to each other while the men watched and took advantage of the impromptu show to regain their strength. Even so, there still seemed to be more than just Gala's hands working on her as she lay buried between her friend's thighs, savouring the variety of tastes to be found there.

She was glad that they were not required to work again until the next evening. The saloon-keeper had been more than pleased with their act the previous night and word had quickly gone round that there would be no rehearsals that day.

As such, she spent the morning and part of the afternoon catching up on her sleep. By the time she was required to start work again she felt rested and refreshed and was looking forward to whatever the evening might bring.

The week passed quickly. All the girls were in demand, although some nights were slower than others. On the busy nights, usually heralded by the arrival of a group of cowboys taking a break from the rigours of sleeping rough out on the range, the girls were not allowed to stay in their rooms with a guest for more than an hour. Only when the saloon was locking up for the night could they invite someone to stay.

Towards the end of their second week came the news that a steamer was due in the next day. Pooki had discovered the jetty and its warehouse on one of her afternoon strolls. The river ran past the far end of town and not a day went by without a wagon or two rumbling down to leave goods for shipment.

The paddle-steamer arrived at midday, announcing its arrival by a series of blasts from its whistle. Everyone who was able to hurried down to watch it make its stately way towards the jetty, whilst its decks were thronged as the passengers stared at the neat little town coming into view.

The boat was due to sail again at midnight, twelve hours being deemed necessary for the taking on and landing of both cargo and passengers. Although the boat was steam-powered, it no longer used wood as its fuel. Nevertheless, a token supply was loaded for the sake of authenticity and a few logs would be burnt to give the smoke a genuine flavour.

The girls were informed that on this particular night they would be doing their show in the stateroom of the steamer for the benefit of the passengers. Townsfolk were welcome to go along as well, but everyone was warned that, whatever else they did, they had to be ashore by midnight.

With this in mind, the girls would do only one show which was scheduled to end at ten o'clock, leaving plenty

119

of time for invitations to visit cabins or find secluded places on one of the decks. The steamer would begin blowing its whistle fifteen minutes before it was due to depart and repeat the signal every five minutes before sailing.

As usual, the show was greeted with boisterous applause. Although some tables in the large stateroom were resolutely occupied by die-hard gamblers, most were taken up by passengers and visitors.

One particular man repeatedly caught Pooki's eye throughout the show. He was tall and lean and was leaning casually against the bar. As the girls left the makeshift stage at the end of their act Pooki began to thread her way towards him. She was just squeezing past a table when a hand caught her wrist.

She looked down into the face of one of the gamblers. He was dressed in black from head to toe. Only his shirt, which was a snowy white, and his waistcoat, which was heavily embroidered in silver, alleviated the blackness.

He doffed his hat revealing jet-black hair. He had long, thick sideburns and a heavy, drooping moustache. Pooki thought he looked vaguely familiar but had no time to think why as he rose to his feet to face her.

'Why howdy ma'am,' he drawled. 'I'd just like to say how much I enjoyed your show and I'd consider it an honour if you'd allow me to buy you a drink.'

He was only slightly taller than she was and physically not a patch on her original target at the bar. She glanced over to see if he was still there. He caught her eye and raised his glass in a reluctant salute, having seen that someone else had staked a claim. Then he moved away from the bar and slipped his arm around Gala's waist just before she was claimed by someone else.

Pooki fumed inwardly. It was bad enough losing what looked like a very interesting man to Gala, but to have to settle for this nondescript gambler just made things worse.

Nevertheless, she smiled at him and accepted his invitation.

He took her acceptance of his invitation for granted and gestured to his card game.

'If you would be so kind as to wait for me in my cabin,' he said, 'I will be with you directly. Here is the key. I will have some champagne sent along to keep you company.'

Pooki did not think much of this arrangement, but was in no position to argue. As graciously as possible she took the key and, with a last reluctant look at Gala flirting outrageously with the man she had earmarked for herself, set off to locate the cabin.

On the way she ducked into one of the many 'rest rooms' the ship boasted. If ever there was a time for aphro-gel, she thought, this was it. Soon, the familiar tingle was beginning to spread and the thought of an hour or so with the gambler was no longer as unappealing as it first seemed.

As she wandered along the thickly carpeted corridors, searching for the cabin, she began to hope that he would be down to see her soon. The gel was doing its work as efficiently as always and she was beginning to feel impatient.

She realised she was lost when, having descended a couple of staircases, the carpet ended, giving way to bare boards. She poked her head round the edge of a door at the end of the corridor and realised she had found the engine room.

A burly engineer, wearing only a pair of greasy dungarees, wandered over to see what she wanted. Pooki explained she had missed her way and was looking for a particular cabin.

The engineer, who had quite a nice smile, she decided, gave her directions.

'Er, before you go, ma'am,' he began hesitantly. Pooki smiled encouragingly. 'Are you one of them dancing girls?'

Pooki smiled even more encouragingly. 'Why yes I am. How clever of you to guess! Did you not see the show?'

'Er, no, ma'am. See, I have to stay here and keep an eye on the steam pressure. There'd be hell to pay if there wasn't enough when it was time to sail again.'

'It certainly wouldn't do to let your pressure drop,' Pooki agreed. 'If there's one thing I like in a man, it's his being able to keep up a full head of steam.'

'Anyway, ma'am, the boys have been talking, see, and some of them reckon as how you girls don't wear no panties.'

'Do they now?'

Pooki was building a fair head of steam herself now. She thought the sheen of sweat that coated the man's muscular shoulders helped set them off very well indeed. His chest, barely covered by the bib of his dungarees, looked as though a head could rest on it quite comfortably.

'Would you like to see for yourself?' she continued.

The man could only gulp and nod wordlessly. Pooki took this to mean he would and slowly began to raise the hem of her dress.

As it rose above her knees, with the man's eyes riveted to its upward movement, she couldn't help but see a growing bulge at his groin. She wondered, fleetingly, if the gambler was waiting for her yet. Serve him right if he is, she thought. This one is most definitely not going to get away.

She was ready for anyone now. In fact she had been for some time, but this man looked as though he would be worth teasing a little. She stopped raising her hem just before his question would have been answered.

So far, he had been treated to the spectacle of the slow

122

revealing of her long, black-stockinged legs. As well as that, he was now able to see the bare skin above her stocking tops and the straps of her suspenders. The moment of truth was now at hand.

With a last smooth movement, Pooki hoisted up her dress and proved, beyond a shadow of a doubt, that the rumours concerning the girls' lack of underwear was true.

The man stared, spellbound, at the blonde fleece and the pink, glistening lips. He ran his tongue over his own lips, still lost for words. Pooki let him gaze at her for about ten seconds before interrupting.

'Well,' she enquired innocently, 'what do you think?'

'Fantastic,' he managed to mumble, licking his dry lips once more.

'OK, so now you know. But what I want to know is, what are you going to do about it?' She looked at him with a mixture of challenge and invitation. 'I mean, if you were to tell your mates you looked but didn't touch, what would they think of you?'

She put her foot on a convenient box. The action served to open her lips invitingly.

'Why don't you touch it? It won't bite, you know.'

Slowly, as if not able to believe his luck, he reached out to cup her mound. At the touch of his hand Pooki shuddered, suddenly swamped with waves of desire.

'That's right, that's right. Now, stroke it gently. Does that feel good?' It feels wonderful, she thought, fighting back the urge to hurl herself at him, biting and clawing at his neck and shoulders, almost desperate to feel his prick stabbing deep between her thighs.

Again he just nodded, still speechless, but growing more confident as his fingers found her wetness and slipped into it. Pooki rocked to a quick climax and pulled away slightly.

'Don't you have something to show me?' she murmured.

It seemed to take him an age to undo his braces but it was worth the wait when he finally produced a long, thick cock and looked at her uncertainly. Pooki just smiled at him.

Suddenly it seemed as if a dam had been broken. With a strangled cry he threw himself at her, groping at her breasts and thighs with his calloused, grease-stained hands. Pooki retaliated in kind, attacking his chest and neck with teeth and fingernails.

When he at last made his entrance it was with a violence that would normally have shocked her. With one thrust of his hips he slammed her back against the door. She whimpered in appreciation as he tore into her. If it hadn't been for the gel, the pain would have been unbearable. As it was it merely added to her pleasure.

Her only regret was that it didn't last very long. She was having one long, body-wracking orgasm after another as he pounded away like a man possessed. All too soon, however, he gave a grunt and his knees buckled under him. He withdrew and collapsed on to the deck, eyes glazed and chest heaving from his exertions.

He just sat there, panting and Pooki realised that his head of steam was gone for a while. She remembered her assignation with the gambler and after dropping a quick kiss on the top of his unresponsive head, headed back down the corridor towards the gambler's cabin.

Pooki had no idea what time it was when she let herself into his room. A bottle of champagne stood in an ice bucket next to the bed, along with a couple of glasses.

She had barely time to open the wine, pour herself a much-needed drink and settle herself comfortably on to the bed when the door opened and the gambler entered.

'I'm sorry to have kept you so long,' he apologised,

'but I'm in the middle of a streak. May I crave your indulgence for just a few more minutes?'

Pooki shrugged her shoulders.

'Just so long as you don't take too long,' she said. 'I'll have to leave at midnight.'

'Just a few more hands and then I'll make it up to you, I promise,' he assured her. 'Have another drink and I'll be back before you know it.'

He backed out of the door and left Pooki to her own devices. She finished her drink and went to pour herself another.

'It must be later than I thought,' she decided, looking at the remains of the ice cubes in the bucket. 'This bottle has been here for some time.'

She spent a few minutes in the cabin's tiny bathroom, tidying herself up, and then, suddenly feeling tired, propped herself up on the pillows again.

Dimly, she heard the ship's whistle signal fifteen minutes until departure, but it wasn't until it sounded again, five minutes later than she realised what the sound signified.

'It's all right,' she told herself. 'I've still got ten minutes. Ole whatsisname's going to be mad though. He's missed his chance and no mistake.'

Somehow, it seemed too much trouble to move just then and even the five-minute warning failed to rouse her. She looked round blearily for her glass. Perhaps if she had another drink it would wake her up a little. The only trouble was she couldn't find it. She must have dropped it.

She pulled herself to the edge of the bed. Sure enough, there it was on the floor. Unfortunately it was broken. Pooki decided she had better find a steward to clean up the glass.

'Someone might cut themselves,' she muttered to herself.

It seemed to take her ages to sit up on the edge of the bed. Standing was even more of a problem but with a mighty effort she managed it. She lurched in the general direction of the door and only realised she had missed it when she hit the wall with a bump.

The pain helped to clear her head for a moment and she was able to locate and grip the door handle. The only trouble was, it wouldn't turn! She rattled it uselessly for a few moments before a wave of dizziness forced her to stop.

She tried to think why the door should be locked and came to the conclusion that the gambler didn't trust her to wait for him.

She felt a surge of anger at being treated this way. She would show him! She looked round. Eventually she managed to focus on the porthole. It was more of a window than a porthole and looked large enough to offer a way out.

She was aware of the whistle sounding, indicating that the boat was about to sail, but the significance failed to register. Instead she concentrated first on reaching the window and then on trying to open it.

The blast of cool night air that rushed in helped to blow away some of the muzziness that was confusing her. She became aware of the lights on the river bank beginning to move away.

'Of course!' she thought. 'It's after midnight. We're sailing.'

She knew she had to tell someone to stop the boat. She leaned out, looking to right and left. Some four feet below her the water was slipping slowly past. To the left she could just make out the shape of the huge paddle at the stern of the boat, churning the water to foam as it tried to grip. To the right, the side of the boat disappeared into the darkness although there were lights higher up on the main deck.

Had she been in her normal state of mind the thought of trying to swim back to the shore would never have occurred to her. She would simply have waited until she was able to leave the cabin and told a crew member. Although Central would not have been pleased with her, she would not have been the first person to find themselves in such a predicament.

But Pooki was not in her normal state of mind. The strong sedative that Krantz's man had introduced to the champagne was clouding her judgement. Gingerly, she hoisted up her skirt and clambered out on to the narrow ledge that ran round the boat just above the waterline.

Once there, perched precariously above the water that was beginning to surge past, she hesitated, aware of the wheel slamming into the water a few yards away.

A voice startled her.

'Hey, you stupid bitch, what are you doing out there?' Come back at once!'

She swung round to see the gambler leaning out of the window. She began to edge away from him but when he started to climb out after her she panicked and tried to run. Her foot, still wearing its high-heeled shoe, slipped on the wet ledge and she pitched head first into the water.

The gambler cursed long and loud as he watched the river swallow her up. Apart from the fact that he would have no chance of finding her if he followed her in, there would remain the problem of what to do with her if he did find her. Not only that, he didn't like the look of that paddle, churning only a few yards away.

Carefully he climbed back into his cabin and wondered how he was going to explain this latest failure to the duke.

The shock of her immersion in the cold water helped to clear Pooki's head still further. Instead of striking out, desperately, for the surface, she kicked sideways and downwards, suddenly conscious of what the paddle-wheel would do to her if she came within its reach.

She felt the turbulence of its passing as she concentrated with all her might on holding what little breath she had managed to grab before hitting the water.

When she finally surfaced the boat was twenty yards away and receding fast. That was no longer her most pressing problem. Although she was feeling almost back to normal, the weight of her dress was threatening to drag her under. At last, she managed to wriggle herself out of it, kick off her shoes and begin to swim to the shore.

It took her about ten minutes to reach the bank and there were times when she thought she wasn't going to make it. Waves of nausea hit her from time to time causing her to tire rapidly.

She sat, gasping, on the bank and then began to laugh. She didn't quite understand what had happened over the last hour or so, but what she did know was that she was alive, apparently healthy again and sitting on a river bank half a mile from town, wearing only a suspender belt and a pair of black silk stockings.

Deciding that the stockings would be of no use at all in protecting her feet, she took them off. There was no point in ruining them. She then thought that just wearing a suspender belt was a waste of time and took that off too.

To the two cowboys, camped just on the edge of town, she was a dream come true. They had arrived too late to catch the show on the paddle steamer and the town's hotels were full, thanks to the passengers who had left the boat.

When Pooki appeared out of the darkness, attracted by their fire and limping slightly as a result of standing on a sharp stone, they gave her a blanket and a mug of scalding coffee.

Despite the fact that they could see the saloon, dimly lit in the distance down the main street, they insisted that her foot was in no condition to be walked on any further that night. They further insisted on her snuggling up to them for warmth, the result being that none of them had much sleep that night and Pooki had one or two aches in other places that quite took her mind off her foot.

Chapter 6

The wind blew in, fresh and salty, over the wide, pebbled beach and up to the village which huddled on the edge of the forest. On the beach, the handful of fishing boats lay upside down, the sea having been too rough for fishing. The weather had eased a little now and some of the farmers were again out in their fields examining the state of their animals.

Pooki paused in the harvesting of carrots from the small garden in front of her one-roomed cottage. Pulling her shawl more tightly around her shoulders she stretched to ease the ache of bending over the rows of vegetables. She looked towards the great hall. Even though she knew there would be a blazing fire in the huge fireplace, there was no sign of smoke from the roof hole, such was the strength of the wind. She shivered, envying Gala her job of helping to roast the ox.

Some of the other women were taking armfuls of logs up to the hall and although the work was hard, at least the exercise would be keeping them warm.

She looked with distaste at the muddy hem of her rough woollen skirt, barely covering the wooden clogs she was wearing. With a sigh, she bent over again and continued pulling up the carrots. At least when she had finished the row she would be able to go indoors to wash and scrape them.

Later on in the afternoon she would take them up to the hall, to add them to the cauldron of vegetables that was to accompany the roast meat. Then she would have a chance to clean herself up a little before the feast began.

What a difference from the last zone, she thought, and not only with regard to the weather. As well as being cold and wet, she was wearing uncomfortable clothes and doing menial tasks.

Central, of course, didn't worry themselves over such details. She had had a couple of easy assignments and now it was her turn to have a less pleasant one.

Since her escape from the paddle steamer she had raised a few eyebrows when the cowboys delivered her, wrapped in a blanket, back to the saloon. Only Gala knew the full story and she was as mystified as Pooki over that night's events. Everyone else just accepted her tale of missing the chance to leave the boat in the normal way and deciding to swim. The rest of her time in the Wild West zone had been uneventful.

She had just finished her harvesting when the church bell began to toll. Startled, she looked towards the sea.

About half a mile out, but approaching fast with the aid of the strong wind, was a Viking longship.

Even as she watched, the large square sail came down as the boat prepared to beach. Already some of the shields along its side were being removed as their owners prepared to land.

In the village there was panic. A dozen or so men, armed with rusty swords, a pitchfork or two and some scythes, made their reluctant way down to the beach. Most of the women began to run to the great hall, hoping that its stout door might keep out the marauders.

Pooki decided to take her chance in the open and began

to hurry towards the forest. Behind her, she heard the yells and screams of combat, punctuated by the clashing of metal against metal.

All too soon, and with the forest still agonisingly distant, the sounds ended. Risking a glance over her shoulder, Pooki saw that the beach was now empty except for some still and bloodied bodies. Coming up the slope at a run were twenty to thirty men wearing round, horned helmets and waving double-headed axes.

Pooki turned round and redoubled her efforts. She kicked off the clogs in desperation and grabbed a handful of skirt in either hand as the loose material threatened to trip her.

As she finally reached the edge of the wood and began to pick a path into its concealing depths, she realised she was too late. Footsteps were now close behind her, too close to allow her time to hide. Spotting a thick branch she grabbed it and turned to face her pursuer.

For a moment they faced each other without moving, both of them fighting to regain their breath. Pooki found herself staring at a big, fair-haired man. His hair streamed out from under his helmet, reaching his bare shoulders. In fact, he was wearing only a pair of tight breeches and some sort of sandals.

Grinning at Pooki's show of resistance, he threw down his shield and short, blood-stained sword. She noticed that the bulge in his breeches seemed to be growing.

Carefully he took a step towards her, then another. As soon as he came within range, Pooki swung at him with her branch. Almost contemptuously he avoided the clumsy swing. Pooki pretended to swing again but changed the swing to a stab. This time she came closer but still missed.

The man grabbed the branch as it slid past him and then began to haul it in, hand over hand. Within a few seconds Pooki would be within his reach. Just before that happened she pushed as hard as she could and then let go. Without waiting to see what happened she turned and ran again.

Behind her, she heard an angry cry and a crash of undergrowth as the Viking fell backwards, but almost immediately she heard again the sound of running feet.

Suddenly she felt a violent push in her back and the next thing she knew she was lying face down in the grass and leaves.

Rough hands turned her over and she lay, panting, looking up at the man. Slowly, he undid the leather belt from around his waist. She watched in fascinated horror as he pulled them down to reveal his erection.

Dropping to his knees, he grabbed her legs and forced them apart, turning his head to one side to avoid her wild punches. Once between her thighs, he used one hand to push her back down and used the other to haul her skirt up to her waist.

He paused to study the sight his actions had revealed. Pooki had, like most of the other women in the village, opted not to wear the rough and itchy woollen pants that were the only form of underwear available. As such she presented the man with an unobstructed view of his goal.

He smiled in appreciation of her plump mound and succulent lips and almost casually leaned foward to bring his rigid prick into contact with them.

Fortunately for Pooki, her fear of the situation and the exertions of the chase, along with her brief show of resistance, had managed to generate some heat in her body and she was in fact sweating lightly. This minimal amount of lubrication saved her from a lot of the pain she might otherwise have felt as he brutally forced his way into her.

Within a very short time, however, her body began to respond and she could feel the familiar wetness start. If

133

he hadn't climaxed so soon, he might well have brought Pooki to orgasm as well.

Withdrawing as abruptly as he had entered, he quickly pulled up his breeches again and hauled her to her feet.

'Where are you taking me?' she gasped.

'To join the others. If you're lucky, I'll keep you to myself. Otherwise some of the boys might take a fancy to you.'

Keeping a firm grip on her arm, he retrieved his weapons and set off for the great hall. The daylight was beginning to fade as they arrived at the huge, studded door. One or two other Vikings were arriving at the same time, also dragging dishevelled women with them. The men grinned at each other as Pooki's captor kicked open the door.

They were greeted by a blast of heat, light and noise.

'Close the door, damn you!' someone shouted as they entered.

In readiness for the night's feast, long trestle tables had been set up on either side of the huge fire that was roaring away in the hearth. In front of it on a massive spit was the ox. Gala, her dress torn to reveal most of her breasts, was diligently basting the carcass as another woman, her dress barely managing to stay on due to the tears, slowly turned the handle.

Against the wall furthest from the fire stood two large casks of ale. Judging from the noise made by the Vikings who were already ensconced, the barrels had been well and truly broached.

The only men present were the invaders. If any of the village men had survived, they were obviously hiding out in the woods or fields somewhere. Most of the village women seemed to be present, however, and most seemed to be showing signs of having been ravished.

Once the door was closed and guarded by a Viking

clutching a huge horn full of ale, Pooki's captor gave her a shove towards the main group of women who were reluctantly proceeding with the preparations for the feast, and went to draw himself a horn of ale.

Soon, to the accompaniment of much raucous singing and laughing, plates of steaming vegetables and big slabs of meat were being served by the women. As the meal progressed, the heat and noise rose steadily. Four of the Vikings had gone foraging and returned with two more casks of ale. Considerable inroads had been made into both.

Pooki, her bottom smarting from all the smacks it had received as she worked her way along the tables refilling the drinking horns, paused to wipe her hair from her eyes. A squeal caught her attention, especially as it was accompanied by a roar of approval.

At the far end of the other table another Viking was claiming the spoils of war. Some of his friends were holding a girl spreadeagled across the table while he calmly pulled open his breeches, proving he was more than ready for what he was about to do.

Taking a firm grip on the girl's thighs, he wasted no time with preliminaries, simply plunging straight into her. Despite the apparent brutality of the assault, Pooki shivered in empathy, remembering her own experience of an hour or two earlier. She was surprised to realise she found the sight arousing, which was just as well, because when she next leaned over the table to refill a horn, a heavy hand pushed her face down amid the remains of the meal.

The men on the far side quickly grabbed her arms and as she felt her skirt being lifted there was nothing she could do except endure.

When her unknown assailant finally shuddered in pleasure she relaxed, waiting to be released. Hardly had the space between her legs been vacated, however, than she felt another rigid bar of flesh stab into its place.

If she hadn't been so uncomfortable lying on a plate and a drinking horn or two, she might have begun to enjoy herself. As it was, she watched the faces of the men holding her arms and tried to guess what was coming next.

From their expectant expressions she could tell there was another waiting his turn. She watched the men gape in surprise just as there was some sort of commotion behind her and the man between her legs gave a grunt and collapsed over her.

Almost immediately he was dragged off and allowed to drop to the floor. The men holding her arms let go and Pooki was pulled to her feet. Looking down briefly at the unconscious man and registering the temporary lull in the roistering, she realised that something slightly out of the ordinary had occurred.

The man who was holding her was a giant. He had to be at least six feet six and was built like the side of a barn. The obligatory long blond hair flowed over his powerful shoulders and Pooki doubted she could encircle his upper arms with both of her hands.

Instinctively her eyes dropped to his crotch. The bulge in his tight breeches seemed in keeping with the rest of his massive frame.

The man acknowledged her glance with a half smile and then turned to face the other men.

'This one is mine.'

No one seemed inclined to argue with him and after a further moment things returned to normal. After all, there were plenty of other women about. Pooki noticed Gala being ravished standing up against the wall. By the way she was wrapping herself around the man it appeared she had come to terms with her situation and was endeavouring to make the best of it.

'Come.'

'Do I have any choice?' she replied as she was half dragged towards the door.

A short laugh was her only answer as they stepped out into the night.

Pooki marvelled at herself. Earlier that day she had wished to be inside, out of the weather. Once inside she had found it almost unbearably hot and longed for just a few minutes of fresh air. Now, stumbling along through torrential rain coming at them almost horizontally on the fierce wind, she felt a longing to be back in that warm, stuffy hall.

The man seemed not to notice the weather although he did raise his voice to be heard above the wind.

'Where do you live?'

Pooki struggled to find her bearings. Already she was soaked to the skin, her shawl and blouse no match for the wind and rain.

'Three more cottages,' she gasped.

The room seemed almost warm by contrast to the air outside, but Pooki was shivering in her sodden clothes. She quickly bent over the fire smouldering on the stones in the middle of the room. A few minutes work with some twigs, followed by some heavier wood and a cheerful little blaze, caused shadows to dance around the walls.

'You're cold.'

'Just a little,' she admitted.

'It's those wet clothes. Take them off.'

He didn't make conversation, Pooki decided, just made statements or gave orders. Nevertheless she quickly discarded the sodden garments and crouched close to the flames, rubbing her arms and legs.

A movement caught her eye and she turned her head to see what it was. The man had removed his own clothing and it was his silhouette that had attracted her attention.

His erection made him look as though he was holding a small tree trunk between his legs. In alarm Pooki turned further to see the real thing.

She was relieved to note it was not as big as its shadow but it was still the biggest phallus she had ever seen. Her brain screamed its fear at her at the thought of that battering away between her legs, although another part of her began to respond to the challenge.

'Come here.'

She turned to face him.

'Look, I'm really grateful for what you did back there, but if it's all the same to you, I'd just as soon try to snatch some sleep.'

As she had already guessed, she was wasting her time talking to him. There was only one way she was going to be allowed to have any sleep and that was when his manhood hung down instead of pointing up.

'Bring the mattress,' he said, pointing to the floor in front of the fire.

With a mental shrug she dragged the straw-filled sack over from the wall to the spot he indicated.

'Skins.'

She dragged a couple of sleeping-skins over and spread one over the mattress. As she bent over to arrange it she was conscious of the view she must be giving him and deliberately took longer than was necessary, managing to wriggle her bottom as much as possible in the process.

'Now,' he said when she had finished and was kneeling submissively, her back to the fire, 'you know what I am going to do. If you need to prepare yourself,' he glanced down at his huge penis, 'be quick.'

Pooki tested herself with a quick stroke of her finger. She was, she noted with a certain degree of pride, as ready as she would ever be.

138

'I'm ready,' she said calmly.

'Then open yourself for me.'

As he dropped to his knees, Pooki lay back and spread her thighs as widely as she could. As the massive purple head began its approach she used the fingers of both hands to pull her labia apart.

Wet though she was and as open as she thought she could ever be, she still gasped in shock as he began his entrance. There was no subtlety involved, no edging in and then retreating before advancing again; there was just a single, steady, irresistible push that Pooki thought would split her in half long before it ended. Then she began to worry that his cock was too long, that its end would be doing all sorts of damage to her insides.

When his thrust finally ended she let out her breath in a gasp of relief. He was in and she was still alive. Now all she had to do was hang on until he came.

As slowly as he had entered did he begin to withdraw, then to thrust again. She felt his balls, as big as oranges, bump against her before the slow withdrawal.

After five minutes of this she was completely relaxed and able to thrust back against him. After another five minutes she realised the tempo of his thrusts was picking up a little and she had her first orgasm. Fifteen minutes and two more orgasms later, she was only semiconscious.

By the time he flooded her with his sperm she had lost count of her own climaxes and was swooning with ecstasy. He waited until she had recovered before withdrawing.

'You did well. Now go and clean yourself up and bring me something to drink.'

She crawled out of bed and spent a few minutes with a bowl of water and a cloth before returning with a bottle of rough cider. He drank half of it with one swallow.

'That is good. Now I want more.'

Pooki was about to point out that the bottle was not empty when she realised he was not referring to the drink.

'Oh no, please, I couldn't, not again, not so soon!'

He answered by reaching for her, grabbing a handful of hair and pulling her head down to his groin.

'More.'

Once more Pooki resigned herself to the inevitable and began to nibble at the soft flesh, her fingers hefting his balls as she did so.

The grip in her hair relaxed and she heard him take another drink. She could taste herself on his shaft, whilst at the head were the slightly salty traces of himself. He was beginning to stiffen again and she had quickly to remove the head from her mouth as it threatened to fill it to the point of suffocation.

She turned her attention to the long, fat shaft and the heavy globes beneath them. She nuzzled them gently, savouring the mixture of odours – sweat, her juices, his juices. When she came up for air she found the monster had reared back up to its full size again.

He made no move to mount her and she realised he was waiting for her to climb on. Despite the battering she had taken last time, she felt herself anticipating the feeling of being stretched to the limit again.

She took the huge engorged head and began to rub it against her lips, coating it with her heavily flowing juices. When she was satisfied with the lubrication she opened herself with the fingers of one hand and guided him in with the other.

She groaned as he entered, a mixture of pain and gratification. As she sank down on the slick thickness, he reached up lazily to cup her breasts. Pooki found herself raising and lowering herself almost without thinking. Each time she settled against his stomach he would squeeze her breasts. As she rose up his shaft he would gently nip her nipples.

Soon her thigh muscles were protesting against the unaccustomed strain imposed upon them, although the giant beneath her seemed perfectly content with the way things were going.

She managed to continue long past her first orgasm but knew she would not be able to for much longer. The man must have sensed her problem, for suddenly he reached up and effortlessly lifted her off. With a quick movement, he rolled on to his knees and, placing her on all fours in front of him, re-entered from behind.

The relief Pooki felt at this change of position quickly turned to alarm as he began to thrust powerfully into her. She began to gasp with the sheer force of each lunge. Soon her moans blended into one long, wailing cry as he showed no sign of stopping.

Finally however, with a series of grunts, he spent himself and allowed Pooki, whom he had been virtually holding up for the last few minutes, to collapse face down into the fur.

Three more times during the course of the night she woke up to find herself being arranged for his pleasure. On the first occasion, she made some effort to help him; on the later ones she was just too exhausted to do anything except lie where he put her and allow him to do as he pleased.

When she awoke the next day he was gone. Pooki could tell by the position of the shadows in the room that the hour was late, but it took her a long time to struggle to her feet.

Her thighs felt as though they had been pulled apart by horses and the soreness she felt between her legs made walking almost impossible. She limped painfully to the chest in which she kept her clothes; the ones from the

141

previous night lay in the sodden heap where they had been left.

Once dressed, she slowly made her way to a partially collapsed cottage across the street. There was little sign of any activity going on in the village. A few dogs were sniffing about and a handful of chickens were pecking hopefully at the stones.

Ducking under a splintered beam she found the trap door in the floor and punched in the password. The door slid smoothly to one side, revealing a short flight of stairs. As Pooki reached the bottom a door opened and she entered the service section.

A technician nodded to her as he went about his business but Pooki was too involved with her own problems even to notice. When she reached the medi-bay she collapsed gratefully into a chair and waited to be noticed.

The doctor tutted sympathetically as she gently examined her.

'No damage done inside,' she reassured the anxious Pooki, 'but you've been well stretched and there's a few friction burns on your labia. What did this guy have, a battering ram?'

'It certainly felt like it,' Pooki said.

'Must have been some party,' the doctor remarked, a touch of envy in her voice.

'I'll swop you if you like,' offered Pooki.

'No, thanks, this guy's a bit too big and rough for my taste.'

'It wasn't that bad.' Now that the doctor had put some cream on and the pain had dulled to a steady ache, the night didn't seem such an ordeal.

'Rather you than me. Right, have some physio for your thigh muscles and then come back. I'll make up some cream for you that will act as a mild local anesthetic as well as making you so slippery down there that he could shove his longship up and you wouldn't notice. OK? Come back in about an hour.'

'Right. Thanks, doc.'

'No trouble.'

It was nearer two hours before Pooki collected her cream, during which time she had had a hot jet-bath, a massage and an hour working out the kinks in her muscles. By the time she emerged into the village again she felt almost normal.

She made her way back to the hall and started helping the women there to clean up the place. It had already been swept out and a cartload of freshly cut rushes had just been dragged up to the door. As Pooki helped to spread them she managed to chat to Gala.

'Hi, how did you get on last night? When I left you were rather occupied against the wall over there.'

Gala grinned wickedly. 'You should have stayed. Between us we could have screwed those guys to a standstill. As it was we ran out of men long before dawn.'

'Where are they all now?'

'One of 'em found some horses so they've all gone off for a ride. They told us to prepare another feast for tonight, but I think I'll water the beer a bit and maybe they'll stay awake a little longer. Hey, listen, what was that giant you left with like?'

'He didn't talk much.' It was Pooki's turn to grin now. 'But he didn't need to. His donger said it all. It would make a horse jealous. I've only just come back from the medi-bay.'

'You're kidding!'

'You want to see the stretch marks?'

'Wow, maybe he'll go for someone else tonight.'

'I certainly hope so. One night with him is like a year with anyone else.'

In the event, Pooki found she was marked down as his

property. During the evening's feasting, several girls were taken as they attempted to serve the food and drink. Pooki noted with some amusement that Gala seemed to be in demand, at one time being dragged under the table by two Vikings at once.

Her 'companion' of the previous night spent the whole duration of the feast with a succession of girls on his knee. Despite this, Pooki didn't even have her bottom felt as she worked her way up and down the room. She noted with some satisfaction that he did not seem to be really interested in the others.

She smiled when Gala, having emerged from under the table, took her turn on the giant's knee. She saw the stealthy grope she gave the man and the look of awe that followed. Pooki could feel the wetness spreading between her legs as she realised he would be having her again that night.

Sure enough, he suddenly rose, spilling Gala from his lap, and snapped his fingers at her before heading for the door. Pooki quickly put down her tray and followed.

She had managed to apply a good quantity of the cream about half an hour earlier and, frankly, was looking forward to seeing how effective it was.

Fully expecting to share her bed with the man again, Pooki had left the fire well stoked, laid in ale and wine, as well as some food, and given the skins a good airing before laying them out in front of the hearth.

As she closed the door behind them and turned to face him, she found he had already loosened his trousers. He reached for her and cupped her mound with a rough hand. Pooki shivered, suddenly glad of the cream.

He released her and stepped back, gesturing for her to undress.

'Wouldn't you like a drink first?' she said. 'Then we could get comfortable near ...'

A huge hand cuffed her around her ear, knocking her to the ground. As she regained her feet, eyes blazing, she launched herself at him, fingers hooked like claws, aiming at his face.

He caught her with one hand, lifting her off the ground and holding her casually at arm's length, while with the other he simply tore her skirt off. Then he pulled her against his chest, positioned himself between her legs and relaxed his grip.

As she slipped down, her own weight impaled her on to him, driving his rigid prick all the way into her. She gasped, partly from shock, partly from pleasurable sensation. All thoughts of attacking him were swept away as she hooked her legs round his waist and began to raise and lower herself.

The man simply stood there motionless as Pooki twisted and writhed around the pole of flesh embedded deep within her. When she succeeded in wringing an explosion from him, he merely grunted before carrying her, still held in position by a prick that showed no sign of softening, to the skins.

Laying her down he began to thrust. Pooki had never experienced anything like it before. It was like a pile-driver pounding away between her legs. If it wasn't for the cream, Pooki knew she would have been rubbed raw. As it was, she was able to climax at least three times before he grunted again and finally lay still.

Shortly afterwards she was directed to bring food and drink. While she was doing so, she took advantage of the opportunity to apply some more cream, knowing from her short experience of the man that his appetites were far from satisfied.

So it proved. Her memories of the night blurred into one vivid recollection of his massive member, driving tirelessly into her, flooding her with its outpourings almost continuously. Occasionally he demanded she take him in her mouth. When the light of day dispelled the gloom of the cottage, she was hard put to decide which part of her felt the more stretched.

When she emerged into the fresh breeze that was blowing off the land for a change, it was just in time to see the longship unfurl its sail as it prepared to sail away in search of fresh lands to conquer.

She sighed, partly with relief, partly with regret as she returned to the cottage and began to gather her things together. By the time she had tidied up and dropped the sleepskins down the cunningly concealed laundry chute, she could hear the hum of machinery as the robot clean-up vehicles moved in.

She paused in the street for a moment to watch the repair crews as they skilfully worked on the mutilated droids still lying on the beach after their futile defence of the village. In a couple of hours they would be reassembled, reloaded with synthetic blood and ready to be massacred by the next boatload of marauders that chanced this way.

Pooki joined the other girls waiting to have an inspection in the medi-bay.

'Hi Pooki, another hard night?' Gala came over to stand next to her.

' "Hard" is the right word. I think that guy was really a droid. He just never stopped.'

Gala gave her a quick once-over and nodded at her swollen mouth. 'Yeah, I can see he left his mark on you.'

'Huh, this is nothing. You ought to see my other lips!'

When it was Pooki's turn to be examined, she found herself facing the same doctor as on the previous day.

'Hello again. Was that cream any good for you?'

'It certainly was. I don't think I would have lasted the night without it.'

146

'Good. Well, let's have another look at you.'

The result of the examination was that Pooki was taken off the active list.

'You can't do anything until your face is back to normal. You could do with resting your pussy as well. It'll be a week at least before you're ready for a man again.'

'You mean I'll be given a week off?'

'Hardly. Just because one part of you is not fit for men doesn't mean you can't be used in other ways,' the doctor chuckled. 'You'll have a couple of days off until your mouth has recovered. After that . . .' The doctor shrugged and began to prepare for her next patient.

Before returning to Central for rest and therapy, Pooki managed to grab a few minutes with Gala.

'So you're having a break then?' she said, on hearing her news.

'At least until my mouth recovers. How did you get on?'

'Clean bill of health,' Gala grinned. 'We're off for baths and massage and then it's back to the village. There's another boat due in this afternoon.'

'I'll see you later then. Good luck!'

Gala snorted. 'It's not me who needs luck, it's those poor suckers on the longship. We're going to suck them dry, ain't that right, girls?'

The other girls who had gathered round to hear Pooki's news and to say goodbye cheered and whistled before drifting away for their treatments. As soon as they had gone Gala became serious.

'Are you sure you'll be all right? We were supposed to be looking after each other.'

Pooki grinned and kissed her on the cheek.

'Don't worry. I'll be all right. So far it's been fun – I've really enjoyed myself. I'll see you soon.'

Once back at Central, Pooki let herself into her room and noticed at once that there was a message waiting for her. She activated the screen and was presented with an image of the controller's assistant. She was to report to Therapy for treatment within the hour and the controller wished to see her first thing the next day.

'No peace for the wicked,' she muttered to herself as she quickly unpacked her things.

She sent an acknowledgement of the message to the controller's office, left a message in the computer telling any other callers where she could be found and headed for Therapy.

Chapter 7

As Pooki walked with Robert along the sand towards the grass hut, she was aware of a slight stiffness and a few twinges of pain between her legs. Things were a lot better than when she left the Viking zone, but she was still decidedly tender. The thought of anyone going anywhere near her bruised lips made her cringe. Fortunately, Central was understanding of her situation, by no means a unique one on Paradise – hence her current assignment.

Now, after a week in the South Seas, she was beginning to wonder if things would ever be the same for her again. Certainly it wouldn't be long before the medics pronounced her fit enough to begin working as before. After her last check, the night before, the doctor had announced that a few more days should see her back on the fully-active list. Pooki wasn't so sure she was ready for it.

The South Sea zone catered almost exclusively to the older visitor. Not for them the danger of the war zones, the rough and tumble of the Wild West or even the free and easy lifestyle of California. Instead, the over-forties tended to opt for the cosseted way of life as provided by the willing and nubile young men and women of the South Sea Islands. (Those who possessed a naturally light skin were carefully dyed a rich mahogany. All hair suffered a similar treatment and Pooki was willing to bet there were few of her friends who would recognise her in her current situation.)

Pooki and Robert were house-boy and girl to a couple who were staying in one of the huts. 'Huts' tended to suggest a simple one-roomed affair with a sandy floor. Nothing could be futher from the truth. They were actually very comfortable four-roomed bungalows. The bedrooms were large and airy. Despite their homemade appearance, in between the inner and outer grass walls was a layer of insulation that was only slightly modified from those used on spacecraft.

The furnishings within the huts had a rustic, handmade look to them but they were some of the most carefully designed pieces ever to be made. Even the chores that Pooki and Robert were required to do were, in the residents' absence, largely done by machines.

On entering the hut early each morning, their first task was to check that the little cleaning robot had done its work properly during the night.

Gliding soundlessly around on its own electromagnetic forcefield, the machine would 'see' and 'smell' any objects that were out of place. Rubbish of any sort would be quietly ferried to the hidden garbage chutes, furniture would be straightened and crockery washed and put away, leaving the humans to give the place a quick once-over before preparing breakfast for the residents.

Pooki had become quite fond of the little machine and never forgot to give it an affectionate pat on its dome before it put itself away under the floor in the kitchen. Then they would check to see what the residents had requested for breakfast, punch in the requirements in the auto-chef and wait the few seconds for it to be delivered, already garnished with an exotic flower, on its tray.

The residents rarely varied their breakfast demands. He would have a large glass of tropical-blend fruit juice followed by a freshly baked bread roll, butter and a jug of coffee. She never had more than a small glass of coconut milk and some slices of freshly picked pineapple.

Once the meals had arrived, they would check that it was not too early and then Pooki would take him his while Robert served his wife. The residents slept in separate rooms and the reasons for this became obvious only after the first morning.

Carefully setting the tray down next to the bed, Pooki gently lifted the light sleep-sheet from his naked body. She stood for a moment looking at it. Despite his age, he was in quite good shape, she decided. Maybe his stomach was beginning to bulge a little too much, but the rest of him wasn't too bad.

As lightly as possible she crawled on to the bed next to him. Then she began to blow, very softly, at the flaccid piece of flesh between his legs. He muttered something and stirred slightly, rolling on to his back and stretching out his legs.

Pooki was never sure if he was awake at this point or not. It didn't really matter as, awake or asleep, she always proceeded in the same way.

Slowly, skilfully, she began brushing his prick and balls with her nipples, undulating her torso above him, increasing by tiny amounts the weight she was applying. As he began to react to the stimulus, she increased the pressure.

Soon he was fully erect and she was massaging him firmly, pulling in her shoulders to trap him in her cleavage, stretching and contracting to make her breasts rub up and down his length.

Although he had quite a slim cock, its length was perfectly respectable and his balls were among the largest and heaviest she had handled in her short career.

Satisfied that his prick was fully erect, she began working on him in earnest. Pinching the loose folds of skin around his balls she began nibbling her way up and down his shaft.

The tension in him was obvious now. He started making involuntary little thrusting motions and she always believed he was fully awake at this point, although they both acted as though he was still asleep.

When he began grunting and rolling his head from side to side on the pillow she guessed he was not far away from his climax. Taking the head of his prick firmly between her lips she began to suck, rubbing one hand up and down his length and cupping his balls with the other.

At last he jerked upwards into her mouth and she began swallowing rapidly as he flooded into her. Only when his outpourings ceased and she finally stopped swallowing did he open his eyes to look at her.

'Good morning, master,' she greeted him. 'Did you sleep well?'

'Very well, thank you.'

He sat up in the bed and waited for Pooki to position the tray across his lap. She then sat beside him so that he could eat and fondle her breasts. Like all the girls in this sector, she wore only a short grass skirt.

From the next bedroom they could hear the wails of his wife as Robert finished waking her up. Pooki had tried to prolong her ministrations so that they finished at the same time, but no matter how hard she tried and how carefully she worked on him, he was always starting on his breakfast before they had finished next door.

Up until now, when he had finished his breakfast he would bestow a perfunctory kiss on each nipple before heading down the beach for a morning swim. The hut was situated on the edge of the tree line. It was nicely shaded

152

by the palms and was a mere twenty yards from the water. Pooki would quickly tidy up the room while he was away.

This morning, however, he showed no inclination to follow his normal routine, lingering over his coffee instead and playing with the butter left on his plate with the knife he used to spread it.

His free hand slid down her side and began to caress her hip above the low-slung waistband of her skirt. Soon it began to delve among the strands of grass until it found her thigh.

Pooki found herself tensing, worried that he might try to go further. Central had assured her that this resident had no particular penchant for straightforward sex, preferring instead to lie back and enjoy the sort of treatment she had just handed out.

'You have a delightful little bottom, my dear,' he said, stroking what he could reach of it. 'I wonder, may I see it?'

Still unsure of what he had in mind, Pooki obediently stood up and undid her skirt. She let it fall to her feet and waited for his next move.

'Turn around, my dear, and let me see it properly,' he commanded.

She turned away from him and pushed her bottom back slightly, accentuating its smooth curves. She heard him sigh appreciatively.

'Come closer so that I may stroke it,' he said.

Pooki stepped back until she felt her knees come in contact with the edge of the bed. His hands began running greedily over the soft flesh.

'Ah, exquisite! Turn around and see what effect you have on me.'

Doing as she was told, Pooki found he was erect again. He pulled himself up on to his knees and began to kiss the cheeks of her bottom, running his tongue down the

153

valley between them. She could feel his breath, hot against her as he tugged her on to the bed and positioned her on her hands and knees in front of him.

Once again he began to kiss and fondle her cheeks and then, easing them gently apart he traced the valley with his tongue until he reached the tight little aperture of her anus.

To her surprise she felt him probing with his tongue. Her surprise soon gave way to delight as her body began to respond. She forgot her fears as her juices began to flow and the novel sensations took her mind off what might yet be to come.

When he started to nibble at her cheeks again, he began using a finger where his tongue had left off. Pooki realised with surprise that he had managed to insert one almost as far as it could go.

She felt herself wriggling against it and pushing back to continue the contact. Abruptly he stopped and, unable to see what he was doing, she tensed, expecting him to explore further between her well-spread thighs.

Instead she heard a rattle of cutlery and, twisting her head round, she saw him dipping his fingertips in the butter left on his plate. His hand moved out of sight but she very soon found out what he intended to do with it.

Firmly, thoroughly, he began smearing the butter over and round her anus. Satisfied with that, he applied some more to its rim and proceeded to work some inside. She felt, rather than saw, him putting the remainder on himself.

She guessed what he was going to do to her and tried to relax as much as possible. Gently, he inserted a finger again, moving it around to prepare her for what was to follow. Then she felt his prick nudging at her entrance. She reached back with both her hands and used them to spread her cheeks as he used one hand for balance and the other to guide himself.

154

Suddenly he was in! He was in no hurry, pushing forwards a little at a time and then withdrawing again, but each push took him a little deeper.

It felt strange at first and incredibly rude. He was such a tight fit that Pooki didn't dare to move. She just held her position and relied on his goodwill to keep things going.

She heard him sigh as he made his final plunge and she could feel his balls nudging her pussy as he completed his penetration. He leaned over her back and began to squeeze her breasts. Her nipples were stiff with excitement and as he began his thrusts Pooki found herself responding instinctively.

Soon he was sliding in and out as though it was a regular occurrence. Pooki was enjoying herself. The feelings were not as intense as if he was in her pussy, but it felt good nevertheless. She started to push back against him and found that if she shifted her weight slightly from one knee to the other she was able to rotate her hips a little.

He seemed to appreciate her efforts and began to spur her on.

'That's it, that's it! Waggle your ass, my little darling. Stars, you're tight!'

'I've ... never ... done ... it ... like ... this ... before,' she moaned, beginning to lose control as the sensations began to drive her towards her climax.

'A virgin!' he gasped, delighted by the fact that he was the first to penerate her in this way. 'I've got myself a little virgin ass!'

'Not any more you haven't,' she gasped in reply as the spasms started to overwhelm her.

Her reactions to his assault goaded him to even greater efforts.

'Oh, you little beauty,' he panted. 'You sweet little

beautiful juicy ass! You're so tight! Take my come! Suck it out of me!'

He was slamming himself against her in a frenzy. She became aware that his balls were swinging against her slit in a way that she thought would have had her screaming with pain had anyone told her what was going to happen. As it was, she realised she was as wet as ever and had he decided to switch targets she would have made no attempt to stop him.

He showed no inclination to do anything except keep going where he was, however. Pooki recovered from her own, rather unexpected orgasm and, finding she was still enjoying the experience, reached back to seize his balls and drive him even more frantic.

Finally, gripping her by the hips with both hands, he buried himself for the last time and, with a triumphant howl, he pumped his appreciation into her before collapsing forwards over her back.

They were brought back to reality by an amused voice from the doorway.

'Enjoying yourself, my dear?'

They looked up to see his wife grinning at them. She was standing with her legs apart, fingering herself as she watched. Robert was behind her, his hands covering her breasts. It took Pooki a moment or two to realise he was screwing her from behind at the same time.

She wondered if they slept apart so that he could indulge his anal fantasies while she stayed with the more conventional pleasures. She made a mental note to ask Robert.

'Ah, good morning! Yes, thank you,' he replied, his breathing still a little ragged. 'I see you are being well attended to.'

There was no reply. She had abruptly sagged back against Robert, her eyes losing focus as her own moment arrived. Robert carefully disengaged and as she regained her composure, Pooki found herself being abandoned as well.

The man waited until his wife had fully recovered and then led her off for a swim. Pooki and Robert quickly took turns under the shower and by the time the couple returned from the beach they were dressed again – if you could call putting on one piece of clothing 'dressed', Pooki thought – the breakfast things had been disposed of and the beds straightened.

They waited to see if their services were required any further but, as usual, they were dismissed for the rest of the day.

As they headed back to their own, much more spartan quarters, Pooki asked Robert about the man's wife.

'Usually she likes me to go down on her first thing,' he admitted. 'Then she rolls me over and climbs on.'

'Normally he just likes a blow job,' Pooki said. 'But this morning he gave it to me in my ass.'

'I thought he was doing something different,' he replied, 'when she said she wanted to watch. He must have told her what he was going to do last night. She got so excited watching the two of you, she wanted to do it again, right then and there!'

They reached the cluster of huts that was the village centre. One was a restaurant, serving food all day for the residents who could just drop in whenever they chose. Another was a bar serving a great variety of tropical specials as well as the normal type of drinks.

Others housed little workshops where the 'natives' carved wood or plaited things from palm fronds. Yet others were the living quarters of the natives. Here they were often visited by residents, especially after lunch, when almost everyone had a siesta.

On the beach, hammocks were strung between palm trees and umbrellas were planted over thin mattresses.

Most were occupied during the afternoon as the residents took a native with them for an afternoon nap.

Pooki changed her skirt, which had suffered somewhat during her breakfast session. Then she took her place in front of her hut and began to weave a basket.

Her afternoon was spent coaxing a retired mining-operations manager into a suitable condition to give them both some satisfaction. Rather to her surprise, and his obvious delight, he managed to perform, to his satisfaction at least, on two occasions.

He staggered off to regale his friends how he had managed to 'roger the little darling twice' and left Pooki feeling pleased with herself but rather hoping she would find a more energetic companion for the evening.

Unfortunately, and this was one of the drawbacks of the South Sea zone, many of the residents were happy to allow the natives to do all the work. Pooki found that having put her all into giving a resident their moment of glory, she was then left high and dry. (Or high and wet, as Gala was wont to declare.)

Pooki found she missed her friend, not so much for the immoral support that she had relied on so heavily a few weeks ago, but for her company and sense of humour. Gala could find something to laugh about in any situation and rarely failed to cheer Pooki up.

She was both pleased and surprised to find she was actually enjoying herself. She found she gained almost as much pleasure from what she did to her partners as from what they did to her. Of course she had already discovered that when she entered fully into the spirit of the thing she could combine business with pleasure. In this zone however, it was almost all business.

The evening was not one of her most memorable. She found herself in the company of two middle-aged women who were either incapable, unable, or just plain unwilling to entertain each other. She spent most of the night alternating between the two, being directed as to what she should or shouldn't do (and how best to do it) and whenever she managed to wring some shrill little bleats of satisfaction from one, she promptly had to do the same for the other. If, for whatever reason, the other failed to find the same degree of satisfaction, she was accused of not trying hard enough, or of favouritism and had to work extra hard to rectify the situation.

Fortunately, the women did not believe in making too late a night of it and Pooki was able to have a reasonable, if slightly frustrated, night's sleep.

The next morning found her in good spirits, wondering if her 'master' had any more surprises in store for her. She felt a familiar tingle between her legs and thought with some relief that it wouldn't be long before she was fully recovered.

As soon as she and Robert entered the hut, she felt that something was not quite right. Everything seemed normal and the place had obviously been cleaned and tidied. It was only when the robot came into sight that they realised something was indeed wrong.

Instead of gliding effortlessly around the room, it moved rather hesitantly. Pooki noticed that it was also leaning slightly to one side, almost as if it were drunk.

Seeming to sense their presence for the first time, it paused and slowly rotated its dome towards them. A little flap, which they had never seen in use before, opened and a curious pointed instrument poked out.

It was Robert who reacted first.

'Get down!' he yelled, pushing Pooki to one side and diving the other way.

There was a sharp little crack, followed almost immediately by an acrid, burning smell.

Pooki found herself on the floor behind a sofa. Cau-

159

tiously, she lifted her head and peered over the back of it at the machine. As soon as it registered her movement, the dome swivelled until the flap was aimed at her. Instinctively she ducked, just as the crack came again. Pooki looked up at the wall behind her to see a little hole with a wisp of smoke drifting out of it.

'What should we do?' she called across to Robert who was still crouched behind a chair.

He glanced round at the open doorway. 'The damn thing's blown a fuse or something,' he replied. 'It seems to respond to our movements. I'll try to distract it while you get out.'

'Fine by me, but what about you?'

'As soon as you're out, wave something in the doorway. If you can draw it outside then I can follow. We can't leave it in here, it might attack the residents.'

'It might have already attacked them,' she pointed out, able to think again now that the initial surprise had gone.

'We'll worry about that later. Now get ready. I think it's starting to come and look for us.'

Pooki raised herself into a crouch and prepared to dive through the doorway. She gave Robert a thumbs-up and waited.

'Don't go till I say,' he stressed. 'We'll have to wait until it turns towards me.'

He rose to a crouch and peered round the edge of his chair. There was the sound of movement from the robot and then, as Robert quickly ducked, he shouted for her to go.

There was no need for Pooki to take a deep breath; she found she had been holding it for some time. As soon as Robert spoke she launched herself for the doorway, her flesh cringing as it anticipated being drilled by the machine. To her surprise and relief, she rolled to her feet in the soft sand and found herself unscathed.

'Are you OK?' she called urgently towards the hut.

'So far, but you're going to have to do a good job. It's in between me and the door now.'

Pooki looked round frantically for a stick or something to wave in the doorway. She could see nothing.

'Pooki, please try to hurry,' Robert's voice sounded calm enough but Pooki could hear the underlying tones of desperation.

Desperately, she ripped off her skirt and, stepping to the edge of the door, began waving it in the space. Almost immediately there was a sharp crack and she felt the skirt twitch. A thin plume of smoke began to rise from it.

'That's it, do it again,' Robert called.

Pooki did so and again there was the crack.

'It's coming towards you,' she heard him yell. 'Start backing away. When I say, drop that thing and run. Now!'

Pooki dropped her skirt and sprinted towards the sea. At the back of her mind she had the idea that it wouldn't be able to swim. About halfway there she risked a glance over her shoulder.

The robot was just emerging from the hut. From the little she had been able to glimpse, it appeared to be adjusting to the brightness. Until its sensors were able to compensate for the extra light it would be unable to locate a target.

Pooki stopped when she reached the water's edge. If the robot didn't follow her, Robert would still be trapped inside and the residents would still be at risk. Another look reassured her on those scores. The robot was just starting down the beach after her. A quick glance up and down the beach showed she was the only person about.

The robot had been heading towards her, but now, as she stood still, it slowed, its dome swivelling to right and left, searching for movement. Pooki realised that if Robert tried to come out now, he would present an easy target.

Hoping the range of its weapon was short, she waved her arms to attract its attention and then, as it started towards her again, she began to wade backwards into the water, keeping her eyes fixed firmly upon the advancing machine.

Robert made his escape when it was about halfway down the beach. Pooki's splashing noises masked any sounds he might have made. Pooki hoped desperately that it wouldn't be able to follow her. Her heart sank as she realised that, even if it couldn't cross water, she was trapped. Any sideways movement she made could be easily cut off.

She didn't really start to panic until, after a moment's hesitation, the little machine began to glide over the water towards her. She knew there was no way she would be able to outswim it and resigned herself to a despairing attempt to swim underneath it and hope she could reach dry land where she might have a chance of outrunning it.

The water was up to her armpits now and she was just steeling herself for her dive when Robert arrived at the water's edge and began splashing and shouting. The machine immediately stopped and turned to consider this new target.

It made a decision and started back towards him. Pooki began to follow. Just as it seemed about to fire, Robert crouched down and stopped moving. Pooki immediately began to splash and shout. The dome started to turn towards her. Before it completed its turn, Robert took a few steps nearer and began to splash again.

Instantly, Pooki stopped all movement. As soon as its attention was fixed on Robert, she began again. Soon they were within ten feet of the thoroughly confused machine.

'We have to disable it somehow,' he shouted, 'or else one of us will make a mistake and it'll get us.'

By way of reply, Pooki splashed an armful of water

over the robot. As it turned to face this new threat, Robert splashed it from behind. By continuing to splash and weave from side to side, they were able to approach quite close. The dome was spinning frantically round as the sensors tried to detect a target through the sheets of water cascading over it.

With a desperate lunge, Robert threw himself on to the machine. His weight caused it to tip over and Pooki could hear the whine of its motors as it tried to compensate. As soon as its weapon was pointing away from her, Pooki hurled herself on to it as well.

The whine of the motors rose to a scream as it slowly began to be pushed down into the sea. Just as Pooki thought it was going to be able to rise back out, there was a series of pops as several circuits blew.

They weren't sure whether it was their weight or the inrush of water that caused the malfunctions. All they knew was that its struggles suddenly ceased and it sank beneath them.

They kept leaning on it until no more bubbles came up. Only then did they relax their pressure. Pooki felt weak at the knees from the strain and would have been happy to leave it on the bottom, but Robert insisted that they drag it out again.

'The tech boys will want to find out what happened to it,' he explained as Pooki objected to helping drag the heavy and awkward object back to the beach.

'All right. We'll pull it out, but I'm not moving it any further than that,' she warned.

They left the robot on the waterline and returned to the hut.

'Yours, I believe?' remarked Robert with a grin, as he handed Pooki her skirt.

Pooki had completely forgotten she was naked, but the way Robert was admiring her brought her back to reality.

She put the skirt on and suggested that she prepare the breakfast while he contacted the maintenance squad.

From his hiding place among the trees, the man ground his teeth in fury as he saw another careful plan foiled. It had taken considerable skill and patience to make the modification to the robot and, considering it was almost impossible to convert a household machine into an efficient hunter, he was proud of his work. He had been convinced that the machine would have been able to take care of the two workers, but had to admit a grudging admiration for the way they had disabled it.

Once again he was going to have to report his failure back to Rontar.

Robert returned with the news that they were to leave the robot where it was and carry on as normal. When they came off duty they were to put in a full report. In the meantime it was business as usual.

The last thing Pooki wanted to do was to serve breakfast in the normal way. Reaction had set in and she was feeling decidedly shaky. Ideally, she thought as she loaded the trays, I'd like to curl up in one of those hammocks with Robert and work off my tension with a good fuck. Tentatively she slipped a finger under her skirt. Things seemed all right again – better than all right in fact. She was actually looking forward to what Gala often referred to as a 'good stiff one'.

Deciding to settle for what she could get, she made sure there was plenty of butter on the breakfast plate.

By the time she left the hut and made her way with Robert to make their report, she was feeling much better. She looked along the beach but there was no sign of the robot. It must have been removed during breakfast. She wondered what the crew thought about the noises coming from the hut. Robert had obviously excelled himself, judging from the cries coming from his room and she had been unable to restrain herself as her 'master' had once again paid homage to her 'juicy, little ass.'

One of the entrances to the service areas was set into the floor of her basket-making hut. Once inside the service area, Pooki and Robert were quickly taken to a workshop where they found the robot stripped down to its chassis.

The technician dealing with it looked up as they entered.

'Who's been tinkering with this machine, then,' he asked them, 'and why?'

There was little they could tell him beyond repeating the events of the morning. He listened carefully but was none the wiser when they had finished.

'I hate mysteries,' he complained, 'and I can tell this is going to remain just that.'

He poked about among the bits he had disconnected and held up what Pooki recognised as the machine's weapon.

'This is not standard equipment on a mark five domestic cleaner,' he began.

'What is it then?' asked Pooki.

'It's a high voltage stunner,' he replied. 'It shoots an electrical charge about ten feet. It wouldn't kill you, but it would knock you out and leave a nasty burn. They're normally used to control some of the larger types of cattle found on certain planets. Somebody, somewhere, has got a grudge against one of you two or against your residents. Any ideas?'

They both shook their heads.

'Which leaves the residents. I've been in touch with Security and explained what has happened. They're running checks on all four of you to see if they can find a motive. Could be a crank of course, or someone's idea of a joke, but I doubt it. This was a pretty competent job, one that needed more than a little thought and a lot of expertise.'

He shook his head in annoyance.

'Anyway, Security will be keeping a watch on you all to make sure nothing else happens. We'll let you know if anything turns up. Thanks for your time.'

Pooki spent the next few hours racking her brains trying to think of a reason why someone would want to set a robot on to her. She knew that as a member of Rontar's royal family she was a legitimate target for some people, but it was in fact some thirty years since anyone had attempted anything more violent than a derogatory speech.

She gave a mental shrug. The attempt was obviously aimed at the residents and it was fortunate that it had been foiled. Security would ensure that nothing else would happen. She would forget the whole matter.

This was made easier for her when she was called upon to help prepare for the evening's festivities. There was to be a beach party. The natives were going to put on an entertainment for the residents. There would be dancing and feasting, and the rest was up to each individual.

While most were having their siestas, Pooki and a handful of others were putting up tables, preparing barbecue pits and stringing up more hammocks. When darkness descended, the residents began to follow the flares down to the beach area in front of the village. A band was beating out soft and gentle rhythms that blended perfectly with the lapping of the waves.

The air was filled with the scent of the night flowers and the rich aroma of a variety of foods. The flickering of the torches cast a constantly changing pattern of shadows, whilst the warm breeze, barely noticeable, brought with it a slight tang of salt.

166

As the food and drink were being served, Pooki and some of the other girls swayed around in what they had been told was a traditional dance. After an hour or so the remains of the food were cleared away, leaving just a few pieces of meat sizzling over the fires. One table was left, providing an endless supply of exotic fruit cocktails guaranteed to bring the foolhardy to their knees.

The tempo of the drums increased now and the dancing became slightly more suggestive. The girls were still wearing their grass skirts but they had added garlands of flowers around their necks. These were now presented to the residents who were encouraged to join the dance.

Then, whilst a couple of the men held a pole, the natives bent backwards to pass under it. As the pole was lowered they had to bend further and further back. In order to balance themselves they had to shuffle forwards, squatting almost on their heels, their knees well apart.

The grass skirts worn by both sexes were unceremoniously parted for ease of movement and the resulting view that was offered drew admiring applause from the watchers. If anyone brushed against the bar or fell backwards they had to drop out.

Pooki managed to pass under the bar several times but was eventually eliminated. Soon only Robert and another girl were left. With the sweat gleaming on their dark skins, they looked magnificent as they wriggled under. Both might as well have been naked for all the concealing their skirts did and Pooki noticed several of the residents were conducting comparisons with their own native companions.

When she felt a hand slip under her skirt and begin to feel her bottom, she knew without having to turn round who it was. As the competition ended in an honourable draw, Robert and the girl congratulated each other.

As the applause faded away, so did most of the

spectators. Robert had been quickly claimed by his mistress and the four of them strolled slowly towards their hut.

Pooki could tell by his uneven gait that her master had had a lot to drink. By the time they reached the hut she was having to support him. His wife was in an even worse condition, and Robert was virtually carrying her. By the time they had been put to bed they were both snoring softly.

Pooki was joined by Robert as she sat in the doorway watching the moonlight dancing on the tiny waves.

'It's beautiful,' remarked Pooki, looking up at him as he stood by her shoulder.

'So's yours,' he replied, sitting next to her.

'How did you know I was referring to this?' she asked reaching under his skirt.

'I saw you watching me going under the bar,' he smiled. 'And it wasn't my face you were watching!'

'Fair's fair,' she protested. 'You had a good look at me this morning!'

'I know,' he grinned. 'I just wish it wasn't so dark so I could see it again.'

'Would you settle for just feeling it?'

Pooki already knew what the answer would be. There was only one way the thing she was holding in her hand would be quietened. Actually, she could think of several ways, but the result would be the same in each case.

'Only if I really have to.'

He leaned towards her and they kissed. It was a long, deep affair, after which Pooki knew he had a tooth missing at the back of his mouth. It was the sort of kiss which said, 'I've waited a long time for this and now the moment's arrived I'm not going to rush things.' They kissed a few more times just to check that the message hadn't changed.

By the time they decided it hadn't they knew quite a bit more about each other.

He knew that she liked having her nipples rolled between finger and thumb, for example, and Pooki had discovered that if she ran a fingernail carefully down the length of his shaft it made him shiver.

They decided to suspend further discoveries until they found somewhere more suitable. Although their residents had no use for them that night, strictly speaking they were still not supposed to entertain a fellow employee. Thus they decided not to use their own huts. The hammocks were discounted on the grounds that they would be too easy to fall out of and all the mattresses they could find seemed to be occupied, some very actively. Pooki was rapidly running out of patience. She was just about to suggest she leant against a tree as an interim measure when Robert remembered that the hut next to theirs was vacant.

'The residents checked out this morning. The guy who worked there said they were called back to their planet unexpectedly.'

'That would be ideal, but won't we set off some sort of alarm somewhere?'

'Not if I disconnect it first,' he said with a smug grin.

Five minutes later they were all over each other in a large, cool bed. When he slid himself snugly into her eager slit she found that it had made a complete recovery. So keen was she to make up for lost time that he finally had to beg her to let him go to sleep, but not before she had encouraged him to check her reactions at least three times. He had been forced to put his hand over her mouth more than once to stifle her cries of passion and she fell asleep, content with the knowledge that her cries had been from pleasure and not from pain.

Chapter 8

When Pooki finally stepped out of the ultra-shower she had to admit to herself she was feeling good. Her skin, scrubbed clinically clean by the ultra-sound and lightly oiled and scented by the spray, glowed with health and vitality. More than that, the aphro-gel in the oil had induced a gentle tingle that would, under the right circumstances, inflame the nerve ends until only repeated sexual release could douse them.

She looked at herself in the full-length mirror. She looked good, she told herself, and she felt good. What a difference between herself back on Rontar and herself now! Her hips seemed a little more rounded and her breasts a little fuller than they had been then. Not really surprising, she thought. They had been through a lot in the few months she had been on Paradise.

She cupped her breasts experimentally, feeling the weight and texture and gently rolling the pink tips between thumb and forefinger as they squashed together. The aphro-gel immediately helped them stiffen, sending ripples of desire surging through her system. She stopped before the ripples became waves. There would be plenty of time for that later, although it would be nice to give herself just a little thrill before dressing.

170

Reluctantly she decided not to and she pouted in mock annoyance at her reflection. An onlooker would have noted, if such a person was able to tear their gaze away from her gorgeous body, how the expression transformed her face from beautiful to sexy. The sleepy blue eyes looked innocently up from under their long silky lashes.

Deciding that her body was standing up to the rigours demanded of it, she began to dress. First, a subtle application of scent: two dabs between the legs, one on each side of her lips. She wanted the perfume to compliment her own natural scent without masking it. The idea was to create an intoxicating blend that would entice and stimulate.

After a moment's hesitation she added a third dab. This one was further round, just above the tight little anal opening. Who knows, she thought, just what the evening would bring? She giggled at the thought of what the Pooki of six months ago would have said to such an idea.

She put a spot behind each knee and one on the inside of each ankle, just below the bone. A couple more on her neck, one at the base of her throat and finally a dab between her breasts, and she was ready to start dressing.

Although this was to be a formal ball and she had already chosen her gown, Pooki was still undecided as to her choice of undergarments. The silk stockings were, of course, essential. As she carefully rolled them up her smooth legs she made up her mind about the rest.

Quickly, as though she were afraid that she might change her mind again, she stepped into a pair of loose-legged, pure silk knickers. A chemise, again of silk, slipped easily over her head and then she was ready for the dress.

Once the gown had been adjusted to her satisfaction, there remained only the need to step into her shoes and wrap the heavy cloak with its satin lining around her shoulders.

She left the room, descended the stairs and went out through the front door. The horse and carriage were waiting, as was the servant who helped her in. As soon as the door was closed, the carriage moved off towards its destination.

Pooki had not been invited to the dinner that preceded the ball. Her role was to be present afterwards, to dance with anyone who wanted her as a partner, and to be available for just about anything both during and after the ball.

When the other guests made their appearance, Pooki and the others in her situation were positioned in readiness. They were arranged in elegant little groups, chatting about this and that and holding, but not drinking, long-stemmed glasses of wine.

Soon the guests had broken into these groups. The men whisked the women away on to the dance floor and the women were offered drinks and titbits by the male extras.

Pooki found herself being courted by a succession of men. She would be allowed a choice only if there were no other girls available. At this stage in the evening, few liaisons had been formed, and the wise girls tried to catch a partner of their choice early. Sometimes of course, such a plan would backfire. The chosen one would whisk the girl away to one of the many available places, have his way with her and then return to look for another partner.

On this occasion, however, Pooki was in luck. A man in his early thirties, dressed as a cavalry officer, seemed captivated by her charms.

In between dances he was attentive to her every whim, supplying her with food and drink and entering into lively conversation. During the dances he managed to let his

172

hands stray, brushing her shoulders, her back, and once, her breast.

After an hour or so he suggested they take a walk in the gardens.

'It's becoming warm in here. Don't you agree, m'lady?'

'I do indeed, sir,' she replied demurely.

As they strolled through the gardens, they passed many couples who had had the same idea. There were many discreetly positioned benches secreted in dark little nooks behind bushes and hedges. From these came the sounds, clearly carrying on the still warm air, of clothing being rustled, of whispered endearments, of heavy breathing and the moans and cries of passion.

Combined with the scent of the thousands of flowers planted in the ornamental gardens and the gentle strains of the music, the effect was stimulating. Add the lasting stimulus of the aphro-gel and a good-looking man, and the effect was to make Pooki feel decidedly horny.

She chose a secluded alcove and suggested they rest for a moment. Hardly had she seated herself when he fell to his knees in front of her.

Gently he took hold of one of her legs and, removing her shoe, began to kiss her foot whilst caressing her calf.

'Mmm, that feels good,' she murmured, idly twisting a lock of his hair.

Thus encouraged, he kissed his way up to her knee, his hand, meanwhile, moving up to her thigh. For Pooki it was decision time. If she encouraged his advances, which her body was urging her to do, he might look for another partner afterwards. On the other hand, if she managed things properly, she could encourage him to take her to his home where they could indulge themselves for as long as they wished in far more comfortable surroundings.

'You soldiers,' she protested, as his fingers slipped into

173

the leg of her knickers, 'seem to want every girl they see as soon as they see them.'

He paused in his kissing to look up at her. His fingers, however, carried on teasing the very top of her thigh. She could feel his knuckles brushing her lips and knew he was toying with her – her readiness was obvious.

'But what else are women for?' he replied, smiling. 'You make the horrors of war worthwhile. We never know which battle is to be our last, so we take our pleasures when we can.'

Pooki couldn't prevent a little sigh of pleasure as a finger finally began stroking her slit.

'You make it hard for a girl to say no,' she whispered.

'And you, my dear, make it hard,' he replied, taking her hand and putting it on his trouser front.

Pooki could feel the heat of his erection through the cloth and quickly began to undo the buttons. Almost before she had finished his member forced its way free.

'Oh, sir,' she protested with delight, 'your cannon is far too big for me to handle!'

Although she spoke jokingly, she was quite impressed with the size of his weapon. She couldn't see it, but her experienced fingers told her this one was larger than average.

'Nonsense, my dear,' he grinned. 'Allow me to demonstrate.'

Quickly he took both of her legs and put them over his shoulders. As Pooki frantically hoisted her ballgown up and out of the way, he pulled her bottom to the edge of the bench. While one hand eased her knickers to the side, the other parted her lips. He left it to Pooki to guide the head of his rampant prick into her hot wetness.

She began shuddering almost before he was fully inside her. By the time he had thrust three times she was pulling his hair and drumming her heels on his back. Her

174

breathing became ragged and her moans were steadily increasing in volume as he established his rhythm.

All pretence of being reluctant vanished as Pooki urged him on with shrill little cries. She was bare to the waist now as he kneaded her breasts, sucking first on one nipple and then the other. By the time he finally came, she was almost unconscious from the intensity of her own multiple orgasms.

It took her a good five minutes to regain some degree of self-control after he had withdrawn. She looked up to see him puffing on a thin cigar and watching her with admiration.

'That was unbelievable,' he said. 'You were so hot, it felt as though you were sucking me into a furnace.'

Pooki smiled weakly. 'It takes two you know.'

'But are you all right? I mean, can I get you anything?'

Pooki looked at him and gave him the full benefit of the eyes and the pout. 'You could get me into a big soft bed,' she suggested, 'and then I'll show you whether I'm all right or not.'

Twenty minutes later she was quickly tidying herself up in his bedroom while he looked for a bottle of wine. In a cleverly concealed series of pockets in her cloak, she carried spare stockings, knickers, a clean-all, a sachet of perfume and a tiny tube of aphro-gel. By the time Charles returned, it would have taken an expert to detect any difference between her present appearance and her earlier one.

The next morning Pooki half sat, half lay in the massive four-poster bed and slowly sipped a cup of tea, brought to her by an attractive little maid. She ached all over in a most satisfactory way. With each unguarded movement she made, her body sent her a reminder of the excesses it had been subjected to the previous night. She sighed with contentment as she looked round the huge bedroom.

Next to where she lay, the mattress and pillow still bore the imprint of where Charles had snatched a few hours' sleep. Across the room, scattered around the chaise longue, lay the wine bottles they had emptied together. She corrected herself. Most of it had been drunk, but quite a lot had been used to bathe various parts of their anatomies prior to being licked or sucked off. There was nothing quite like having chilled champagne poured over your genitals to reawaken an interest. The way the bubbles fizzed over the tender flesh was virtually indescribable.

Near to the chaise longue, occupying pride of place in the middle of the floor, lay the remains of what had been, only a few hours earlier, a magnificent ballgown. She distinctly remembered the thrill of anticipation she felt when he had begun to rip it from her acquiescent body.

'So tell me, Charles,' she had prompted on his return from his cellars, triumphantly bearing several bottles of wine, 'what is the army's attitude to women?'

'We regard them in much the same light as a military objective, ma'am,' he answered, putting the bottles down carefully and slowly walking towards her.

'Oh really?' she replied, looking with interest at the growing bulge in his trousers. 'And just how do you regard a military objective?'

'We assess the situation, ma'am, and then take the shortest possible route towards it.'

Pooki licked her lips. 'And if you should meet with resistance?'

'We crush it as speedily as possible.'

He took the two short steps towards her and swept her into his arms. After savouring his kiss for a long moment she pulled away feigning indignation.

'That was presumptuous of you, Captain! You took advantage of me in the gardens, when I was feeling a trifle giddy from the effects of the heat and the wine. Perhaps I made a mistake coming here. Maybe I had better leave.'

'I think not, m'lady.'

With one swift movement he ripped open the front of her dress, taking the chemise with it. The thin material split down to her waist. A second tug, and the dress hung from her hips leaving only her arms still covered.

Charles paused to study her flushed countenance, her firm breasts with their stiff nipples before reaching forward for one last, decisive jerk at the defeated fabric.

Letting the remnants fall to the floor around her he waited for a reaction. The speed of his actions had caught her unprepared, but standing amidst the wreckage of her dress and wearing only her stockings and a scrap of silk between her legs, she decided to give in gracefully.

Peeling off the remains of her sleeves she sat on the chaise longue, picked up her glass and crossed her legs.

'Before you remove the rest of my clothing, Captain,' she murmured, 'may I suggest you remove your own. Those trousers look dreadfully uncomfortable and I would hate you to damage your weapon.'

Charles took only a fraction longer to remove his own clothing than he did hers. Despite the tightness of his coat, boots and trousers, they were off in an instant. His weapon, impressive in the dark of the garden, was even more so in the light.

Pooki congratulated herself on her choice as she leaned back and uncrossed her legs. 'I surrender, I surrender,' she sighed. 'Do what you will.'

He knelt by her side and began to unroll a stocking. As the stocking slid down he began to kiss the flesh it revealed. Once it was off he kissed his way back up her leg before crossing over and beginning again on the other.

177

Lifting it, he gently nuzzled the back of her ankle, then he kissed the back of her knee. When he reached the top of the stocking, he allowed his hands to start unrolling whilst his lips continued upwards.

She found her thighs parting involuntarily to allow him to bury his face in her silk-covered mound. She could feel his tongue probing against the thin material as the second stocking fell to the floor.

Now his hands began their assault, working their way from calf to thigh before pausing at the final flimsy barrier. She was moaning softly now, her hands pushing down on the back of his head, hips gyrating slowly as he eased the silk aside to allow access for his tongue.

As he began to lick up and down her slit, a finger made slippery from her copious juices worked its wicked way into her anus. She gasped as it made its entrance and then gasped again as another finger penetrated her cunt. As the fingers began to slide backwards and forwards he continued to suck on her clitoris. His free hand located a breast and began teasing the nipple.

About three minutes of this was all she could stand before shuddering into a climax. He allowed her no time to recover, quickly changing position so that when she opened her eyes it was to be confronted by his prick. She closed them again but opened her mouth.

Now it was her turn to drive him wild. She licked her way down the shaft until she reached his balls. Taking one into her mouth, she teased it gently with her tongue, her hands never ceasing in their stroking of his shaft.

She pushed the ball out and began again on the other. Then she nibbled the loose skin behind them and ran her tongue up and down his crack, stabbing at his anal opening with her tongue before retracing her path back to the head of his cock.

He was forced to pull himself away from her greedy

mouth and positioned himself between her legs instead. She co-operated by hanging one leg over the padded back of the chaise longue and letting the other one trail on the floor.

His entry was effortless, thanks to the position and the preparation. Within three thrusts he was sliding in as far as he could go. After a few more, however, he withdrew and began to reposition himself. Anticipating his intentions, Pooki drew her knees up to her breasts. This time his entry took a little more time but soon he was as deep as ever and she was raising her bottom in encouragement.

A rhythm was established – a slow penetration of her cunt, followed by seven long slow strokes, withdraw, reposition, a slow penetration of her anus, followed by another seven long slow strokes. She found that if she helped guide him into the appropriate opening it kept the rhythm going better and she also found that whichever place he was in, she wanted him in the other.

She couldn't remember where he ultimately spent himself, but it proved immaterial anyway. By the time they had decided that enough was finally enough, he had utilised every orifice of her body as a depository for his offerings, some more than once.

She hadn't heard him leave, but from the lack of his clothing, she guessed that he had. She shifted position slightly to ease an ache and began to plan her day.

She would have to find something to wear for a start. Then, once back in her house, a long hot bath. After that, who knew?

Tapping the gilt-edged invitation against her neat white teeth, Pooki pondered the preparations she would have to make.

The little rectangle of card with its beautifully embossed writing invited her to join the party being assembled at

179

the country seat of the Duke and Duchess of Wargrave. The invitation suggested that she might like to join the party for dinner the following day. That meant arriving during the afternoon, as she would need to settle into her room and rest for a while to recover from the rigours of the journey before dressing for dinner.

Calling Jane, her maid, Pooki issued a stream of instructions. Clothes had to be packed; new ones had to be bought; a coach, horses and driver had to be hired.

As Jane scurried off to begin packing Pooki began to make a list of the extra things she would need for a sojourn in the country. Top of the list would be some riding boots and the clothes to go with them. When the list was complete Pooki waited for Jane to finish what she was doing in order that she might accompany her mistress to buy them. While she was waiting she thought back to their briefing.

The Briefing Officer had not introduced himself but had simply told them they would be going to Victorian London.

'Some of you will be going as downtrodden workers, living in squalid conditions and being abused in a variety of ways by your employers and fellow workers,' he began. 'Others will be servants to merchants, lawyers, other members of the emerging middle classes and, of course, the aristocracy. Some of you', he admitted begrudgingly, 'will be "married" to the aforementioned people and a very fortunate few of you will be granted temporary membership of the aristocracy itself.'

He proceeded to reel off names and assignments. Pooki jumped when she heard Gala's name called. She hadn't realised that Gala was going to the same zone. She had left a message for her but had yet to meet up with her since returning from the South Seas.

She smiled to herself as Gala's assignment was announced – she was to be a music-hall entertainer. Just the sort of role that would appeal to her she thought, remembering their assignment as saloon girls in the Wild West.

Then her own name was called and she felt a trifle smug on hearing that she had been awarded one of the coveted roles of aristocrat.

Once everyone had been given their assignments the meeting broke up to allow them to be given a briefing specific to their role. Pooki joined the handful of 'aristocrats' in a smaller room.

It was their bad luck to have the same Briefing Officer that had opened the session.

'Just because you've been chosen to be aristocrats,' he had snarled at them, 'doesn't mean you sit around all day being waited on hand and foot. You', he pointed at Pooki, 'are the recently widowed wife of the son of the Marquis of Ormsgill. The family don't wish to be burdened by you so you must find yourself a new husband, or a rich benefactor, as quickly as possible. This means,' he leered, 'that you must be available to any offers that come your way. You will be sent lots of invitations to various functions where your suitability will be tested.'

He continued outlining to each person what their role entailed.

Pooki and the other 'aristocrats' needed only to practise horse riding and to be aware of how the aristocracy of those days regarded their social inferiors, and were thus dismissed to punch up the practice schedules and other final details on their computers. Pooki could imagine Gala having to practise her routines several hours a day and congratulated herself at landing one of the plum roles – despite what Old Sour-puss had said.

She noted she was being given a maid and a house in London from which to operate. Her instructions closed with departure details. She checked the time and found she was going to have to hurry to catch her first riding lesson.

Three days later in her allocated compartment she found her 'maid', Jane. She was a cheerful, attractive brunette from a planet unknown to Pooki. As the roboshuttle whispered along the tunnel at its usual frighteningly high speed they chattered about their experiences.

Jane had been on Paradise a month less than Pooki but had signed up for a full year.

'When I've finished here,' she said, 'I'm going home to find a rich husband. My planet is so boring that any girl with a Paradise certificate can have her pick of the men. As long as you keep them happy in bed, they'll let you do whatever you want out of it, even finding yourself something you really fancy on the side!'

Arriving in 'London', they easily found the house, set on the edge of Mayfair, and had barely time to examine its contents before the first invitation was delivered.

The day after her evening with Charles, sitting comfortably on the plush seats of the hired coach, Pooki and Jane trundled out of London and into the countryside. Pooki looked out of the window, trying to anticipate what the next few days would be like.

Two hours later the coach started to climb a long incline and began to slow. About halfway up the slope they entered a wood. Pooki was admiring the trees – there were varieties here that she had never seen before, and she remembered being told that IGX had gone to vast trouble, not to mention expense, to find the same type of tree that had existed back on Earth in the real 'zones'.

Just as the coach reached the top she was startled by an explosion in front of them. As the driver fought to control the horses, a masked man astride a huge black stallion appeared, brandishing a pair of pistols.

The one he had just discharged he reholstered while he waited patiently for the driver to regain control. The horses were too winded from climbing the hill to bolt and were soon standing quietly.

The man gestured for the driver to climb down and then ordered him to open the door of the coach. Doffing his hat with an exaggerated gesture he spoke for the first time.

'I would be obliged if you would step down,' he announced.

Pooki and Jane looked at each other and with a shrug Pooki led the way out of the coach. On seeing the women the man bowed in the saddle.

'Good day to you, ladies,' he said from behind his mask. 'I am sorry to inconvenience you, but I must ask you to hand over any valuables you may have.'

Acting the affronted yet dignified noblewoman was something Pooki was well able to do.

'I shall do no such thing,' she informed him crisply. 'Furthermore as soon as we arrive at Oldfield Hall I shall have the Duke of Wargrave despatch the militia to have you arrested!'

If the highwayman was impressed by this speech, he gave no sign of it.

'Ah, Oldfield Hall eh? I presume you are joining His Grace's party?'

'Your presumptions are of no interest to me whatsoever,' Pooki replied haughtily. 'What is of interest, however, is how long you intend to detain us.'

'Just as long as it takes for you to hand over your valuables,' he replied.

'We have no valuables,' Pooki stated flatly.

'On the contrary, ma'am,' he contradicted her, staring admiringly at the proud swell of her breasts, 'I can see at least two from here!'

He grinned and then produced a length of rope from his saddle and threw it to the ground in front of Jane.

'You, girl,' he commanded, 'tie one end of that to his wrist.'

He pointed at the coachman. When Jane, at a nod from Pooki, had done so, he added, 'Now pass it round that tree and tie it to his other wrist.'

As soon as Jane had done so he dismounted lightly and checked the knots. Satisfied, he put away his remaining pistol and turned his attention to the women.

'Seeing you are so disobliging, I am forced to search the coach myself. If you will excuse me?'

So saying he ducked into the coach and could be heard rummaging about. When he emerged he was shaking his head ruefully.

'Dear me, ladies, it seems you were right. You have no valuables other than those God gave you, but you have put me to considerable trouble and I shall not leave empty-handed.' He looked them both up and down, insolently. 'From you, my lady, I shall take those fine lace gloves ...'

He held out his hand while Pooki reluctantly removed them and handed them to him. He switched his gaze to Jane.

'Now what shall we have from you, my dear? Ah! I have it!'

The way he was looking at her left her in no doubt as to what he wanted. Jane blushed as he tucked the gloves into a pocket and then indicated she should precede him into the coach.

'You wouldn't!' Pooki protested.

'Ah but I would, and will,' he said cheerfully, following Jane inside and closing the door. He pulled the curtains across the windows and Pooki was left to stand and listen.

As soon as she heard Jane raising her voice in protest

after an ominous ripping sound, she hurried to try to untie the driver. If they could start the coach moving he would be forced to jump out or risk being delivered to the authorities.

As she wrestled with the knots she could hear Jane's sobs from inside the carriage. These were abruptly cut off by a sharp cry, which in turn gave way to a series of lesser ones, each a little softer than the one before. Just when they ceased to be cries and began to be moans, Pooki could not be sure.

She looked over her shoulder. The coach was rocking steadily and Jane's moans were becoming louder and going through another change. By the time Pooki had managed to free the driver the moans had become gasps.

As the driver stumbled back towards his perch, massaging his wrists as he went, the gasps, which had been coming steadily faster and faster, reached a crescendo and burst into a long wail. The coach stopped rocking and Jane's wail died away.

Just as Pooki had managed to scramble up beside the driver, the highwayman jumped nimbly out. His horse, which had been grazing a few yards away, pricked up its ears. With a graceful movement he remounted and, with an ironic bow to Pooki, he wheeled round and vanished into the trees.

Climbing down again, Pooki re-entered the coach. Jane was slumped against the back of the coach. Her skirt was still bunched up around her waist, whilst on the floor lay the torn remains of her knickers.

'Are you all right?' Pooki asked in concern.

Jane roused herself and, realising her disarray, quickly pulled down her skirt.

'Yes, thank you, m'lady.'

She spoke slowly and it was the gleam in her eye rather

than her words that reassured Pooki. Judging from the noises she had been making, the highwayman wasn't the only one who had enjoyed himself, Pooki decided. She rapped sharply on the roof and the coach lumbered forwards once more.

'We should be at Oldfield Hall soon,' Pooki said. 'I shall tell His Grace at once and he can organise a hunt for that man. You must rest of course.'

'Thank you, m'lady. I'll be all right soon,' Jane replied.

They sat quietly for a few moments before Pooki couldn't resist asking, 'What was it like?'

Jane grinned at her. 'It was a bit painful at first because I wasn't ready for him. But after a few moments I began to enjoy it.'

'Yes, you certainly sounded as though you did,' Pooki remarked dryly.

'Oh no! Was I noisy? I always seem to get carried away somehow.'

'You made me feel quite jealous,' added Pooki, suddenly realising that what she had heard had aroused her. 'I just hope that if we meet him again, he chooses me next time!'

Oldfield Hall was an imposing building, looking down a long drive which wound over beautifully kept lawns before entering patchy woodland. The house was visible only for the last half mile of the drive but once in sight it dominated the landscape from the top of the small mound on which it was built.

No sooner had the coach drawn to a halt than a footman was holding the door open and offering his arm to Pooki.

Once inside, a solid-looking butler greeted her and suggested she settle into her room. He would arrange for refreshments to be sent up and she could rest before dinner when she would make her introductions to the Duke.

'I'm afraid I must insist on seeing His Grace at once,'

Pooki stated. 'My servant has had a dreadful experience and I must inform the Duke.'

The butler acknowledged Jane's presence with the briefest of glances before bowing to Pooki.

'Very well, m'lady, I will see if His Grace is available.'

He left them in a reception room and disappeared. When he returned some ten minutes later he asked them to follow him and after a short walk ushered them into a large but comfortable library.

A fire was blazing cheerfully in the grate and seated comfortably in a large leather armchair in front of it was the Duke.

He sprang to his feet when they were announced and his eyes twinkled appreciatively at the sight of the two attractive women. He casually threw the book he had been reading on to a large table behind his chair and stepped towards them.

The Duke was a small, neat man of about forty-five, Pooki guessed. He was immaculately dressed and his thinning grey hair was neatly swept back, exposing a broad forehead.

Once the introductions had been made, Pooki gave him a short but accurate version of what had happened, finishing with, 'And as you are doubtless the local magistrate, I thought I had best inform you as soon as possible so that you may take whatever steps you think are necessary to apprehend this monster.'

'Yes, of course, quite right. Dear me, how distressing! Something must be done at once. Jarvis!'

The butler who had been standing like a statue throughout Pooki's story took a step forward.

'Your Grace?'

'Show Lady Croston to her room and see she has everything she needs. You, my dear - er, Jane, is it? - you must stay for a little while longer while I ask you some questions. I need to be absolutely sure of the facts before I start things moving.'

He nodded his dismissal to Pooki and went to pick up a sheet of paper from the table.

Jarvis showed Pooki to her room which was at one end of the first floor. Each suite was referred to by a colour and Pooki's was the Lilac Room. Once inside it was easy to see why.

All the decoration, from carpet to curtains to bedspread, had shades of lilac as their dominant colour. The room itself contained a large four-poster bed, a pair of easy chairs on either side of the small but cheerful fire, and a small table. In one corner stood a washstand. The window looked over the lawns to the side of the house, revealing a small lake the far side of which reached the edges of the woods.

A door in one corner of the room led to Jane's room and contained a small bed, a large wardrobe and its own door back on to the corridor.

Pooki had barely finished looking round when a knock announced a pair of servants. The first brought in a tea tray and some sandwiches which she put on the small table next to one of the chairs.

The other brought a jug of water, a bowl and some towels which she placed on the washstand.

'Will you require anything else, m'lady?' she enquired.

'Not for the moment, thank you,' Pooki replied.

The other servant finished pouring the tea and, with a bow, joined the other as she left. Pooki settled herself in a chair and sipped her tea.

About half an hour later there was a discreet knock on the door and Jane entered. Seeing Pooki was alone, her face split into a huge grin.

'What's the matter with you?' Pooki asked, pouring her a cup of tea and gesturing to the other chair.

'I've just been fucked by the Duke!' Jane said, sitting down gratefully.

Pooki nearly dropped the cup she was holding out. As it was, some of the tea slopped on to the carpet.

'I don't believe it,' she declared.

'It's as true as I'm sitting here,' Jane swore.

Pooki looked at her 'servant' with interest.

'Well, are you going to tell me about it, or are you just going to sit there looking smug and drinking my tea?'

Jane pretended to have been put in her place. 'I beg your pardon, m'lady, but it was like this. As soon as you had gone the Duke came and took me by the hand and made me sit down in that big chair in front of the fire.

' "Tell me what happened, my dear," he said, still holding my hand. So I told him again, just what you had said, but he wasn't too interested in those details.

' "But what did he do to you?" he asked, pulling up a stool so he could sit next to me and keep holding my hand.

'I pretended to be embarrassed and shy but he kept pressing me to tell him so I said how the man had made me go into the coach with him.

' "Yes, yes," the Duke said, "but what did he do to you?"

' "He made me lift up my skirt," I said, "and when I refused he threatened to hurt me. So, reluctantly, I did and he started to feel my bottom and tell me how nice it was and how smooth it felt."

'The Duke had started to go a bit red in the face by now and when he insisted that I lift my skirt again to show him exactly how it had happened I began to guess where it was all leading.

'I pretended to be surprised by this and asked him if it was really necessary.

189

' "Oh yes," he replied, waving vaguely to his piece of paper on the table, "I need all this for my report."

'So with another show of reluctance I pulled up my skirt again.' Jane chuckled at the memory. 'I thought he was going to have a fit when he discovered I had no knickers on. He certainly had a hard-on, that was obvious!'

Jane stopped to have another drink of tea.

'Go on,' urged Pooki eagerly.

' "You see, Your Grace," I said, "the monster tore my knickers off."

' "So I see," he replied, "but he fondled your bottom you say?"

' "Yes m'lord," I said.

' "What, like this you mean?" he said, starting to run his hands over my ass.

' "Why, yes, Your Grace," I replied, "just like that. And then he started to feel between my legs. I didn't want him to, but he was so big and strong he just did it anyway."

' "You poor girl," he said, still stroking me, "you mean like this?" and the randy old goat started fingering me.

' "Yes, m'lord," I said.

' "Mmn, that was very wrong of him," said the Duke. "And that was all he did, was it?"

' "Why, no, m'lord," I said and made myself blush, "but I don't like to say."

' "Nonsense," he said. "You must tell me. How else can we bring the scoundrel to justice?"

' "Well, m'lord," says I, "I'm ashamed to admit it but he made me undo his trousers and pull out his thing."

' "What!" he cried, "I can scarce believe what I'm hearing. Show me exactly what you did."

'So I bent down, opened the ducal trousers and hauled it out,' grinned Jane. 'Let me say right now, for a little chap he had an impressive tool.'

Pooki was enjoying the story, so much so that she began to wish it was her bottom that was being fondled. She shifted her position in the chair, aware of the heat beginning to build in her own loins.

'And then?' she prompted.

'Oh, and then I had to show him just how the highwayman made me sit on his lap and put his weapon in my sheath,' Jane said.

'And of course you had to jiggle up and down like the villain made you do?' said Pooki.

'Of course.' Jane chuckled again. 'And in the interests of accuracy we both had to come just like in the coach.'

'What did he say afterwards?' Pooki wanted to know.

'He thanked me for my cooperation and suggested I find you and maybe had a little rest. "I have enough information for my report now," he said, "but I may need to check on a few of the points sometime so I would like you to try to remember everything and should you recall anything that you have forgotten to tell me, you must let me know at once." So here I am,' she finished with a laugh.

'I don't know,' Pooki shook her head. 'We've only been here an hour and you've already screwed our host!'

'And been ravished by a highwayman,' Jane reminded her.

'I'm definitely jealous,' declared Pooki, 'but I'll make you a wager. I bet I'm laid by more men – or women,' she added as an afterthought, 'than you, while we're here.'

'You're on,' cried Jane. 'But don't forget I'm two up already.'

'You may have had two up,' replied Pooki, 'but the first one doesn't count. That happened before we arrived. What's more, if our host has you again that won't count either. The bet is on different men or women, not number of fucks.'

'All right,' Jane replied cheerfully. 'What does the winner receive?'

'Damned if I can think of anything,' Pooki said. 'We'll leave it open. If either of us has an idea we'll talk about it.'

'Fine. Now if you don't mind, m'lady, I'll go and clean myself up and find another pair of knickers. What's more, you had better start preparing for dinner yourself.'

There were eighteen other guests invited to the house. About a third of them, like Pooki, were employees of Paradise. The seating arrangements were cleverly worked out so that no employee sat next to another.

During the pre-dinner drinks they had carefully identified themselves to each other using the signals Briefing had given them to ensure they didn't pair off with each other and leave the guests 'short'.

Some of the guests might well choose to liaise with another guest or perhaps with one of the servants. If an employee found themselves free, he or she was supposed to find a guest who had chosen to be with a servant and initiate an alliance.

Thus serving wenches would find themselves ravished by the young masters and footmen would be called upon to pleasure their mistresses.

During the meal, conversation quickly began to flow freely, helped, no doubt, by the excellent food and copious wine. Apart from announcing that there was to be a hunt the next day, the Duke contented himself with speaking only to those close to him at the end of the huge table.

Pooki was sitting towards the other end and quickly found herself monopolised by the powerfully built man on her left. He had been introduced to her as Michael Fitzallen and by the end of the meal, during which he had maintained a steady flow of conversation, he had managed to persuade her to let him raise her dress above her knees and was gently stroking her thigh under cover of the snowy-white cloth.

His hand had just arrived at the bare skin above her stocking when the meal ended and the ladies withdrew to leave the men to their brandy and cigars.

Pooki shared her new friend's reluctance to end his exploration under her dress, but she had managed to inform him earlier that she was in the Lilac Room and that her maid would almost certainly have been dismissed by half-past ten.

When the men rejoined them some thirty minutes later, Pooki found herself staring at another guest. This one was taller but not so powerfully built as Michael and there was something vaguely familiar about him.

She hadn't really noticed him before, as Michael had claimed her attention early on and she had been too busy enjoying his furtive gropings to pay much attention to anyone else at dinner.

He noticed her stare and made his way towards her, smiling faintly.

'May I introduce myself, m'lady?' he said, bowing. 'I have the honour to be the Earl of Bowerham, Andrew Forsythe.'

Pooki acknowledged him with a gracious inclination of her head.

'I am the daughter-in-law of the Marquis of Ormsgill,' she replied, 'but you may call me Pooki. It's a nickname I picked up long ago and I prefer it to my proper name.'

She noticed Michael looking anxiously at her from across the room. She smiled and raised her glass slightly to reassure him before returning to the puzzle of where she had met Andrew before.

'You seem puzzled, m'lady,' he smiled at her.

'It's just that you seem familiar to me,' she said frankly. 'The only trouble is, I can't for the life of me think why.'

'It must be my inherent charm,' he decided. 'Either that or you think I'm the most attractive man in the room. I hope you do,' he added, 'as I think you are definitely the most desirable woman here.'

Pooki looked up at him from under her eyelashes, pretending to be disconcerted at his openness. Before she could say anything, however, he rushed on.

'Since the moment I saw you I knew I would not be able to sleep unless you were by my side,' he confessed.

'You mean you want me to sit at your bedside until you fall asleep?' she said, pretending to be astonished.

'That's not what I mean at all,' he protested. 'I want to take you in my arms, smother you with kisses, peel off your clothing little by little and kiss each newly revealed piece of flesh until you beg for more!'

'Stop!' Pooki pretended to be shocked. 'That's all very well, but what makes you think I would want you to do such a thing?'

The thought of him doing all that was an exciting one, however, and she could feel the dampness, started by Michael's attentions, spreading between her legs as Andrew continued, unabashed.

'I want to caress those perfect little breasts until their rosy tips are ready to burst,' he declared, 'and when you part your gorgeous thighs for me . . .' he stopped as words finally failed him.

'Yes?' she prompted, eager to discover what plans he had for her most personal possession.

'Ah,' he smiled slyly, 'tell me where your room is and I will show you.'

Pooki thought fast. She had no intention of cancelling her assignation with Michael, but Andrew was certainly someone it could well be worth dallying with.

194

'I'm in the Lilac Room,' she told him, 'but you must not visit me there, not tonight anyway.'

He looked crestfallen.

'Someone has already claimed you,' he said mournfully. 'Tell me who it is and I'll fight him for you.'

'You'll do no such thing,' replied Pooki. 'I have, as you have guessed, already made a prior engagement. If you wish I will keep tomorrow evening free for you.'

'Tomorrow!' he cried. 'How can you be so cruel as to keep me waiting until tomorrow?'

Pooki shrugged. 'Tell me which room you occupy,' she said, 'and maybe I shall come to visit you. We can discuss this passion you seem to have developed for my body. It won't be until after midnight though,' she warned.

This could turn out to be a busy night, she thought cheerfully. I just hope I can persuade Michael to leave before then.

'I'm in the Golden Room,' he told her, 'and I shall count the seconds until you arrive.'

With that, he took her hand and bowed over it, pressing it to his lips as he did so. Pooki could feel the intensity of his kiss long after he released her hand and left to mingle with the other guests.

She doubted very much that he would be content to sit and wait for her to show up at his door. Despite his protestations to the contrary, there were too many other equally attractive and available women present. She decided to visit him only if Michael proved a disappointment.

When Michael tapped discreetly on her door promptly at ten-thirty she was ready for him. If she was honest with herself, she was ready for anyone. The two episodes Jane had enjoyed had started something smouldering inside her. Michael's hand on her thigh during dinner had caused a flicker of flame to break out and Andrew's words had

195

fanned the flame into a fire. It would not take much to turn the fire into an inferno that only one thing would quench, and even then, only after repeated applications.

She had spent some time considering how he should find her and decided to appear as though she was preparing for bed – as in fact, she was!

Michael halted on the threshold of her room and gazed at her in admiration. It seemed as if he had interrupted her in the act of removing a stocking. She had one of her feet on the seat of a chair and was bending over it rolling down the flimsy silk. Her pose, which she had been holding for some time waiting for his knock, allowed him to appreciate her long slim legs.

The strapless, peach-coloured basque revealed her graceful shoulders and made her breasts seem fuller than they really were. At the same time it was not long enough to hide the fact that she had already removed her french knickers and he was able to feast his eyes on the smooth roundness of her bottom.

'Why, Michael!' she exclaimed as though his visit was a surprise. 'How nice to see you.'

'It's certainly a pleasure to see you,' he replied meaningfully, hastily closing the door behind him.

'I'm not quite ready to receive you,' Pooki lied. 'As you can see, you have caught me in the middle of changing.'

'Perhaps I can be of assistance,' Michael suggested, stepping forward quickly and kneeling by the chair.

Without waiting for a reply he continued rolling the stocking down her leg, stroking the soft skin as he did so. When he reached her ankle Pooki lifted her foot to allow him to remove the stocking. This done, he looked up, intending to ask her to let him help with the other stocking, but found, instead, his attention caught by the sight of her loins.

From where he knelt, the little patch of blonde fur did

nothing to hide the glory of her glistening lips, lightly rouged to make them appear more prominent. Not yet fully aroused, they still pouted invitingly, challenging him to part them and reveal even greater delights.

Pooki, knowing full well the sight she was giving him, allowed him to look for only a few seconds before putting her foot on the floor and raising her other leg. Reluctantly, he tore his gaze away and began to roll down the remaining stocking. This time, his hands were trembling noticeably as they did their work.

Once the stocking was off, Pooki seated herself on the chair. She wriggled her bottom forwards slightly so that what Michael had been gazing at a moment or two before was now only inches away from his face.

As Pooki had intended, the invitation proved irresistible. With a groan of desire he slid his hands along her thighs until they met at her damp softness. Almost fiercely parting the succulent lips with his thumbs, he buried his face in her flesh.

As his tongue flickered on and around the little, rapidly stiffening stub at the top of her slit, he slipped first one and then two fingers into her.

Pooki sighed with pleasure and lay back in the chair, pushing herself more strongly against him. She reached down to hold his head firmly in place, and as the first waves of the rapidly oncoming climax approached began to rotate herself against his fingers and mouth.

With a long, shuddering moan she spent herself, locking them both in position by wrapping her legs around his neck as she arched her back in ecstasy.

Pooki had been on edge for hours, ever since she had listened to Jane being pleasured in the coach. Subsequent events had served only to heighten her tension and the release, when it finally came, made her feel so good that she simply howled with pleasure.

Michael gently disentangled himself and sat back on his heels to look at her. Her face and chest were flushed and her expression was one of partially sated desire.

'Why don't you help me out of this,' she murmured, running her hands languidly over her basque, 'and then I'll help you out of your clothes. You're beginning to look rather uncomfortable.' She looked pointedly at the bulge in his trousers.

Instantly, he was on his feet and bending over her. She leaned forward to allow his fingers to fumble with the hooks and eyes that ran the length of the basque. As they came undone he bent further to kiss her shoulders and neck, almost beside himself with eagerness to explore her body more fully.

When at last the garment fell to the floor, his hands quickly found their way to her breasts with their hard little nipples. Pooki firmly pushed him away and rose to her feet.

'You'll have plenty of time for that in a moment,' she promised him, 'but I want something to play with as well.'

As she spoke she deftly began removing his clothes. Soon she led him to the bed and they eagerly climbed into its inviting softness.

Michael was far too aroused to spend much time with preliminaries and his urgency was beginning to affect Pooki. She let him roll her on to her back and obligingly spread her thighs to allow him entry.

Even before he had inserted himself fully, she found herself urging him into a series of hard, driving thrusts. She began biting his neck and clawing at his shoulders as he quickly raised her passions to fever pitch.

This time his cry of release almost matched her own as they climaxed within seconds of each other.

It was half an hour later before he entered her again – half an hour during which they had explored every inch of each other's bodies with fingers, lips and tongues. This time it was a much slower, more relaxed coupling and the result, whilst not being as explosive as the previous one, was every bit as satisfying.

They lay quietly for a while, savouring the memories of the past hour or so while sipping vintage brandy. Michael seemed to want to doze a little but Pooki still wanted more. She decided to take the initiative and wriggled down the bed until she was on her hands and knees between his legs.

Michael settled himself comfortably, hands behind his head, eyes closed, as Pooki set to work. She took his limp member in her hand and considered it thoughtfully. What a difference between its condition now and when it was full and stiff and urgently seeking a repository for its offering!

She bent her head and took its end into her mouth. Sucking on it gently, she teased its little slit with her tongue. She could taste the remnants of his last emission mingled with the traces of her own juices.

Slowly the head began to swell as it responded to her treatment. She switched her attention to the thickening shaft, running kisses interspersed with tiny nips from her teeth up and down its length. As she did so, she used her other hand to fondle the heavy sacks below his stem.

She rolled the loose skin between her fingers, pinching it gently from time to time. He was stiffening in a most satisfactory way, she thought, and she felt herself beginning to moisten again, in anticipation of what was to follow.

When a pair of hands began to stroke her buttocks she almost bit a piece out of him in surprise. She had been so engrossed in coaxing Michael back to a useful hardness that she had been unaware of anyone entering the room.

She glanced quickly at Michael as he lay there, wondering if he was aware that they were not alone, but he was still lying with his eyes closed, enjoying her attentions.

The hands, having kneaded her buttocks, began to explore further. Pooki decided to carry on with what she was doing and to wait for further developments. She began to slide her hand up and down the bar of flesh she had resurrected, sucking more strongly on its distended end.

Meanwhile, between her own legs, questing fingers had discovered her readiness and were slipping gently in and out of her. Guessing what was going to happen she raised her bottom as high as she could.

The invitation did not go unanswered. The fingers withdrew to be replaced by something much more satisfactory. She hid her involuntary moan of appreciation by taking as much of Michael into her mouth as she could.

She quickly revised her plans. There was now no need to hold back on Michael. Her own needs were being taken care of by her unknown assailant. What she had to do, she decided, was to try to time things so that Michael and she climaxed at the same time.

Whoever it was behind her was screwing her with such care that she was able to continue pleasuring Michael without giving the game away. Since he had entered both her room and then herself without so much as a by-your-leave, he would just have to look after his own crisis without her help.

It didn't take long for Pooki to be brought to the edge. She had discovered she enjoyed fellatio soon after she had first been expected to perform it. Her newly acquired skills had been honed in the South Sea zone and she found the whole exercise highly exciting.

To be fellating someone who was unaware that she was being fucked at the same time was even more exciting.

To not know just who it was that was doing the fucking made the act seem deliciously rude at the same time.

Her climax was not long in coming, and recognising its imminence, she redoubled her efforts on Michael. She could sense that he was not far away himself. Dimly she realised that the novelty of the situation must be reaching the man behind her, as his thrusting became harder and faster.

She slipped a finger between her legs and gave it a coating of her own freely flowing juices. Then, as the strokes behind her became shorter still, she stabbed it into Michael's anus. He groaned and bucked under her as he flooded into her mouth. Swallowing quickly Pooki felt her own climax surging round her body at the same time as she felt the man behind give one last thrust. She could feel, through the pounding in her veins, the twin spasms of the men, one in her mouth, the other in her cunt.

Such was the intensity of her own spasms that she was unaware of the unknown man's withdrawal. She was a trifle worried that when Michael opened his eyes to grin at her they would widen at the sight of someone behind her. In fact he just reached up to pull her down on to his chest, flicked the covers over them both and promptly fell asleep.

When Pooki awoke the next morning she found herself alone in the bed. Jane was pulling back the curtains and it was this that caused her to wake.

'Morning m'lady,' Jane greeted her with a grin. 'How did you sleep?'

'Very well, once I was allowed to,' she replied, accepting the tray with its plate of bread and butter and cup of coffee. 'What's more, unless you found yourself in demand last night, I'm one up on you.'

As Pooki ate, she related the events of the evening to Jane who listened with interest.

'I can see that while you're out hunting this morning, I'm going to have to do something to even the score.'

'The hunt! I'd forgotten all about it,' gasped Pooki.

'Don't worry, there's plenty of time. You'll even be able to have a proper breakfast downstairs.'

'Mmn. I wonder what time Michael left? I certainly didn't hear him go.'

Jane was right. It was over an hour later that Pooki was handed the reins of a horse by a groom who looked at her hard for several seconds, apparently deciding if she was the right size for the creature.

If Pooki had returned his stare, she might have realised there was something familiar about the man. As it was she was busy looking round for Michael.

The groom gave the girth a last tighten before standing back and watching her join the other riders who were trotting up and down, warming up their animals.

Pooki continued looking round for Michael but he was obviously not going to join the hunt. Neither was Andrew, as far as she could see. She was almost certain it had been him who had taken liberties with her the night before, but she would like to have had her suspicions confirmed.

She was still looking for either of them to appear when the hunt started. Pooki was in no hurry to charge after the hounds as the others were doing. Her only experience of horses was in the briefing for this and the Wild West zones.

The day was turning out to be a hot one and seemed too pleasant to be spent galloping madly after a pack of dogs. Nevertheless she urged her horse into a canter so as not to be left too far behind.

Her groom watched her go. Once she was about halfway across the meadow leading to the woods, he casually slipped his hand into the pocket of his rough tweed jacket. His fingers closed round the transmitter and his thumb located the on/off switch. His face expressionless, his thumb pushed the button to the 'on' position.

The effect on Pooki's horse was electrifying. With a shrill whinny it reared up on its hind legs, almost unseating Pooki and then, back on all fours again, it wheeled and galloped off at a tangent, away from the others but still towards the woods.

Although Pooki had no control over the horse, staying on wasn't a problem at first. It was only when the horse plunged headlong into the woods that she began to feel frightened. She had thought that the horse would soon recover from whatever had spooked it, but even as it blundered through the undergrowth, swerving round trees only at the last minute, it showed no signs of slowing.

Pooki knew it would only be a matter of time before she was unseated – either by the erratic motion of the horse or by being hit by a low branch. She tried to screw up the courage to jump off but she was being jerked about so much that she was unable to coordinate her movements.

Suddenly they emerged into a small clearing. Almost before Pooki was aware of it happening, a familiar figure astride a large black stallion appeared at her side. A strong arm swept her out of the saddle and then, as the black horse slowed, she was put down on to the long grass.

Pooki stumbled and by the time she had regained her balance the man was urging his horse after Pooki's, which was just re-entering the wood. A few seconds later Pooki was quite alone. Even the sounds of the horses had faded. She stood breathing deeply, trying to recover her wits. The sound of running water attracted her attention and she headed towards it.

At the edge of the clearing ran a stream. Idly, still trying to clarify the events of the last few minutes, Pooki wandered along the bank. She re-entered the wood without realising and stopped only when the stream widened out to form a small pool. A large rock, half in and half out of the water, offered somewhere to rest.

As she sat there in the hot sunshine, she was still unable to understand what had happened. One moment a gentle canter, the next a mad gallop and then, from nowhere, a dramatic rescue.

She suddenly felt hot and sticky and looked at the pool consideringly. Two minutes later she was splashing happily in the cool water and feeling much better. It was cold enough to be refreshing without chilling her. The pool was quite deep in the middle and she was able to swim a few strokes backwards and forwards.

She ducked her head under the water for a few seconds. When she surfaced it was to find Andrew smiling down at her from the rock where she had left her clothes.

'Are you all right?' he enquired. 'You seemed to be, so I left you to try and catch your horse before it injured itself.'

'I'm fine, thanks to you. You probably saved my life. But where did you come from?'

'I went out early for a ride and was just returning when the hunt started. I was waiting on the edge of the wood when I saw you having trouble with your horse. The trees prevented me from reaching you so I couldn't catch you until the clearing.'

'I'm glad you did,' Pooki said, sincerely. 'By the way, how is my horse?'

'He took a devil of a lot of catching and even then he wouldn't stand still. It was only when I removed his saddle that I found out why.'

He held up a small disk, about as thick as his finger. Pooki waded over to see and had to ask twice to be shown the disk, so distracted was he by the sight of her splendid nakedness.

'You really are gorgeous, aren't you?' he said as she picked up the disk.

Pooki didn't answer. She was too fascinated by the two wicked little needles that were taking it in turns to extend and retract from inside the case.

'This was under my saddle?' she said.

'What? Oh yes.' He tore his gaze away from her and looked at the two needles as they appeared and disappeared. 'As soon as this was turned on, by some sort of radio control I would guess, your horse would think it was being stung. It was just trying to run away from whatever was stinging it.'

'I wonder who put it there,' Pooki mused.

'And why,' added Andrew.

'One thing is sure,' said Pooki. 'If you hadn't rescued me I could have been badly hurt.' She switched on the full power of her eyes. 'Thank you very much for saving my life.'

'It was nothing.'

'No, really. How can I ever repay you?'

He ran his eyes over her more slowly this time, lingering on her breasts and again on her plump little mound.

'There is a way,' he answered thoughtfully, licking his lips which had suddenly gone dry.

Pooki remembered the events of the previous night.

'I thought you had already helped yourself to that,' she said glancing down to see where he was looking.

'Can you blame me?' he protested. 'You say that you might visit me. When you don't come and I try to find you, I find that you are devoting all your energies to some other person. Your bottom looked so enticing from your doorway that I just had to stroke it. Then your lips seemed so soft I just had to caress them. At this point you lifted yourself and showed me the gateway to heaven.' He shrugged. 'Can you blame me for going in?'

Pooki smiled and splashed back to the deep part of the pool. She turned to face him again.

'And now that you've been there?'

He began to tear off his clothes.

'I want to go there again. Only this time with your full cooperation and undivided attention.'

He started to wade towards her. Pooki noted with interest that the cool water seemed to be having absolutely no effect on his erection.

He grabbed her and pulled her into an embrace made clumsy by the water. As their lips met in a long kiss Pooki could feel his hardness pressing against her belly. She frowned. This was not where she wanted it to be.

Without breaking off from the kiss, she locked her arms round his neck and then wrapped her legs around his waist. Now she could feel him nudging the tops of her thighs.

Andrew needed no further encouragement. Using the fingers of one hand to open her, he guided himself in with the other. Pooki sighed with delight and allowed herself to slide down on to him. With Andrew bracing himself as best he could, she raised and lowered herself sending waves of pleasure through them both.

She could feel the familiar sensations beginning to build and was close to her orgasm when Andrew suddenly jerked himself hard against her and Pooki found herself underwater as his legs buckled and he collapsed under her weight.

They surfaced, laughing and spluttering, but Pooki had been too near her climax to be able to relax. Andrew understood her problem and after making a bed for her out of his clothes on a nearby patch of grass, quickly resolved it for her with a skilful application of fingers and tongue.

'I'm sorry I am unable to do more for you,' he apologised, 'but I think we ought to be returning to the Hall soon, before they send out search parties.'

In fact they only just returned in time. Pooki's horse had made its way home, minus a saddle and riderless. The groom had quite properly notified the Duke and a party was almost ready to start searching. The groom was the only one who did not seem pleased at Pooki's safe return.

He was beginning to feel desperate. Each time it took him a long time to find out where Pooki was going to be. He had to be careful not to arouse anyone's suspicions. Each time he located her, he had to spend time trying to formulate a plan. She seemed blessed with uncommonly good luck. This latest scheme was not the smooth one he would have preferred. He had slipped the disk under her saddle and counted on her being thrown. He then planned to take advantage of her condition to be able to spirit her away. Certainly he had little chance of doing so under normal circumstances. He sighed and wondered what he was going to do next.

After lunch, Andrew insisted that Pooki ought to rest after her ordeal and escorted her to her room to make sure she did so. In the event, Pooki certainly went to bed but gained little rest. On the other hand, she reflected cheerfully, she was able to thank Andrew properly for saving her life, while he was able to show his appreciation of her efforts in a way that left them both tired but satisfied.

As he left to change for dinner he reached into his pocket and pulled out her lace gloves.

'Perhaps I ought to return these?' he said.

'I wondered if you would,' Pooki replied with a grin. 'I thought I'd seen you before and when I saw your horse I knew you were the highwayman. Not content with having my maid, you had to have me as well eh?'

Andrew just grinned at her as he closed the door.

A week later, rumbling back to London in their coach, Pooki brought up the subject of their wager.

'Four,' admitted Jane, 'the Duke, one of his guests, you know, the dark one with the curly hair, a footservant and the head gardener.'

She sighed at the memory.

'The gardener kept inviting me to see his flower beds but the only bed I saw didn't have flowers anywhere near it! I sort of stuck with him for most of the week. How about you?'

'Same as you,' Pooki laughed, 'four. Michael and Andrew shared me for the entire week.'

'What about the other two then?'

'That was the Duke and his wife,' explained Pooki. 'The day after the hunt they invited me for afternoon tea in the conservatory. Of course it was very warm in there and they kept removing articles of clothing and suggested I do the same.' She smiled. 'It seemed the butler had forgotten the plates when he served the sandwiches so the Duke very courteously suggested I use his knee. Naturally I had to let the Duchess use my thigh as her plate and, you'll never believe this, but she didn't use her fingers, she just bent down and ate them right off my leg. The Duke said he thought that looked a good idea and why didn't I try it? I won't tell you where he put the second sandwich! By the time they had finished with me we were all covered in food.'

'Sounds like fun,' remarked Jane.

'I'll say. I'll never be able to eat another sandwich without remembering, that's for sure.'

They returned to London and a few days later were recalled to Central for a briefing prior to leaving for a new zone.

Chapter 9

The swords clashed noisily in the dusty air. For a moment
Pooki thought her master had been injured but he recovered his balance and managed to deflect the next
thrust, a wicked stab that would have disembowelled him
if it had reached its target.

With a grunt of effort, Marcus brought his sword round
in a sweeping arc. It caught his opponent just between
neck and shoulder, biting deep and causing a gush of
blood to spurt out. The other man crumpled instantly,
falling with a clatter of armour into the dust.

Marcus paused for a moment, breathing deeply, and
looked down at his victim. After a moment or two he
lowered his sword and turned away. Pooki hurried over
and he allowed her to begin removing his armour.

He was sweating heavily, little rivulets washing
lines through the dust which coated his chest and
thighs. She inhaled the male odour and found herself
responding to his masculinity. It had been a hard and
exciting fight but she had always been confident of the
outcome.

As soon as his armour had been removed, Pooki helped
him to put on his cloak and then, without so much as a
backward glance at the motionless figure a few feet away,

he strode away from the practice ground, back towards his villa.

As soon as he had disappeared, a tech-crew emerged from one of the buildings and carried the droid into a lift. Once underground it would be repaired and fitted with a new skin and blood sachets. It would then be ready to be programmed for its next fight.

Marcus was feeling pleased with himself as he led the way home.

'Well, girl,' he demanded over his shoulder to Pooki who was having to hurry to keep up with him, 'what did you think of that?'

'You fought well, master,' she replied dutifully.

'More than well,' he said, 'brilliantly! That one knew some tricks I hadn't seen before and if I hadn't been on my mettle he might have defeated me.'

'Yes, master.'

'I rather think I might enter the games next month.'

They continued in silence after that, he dreaming of winning in the Colosseum, she wondering how much she really believed his victory was down to his skill rather than that of the programmer.

In their briefing before being sent to Ancient Rome, the principles of the fights had been explained to them. Any would-be contestants had to undergo a range of tests to ascertain their levels of skill and endurance. The droids they fought were then carefully programmed to test these levels to the full.

At crucial moments in a fight, when it looked as though the droid was gaining the upper hand, it would slip or its thrust would not quite be hard enough. The human would come away believing he had been fighting for his life when, in reality, the only danger was of slipping himself and falling on to his own sword. Even if the human were to just stand still and make no effort to defend himself, the droid would not harm him. It would find its sandal had come loose, or it had something in its eye. The illusion was brilliantly executed, however, and no one ever seemed to realise that he had been tricked.

Returning to the villa, Pooki handed Marcus's cloak to another girl and followed her master into his bathroom. The bath was the size of a small swimming pool, with a second, much smaller one next to it.

Marcus allowed Pooki to remove his loin cloth before stepping into the tub. Pooki quickly removed her own shift before joining him. Using the cloths and oils nearby she carefully washed off the sweat and dust of his morning's exertions.

He had a good body, she thought as she worked the oil into his shoulders. And that's not all, she reminded herself as she worked down his back. She felt the twinges of excitement building between her legs. When he turned round she saw he was already hard and was waiting impatiently for her to finish.

But this was a routine they had been through several times before and Pooki made no attempt to hurry. Slowly, methodically, she scrubbed her way down his body. Neither of them said a word as she carefully washed his erection and gently sponged his balls and between his legs. When she finished and moved down on to his thighs he couldn't restrain a sigh.

Once the last traces of the morning were removed they climbed out and moved into the main bath. The water was still warm, but cooler than that of the tub. Pooki felt her nipples stiffen as she ducked under the surface.

Marcus had lost none of his hardness through the change in temperature. Almost before Pooki had resurfaced he was pulling her towards him. His hands seemed everywhere as his mouth devoured hers. She knew from previous experience that he didn't expect her to do much.

He had been ready for her for some time now, virtually since finishing his fight, and almost as soon as she came within reach he was nudging at her slit.

Partly supported by the water, Pooki wrapped her legs around him and lay back, paddling gently to keep herself afloat. Marcus stood between her legs, holding her hips, setting his own rhythm which sent little waves rippling across the bath.

At times like these she knew he wanted a quick release and the most practical form of encouragement she could give him was verbal.

'Oooh, that feels good,' she murmured. 'I love the feeling of your prick in my cunt. It feels so strong.'

His rhythm intensified and she found, as usual, that her words were having a similar effect on herself. The future queen of Morex, she thought, using language like this.

'You're so big!' she cried. 'You're filling me up! Oh slide it in, slide it in! Harder! Harder! I want you to come inside me. Oh fuck me, fuck me, fuck me!'

The water was slopping on to the sides of the pool by now and Pooki was hoping he would last just a little longer as she was almost ready to come herself. Suddenly, however, he groaned with relief and she could feel him emptying himself into her. Almost immediately he withdrew and she had to ignore her own feelings and climb out to dry and dress him. Then she was dismissed while he went to tell his friends about his prowess earlier that morning.

It was fortunate for Pooki that as she headed towards the kitchens she met one of the guests. His eyes lit up as he saw her. Her hair was still wet and, because she hadn't had time to dry herself properly, her shift was sticking to her breasts and hips.

'Come with me, girl,' he commanded, leading her into his bedroom.

Lifting the hem of her shift he pressed his hand to her slit. Finding her still wet he produced a stiff prick, pushed her down on to the bed and thrust it into her. The entire episode lasted less than five minutes but it was just long enough to allow Pooki to finish where Marcus had left off. When she arrived in the kitchens it was with a satisfied grin on her face.

Throughout the day, Marcus and his house guests were fond of having several short encounters with whichever of the 'slaves' caught their fancies. Pooki and the others were constantly finding their short, white shifts being lifted regardless of what they were doing, and they all kept themselves ready with tiny dabs of aphro-gel.

One girl had them helpless with laughter when she recounted how a guest had found her in the lavatory. Despite her admittedly half-hearted protests, the guest had watched with interest until she had finished, made her hold him while he relieved himself and then bent her over the seat while he relieved himself in a different way.

The evenings were a different story. After (and often during) the leisurely meal the arousal process was spun out for as long as possible. The girls would move round the couches, their shifts only just hiding their charms. As they poured the wine or offered food, they would be fondled quite intimately. On several occasions, guests had had wine poured over themselves or food dropped in their laps as the slaves found it impossible to remain composed.

Marcus had five guests – two men and three women – with him in the villa at the moment. By the time the meal ended, often two or even three hours later, they would retire to their rooms with a number of slaves. Pooki found the days tiring as she was in a perpetual state of arousal, but the nights were easier as there was always another slave helping to satisfy the master or mistress.

Marcus went to the gladiator school three times a week. Sometimes some of the other men accompanied him but usually they preferred to remain in the villa and practise a different type of sport.

He always took one of the girls with him and always went through the same routine on his return. The girls liked going with him as it gave them a chance to savour some fresh air and have a look round. Usually they had to remain in the villa for the benefit of the guests and the only sights they saw were the ceilings.

When Marcus announced that he was throwing a party at the end of his month's tenure, everyone knew what that meant.

'An orgy!' stated one of the girls, licking her lips. 'It's about time too! I thought I was going to finish my time here without so much as a sniff of one.'

Pooki found herself looking forward to it as well. The encounters she had had so far in this sector did not stand comparison to those of the other zones. She decided she preferred quality to quantity and no matter how many quickies she was notching up, there was not much to compare with a good, long night of lust.

However tired and sore she might feel the next day, there was a certain satisfaction to be found in falling asleep covered in sweat and juices, knowing that she had fucked her partner (or partners) to a standstill.

She was beginning to understand what drove Gala to her many excesses and although she couldn't ever see herself chasing an orgasm quite so casually (or quite so frequently) as her friend, she was fully prepared to admit that it was invariably worth the effort.

The sex that she and the other girls were experiencing was not particularly satisfying, though. It was exciting enough in its way – never being sure when or where you would next be called upon to perform – and it was undeniably pleasant, but for satisfaction it fell far short of a solid night of uninhibited lust.

The arrangements for the day of the orgy were simple. Extra slaves would arrive early in the morning to help make everything ready. They would stay for the day and the night as well, serving at the feast and joining in with the entertainment.

The half-dozen or so guests that Marcus had invited would arrive shortly before noon. After some light refreshments they would all go with Marcus to the Games. Pooki and some of the other slaves would go too, carrying bread, fruit and wine in case the spectators became hungry during the afternoon.

Once the Games had ended, Marcus would rejoin his party, having triumphed over whatever adversaries he had been pitted against, and they would return to the villa to bathe and prepare for the feast.

For the three days left before the Games and feast, the villa was a hive of industry. As well as giving the place a thorough cleaning, the water in the baths had to be changed. This was done one bath at a time so that there were still two available for the residents.

Pooki had just left one of them after scrubbing the tiles before it was refilled, and was looking forward to a bath herself when she was stopped by two of Marcus's guests.

'Now where d'you think this little chicken is off to?' one of them remarked.

'I've no idea, but she looks rather hot, doesn't she?'

'So she does. Hot and wet.'

'I wonder if she feels hot and wet?'

The man slipped his hand between Pooki's thighs. She was slippery with sweat all over. That and the effects of the ever-present gel gave the man the impression that he had slipped his finger into a furnace.

215

'By Jupiter, feel her heat,' he said to his companion, stepping back.

Pooki allowed her temperature to be taken by another finger.

'By the gods, you're right! This is too good to miss.'

He promptly parted the folds of his toga and produced his prick. His companion quickly followed suit.

'Now then, my little Vesuvius, which one would you like first?' one of them asked.

Pooki eyed her choices with interest. There didn't seem a lot of difference between them and as it was inevitable she was going to have them both it didn't matter to her who went first.

'It's a difficult choice, masters,' she replied tactfully, reaching out to take hold of them, one in each hand.

She pretended to consider them, checking their lengths and thicknesses and lightly hefting their balls whilst they stood confidently in front of her. Finally she looked at them with a wicked grin.

'I'm not sure, masters. Do either of you have a coin?'

They laughed, pleased that she hadn't chosen one over the other.

'You go first, Claudius,' said one. 'You saw her first.'

'Very well, but there's no need for you to have to wait. Turn round, my dear.'

Obediently, Pooki turned her back on Claudius and bent forwards. The other man promptly positioned himself in front of her.

'Hang on to me,' he suggested.

There was method in his madness Pooki discovered. As she spread her legs and leaned over, taking hold of the man's hips, she found her mouth inches from his erection.

She waited until Claudius completed his penetration and then took the other in her mouth. It was difficult trying to concentrate on what she was doing with Claudius slamming into her from behind. He was giving her some delicious sensations and the temptation was simply to enjoy them.

On the other hand, the prick she had in her mouth was rather tasty as well and once she adjusted to the rhythm Claudius had established, she found she could manage to enjoy herself twofold.

All too soon Claudius made his last thrust. She could feel his flood splashing into her as he pulled her back against him. As soon as he released her she turned round and offered herself to his companion.

This time she had to lean against the wall, as Claudius was in no condition to support her. She was so slick that the man slid into her effortlessly. Soon he was pounding away at her also.

This time, she was better able to respond having a firmer support to lean against. She was able to rotate her hips as he drove into her and they were both soon gasping with pleasure.

Once again she felt the explosion against her insides and this time she managed one of her own.

She had to go straight to her room afterwards. Her shift, already damp, was now soaked with sweat and the offerings she had received were trickling down the insides of her thighs.

She peeled off her tunic and picked up a cloth, ready to sponge herself down, when a voice halted her.

'So you're the little volcano I've just been told about.'

She turned to find Marcus standing in the doorway. He stared with admiration at her glistening body. His gaze dropped to the damp and matted hair between her legs.

'And I do believe you've started to erupt! I can see the lava on your thighs. I wonder if you're still as hot as Julius said you were?'

Pooki dropped the cloth and lay back on her bed, and in an instant Marcus was between her parted thighs. Once again, the entry was as smooth as a hot poker sliding into soft butter, and Pooki found her excitement matching that of the man on top of her. She felt the hot jet of an ejaculation and felt herself responding in kind.

This time she was glad he left her quickly. She lay there gathering her strength. Although all three episodes had taken less than fifteen minutes, she felt worn out by the speed at which they had all taken place.

On the day of the feast everyone was up and about early. For once the slaves felt at ease. Marcus and his house guests were saving themselves for the evening and thus there would be no quick interludes to be ready for. Pooki felt strangely calm without the customary dab of aphro-gel to keep her in a state of readiness.

No sooner had breakfast been cleared away than the extra slaves arrived and Pooki had a double shock. She found to her surprise and delight that one of the girls was Gala. She was just about to whisk her friend away so that they could exchange gossip as they swept out the bedrooms when the sight of one of the male slaves stopped her dead in amazement.

'Sonus!' she cried. 'No, surely it can't be?'

Sonus looked equally thunderstruck at the sight of her.

'Pooki?' he ventured doubtfully.

Forgetting her situation for the moment she hugged him warmly.

'But what in space are you doing here?'

He looked wryly at her short shift with its low cut neckline.

'The same as you I imagine. You remember I told you at that party that my parents were sending me on a tour to finish my education? Well, this is where they sent me. I was too embarrassed to tell you the truth.'

Pooki laughed.

'Me too! And all the time we've both been here, "broadening our outlook on life".'

There was no time to talk further. Sonus was sent with one of the regular slaves to collect some barrels of wine and Gala was despatched to the kitchen to help with the food.

Pooki cleaned rooms with her mind in a whirl. She had never forgotten Sonus, although his memory had dimmed a little. Seeing him again had brought them all flooding back however. He was even more attractive than she remembered and she wondered how he thought she looked.

Later in the morning she managed to spend some time with him and the first thing he did was to reassure her on her appearance.

'You're looking great, Pooki,' he told her. 'You seem much more confident than you did at that party. More beautiful too, if I may say so.'

'You may, you may, but you're looking good yourself. You seem to have filled out.'

She was finding it hard not to touch him as they spoke. His shoulders and chest seemed broader than when they met, she thought, although she was aware that she had filled out a little too.

'Speak for yourelf,' he grinned. 'I just wish I was one of the guests rather than an employee. I know who I'd choose to spend the night with.'

Pooki grinned back at him.

'Thank you, kind sir! But tell me Sonus, how long are you here for? I've only got a few more days and then my contract expires. Why don't we travel back together and make up for lost time?'

'That sounds great, but before we decide anything I have a confession to make. Sonus isn't my real name. I'm actually called Janus and my father is king of Morex.'

219

If he expected to surprise Pooki with his statement he succeeded beyond his wildest dreams. She stared at him, flabbergasted. They were sitting in a corner of the central courtyard of the villa and Pooki was convinced that if they had been standing, she would have fallen over.

'You're kidding!' she shrieked. 'Say that again!'

Surprised by her reaction to his statement, Sonus repeated it. It was his turn to be amazed when Pooki began to laugh.

'What have I said? What's the joke?' he asked, confused.

It was several minutes later before Pooki, eyes still streaming with tears of laughter, was able to explain.

'You are Prince Janus of Morex?' she demanded, wanting to have it confirmed one last time.

'Yes.'

'Shortly to marry the Princess of Pulkrington, daughter of the King of Rontar.'

'Yes.'

'Well, that's me, baby! Pooki, Princess of Pulkrington.'

It was his turn to be struck speechless until the humour of the situation dawned on him and he joined Pooki in a fresh burst of laughter.

'So our parents sent us here to grow up a little before introducing us and not only had we already met but we liked each other!'

'That's right,' agreed Pooki, 'and personally speaking, I'm rather looking forward to the honeymoon.'

'Hey, me too. Where shall we go?'

They were called back to work before they were able to talk further and although Pooki managed to speak to Gala, she didn't even see Sonus again before it was time to go to the Games.

Gala managed to have herself included on the trip and the two friends spent the afternoon catching up on each other's gossip, in between keeping the guests supplied with food and drink.

Gala had been sent to the villa independently from Sonus and so had not realised who he was. She took the news far more calmly than Pooki had.

'There you are then. Everything's going to work out fine. If I were you, though, I'd start thinking about tonight. You realise, don't you, that he's going to see you being screwed by all those randy Romans while you'll probably see him giving it to their wives?'

Pooki hadn't thought of that, but after a while decided to be positive about the whole thing.

'Well, at least he'll get a good idea of what he's going to get,' she said, 'and he'll see that I'll be able to be a good and supportive queen.'

'Right! And you'll see what you're going to get,' Gala chuckled. 'If it's anything like the rest of him you should be all right.'

The party returned to the villa in a state of rising excitement. Marcus had done well in his fights, despatching two lions and three humanoid opponents.

The villa was ready for the feast which was due to begin after everyone had had a chance to bathe and change. Marcus took Pooki and Gala with him to help him prepare and for once he was prepared to forgo his customary post-fight wind-down. The girls barely had time to prepare themselves before the gong summoned them to the feast.

Crisp new shifts were waiting for them once they had hurriedly bathed. Before putting them on the girls applied rouge to themselves from the little pots provided. Having reddened their lips and cheekbones they studied their reflections in the polished silver sheet that acted as a mirror.

Gala decided that her nipples could stand a little rouge and carefully applied some. Liking the effect, Pooki followed suit and then with a dash of recklessness decided to paint her other lips also.

'Wow!' Gala was impressed. 'That really draws attention to your little honeypot. Here, do mine!'

Both girls were delighted with the results. They put on their shifts and practised bending over to reveal their bright red nipples and raising their arms which lifted their hems until only a blind man could fail to notice the succulent lips previously hidden.

As the echo of the gong faded they entered the dining room. Quickly they took up their positions, Pooki with a jug of wine, Gala with a tray of meats. Sonus was with another male slave filling the jugs from the barrels in the corner.

The room was large and airy. The doors opened on to the courtyard and the evening light was only just beginning to fade. Torches had already been placed in sconces all round the room and outside around the courtyard, but as yet there was no need for them.

The room contained a dozen couches. Each had a raised end and no sides. They were grouped in fours around stone plinths, almost groaning under the weight of plates of meat and fish as well as bowls of fruit.

The guests strolled in, chose a couch and sprawled themselves on it. Marcus looked round to ensure that they were all comfortable and then clapped his hands sharply together. Immediately, Pooki and the other serving girls moved forwards and began offering the guests food and drink.

At the same time some scantily clad dancers appeared in the doorway and began to sway about in time to the music strummed on a lyre and punctuated by the tinkling of tiny cymbals.

The dancers gave way to some jugglers who also performed a few acrobatic feats in the limited space. Then some actors appeared and gave a spirited performance of a rather lewd story concerning a widow and her efforts to make ends meet.

By the end of the first hour everyone, guests and slaves, had relaxed. The feast was going well. Sonus had already had to replace one empty barrel. The guests were obviously enjoying themselves, shouting comments to each other regarding the merits or otherwise of the performers and Marcus was recounting yet again how he feared that one of the lions had been about to bite off his arm.

The dancers reappeared. This time they were fairly well covered, apparently with a great number of silk scarves. Wending their way around the couches they encouraged the guests to pull them off one at a time. Within a very short while the dancers were naked.

At this point the music became rather slower and more rhythmical. One of the musicians began beating a large drum and the female dancers started to swing their hips and jiggle their breasts. They carefully avoided the grasping hands of the guests to start with, but as their movements became more abandoned they began to allow themelves to be stroked and fondled.

As there were only four dancers, three girls and one man, there were not enough to go round. Soon the other slaves, male and female, were being fondled as well. Pooki noticed at least two of the women guests had allowed their togas to fall away on either side of them, revealing their own breasts and thighs.

Her own rouged nipples had been noticed and admired for some time and were now stiff from all the attention they had been receiving. As Pooki leant over Claudius to fill his cup she heard a murmur of approval from his wife.

'Is this the little volcano you told me about?' she asked her husband.

'Why, yes, it is,' he confirmed. 'But why do you ask?'

'From the look of her cunt she's ready to erupt again,' was the reply.

Pooki felt her shift being raised so Claudius could see the scarlet lips.

'By Jupiter I see what you mean! Let me have her!'

'Not so fast, Claudius, there's something I want to do to her first.'

Pooki shivered as a tongue began lapping between her legs. She looked round to see similar activities beginning all round the room but then, as the sensations she was receiving began to build, she gave her full attention to matters closer at hand.

With only the slightest demur, Claudius's wife was persuaded to pause long enough for Pooki to arrange things a little more comfortably. Now, with their heads buried between each other's legs, they were both able to give and receive maximum pleasure.

Soon they were gasping and moaning as a result of the things they were doing to each other until finally Pooki's partner was forced to call a halt.

'That was wonderful, my dear,' she sighed, 'but I think I'm ready for something rather more substantial.'

Pooki knew exactly what she meant. She was more than ready for a stiff prick herself. She could imagine only too well how it would feel, sliding deep into her well-prepared slit.

A passing slave caught her fancy. He was tall and well muscled. His torso had been lightly oiled and it gleamed faintly in the fading light. What really caught her eye, however, was the fact that, somewhere along the way he had lost his loincloth. His prick, waving gently in front of him, was obviously in need of a haven.

Even as she was licking her lips at the thought, a greedy bejewelled hand reached for it and almost yanked him round.

'Come here, slave!' Claudius's wife commanded. 'There's something I want you to do for me.'

The slave had no need to ask what it was. She was lying almost as Pooki had left her, one leg trailing down to the floor, the other raised and bent at the knee. Her toga was only just clinging to her shoulders and her large soft breasts rolled enticingly as she pulled the slave towards her.

Pooki moved away from the couch and let the slave take over. As she passed another couch an arm encircled her waist. She turned to find one of the guests, still respectably covered from neck to knee, smiling at her. He gestured to his empty cup.

'Why don't you find us both some more wine and come sit beside me?' he suggested.

Pooki smiled agreeably and went over to ask Sonus for two cups. On the way she had a more leisurely look round.

The first person she noticed was Gala. She was squatting over a rather portly guest, gently raising and lowering herself on his rather portly prick. He was lying back with his eyes closed and a blissful expression on his face. Gala was taking full advantage of his lack of attention and was almost swallowing the long cock of another guest standing next to her.

Elsewhere, two other girls were sitting facing each other, kissing passionately and playing with each other's breasts. A second glance showed that while one was being thoroughly licked out, the other was being screwed, both by the same man. Pooki wished she could change places with one of them.

The three dancing girls were entwined in a complicated-looking arrangement with two other guests. Even as she looked another guest found the unoccupied cunt and promptly rectified the situation.

The room was filled with the moans, groans, gasps and cries of passion.

She smiled at Sonus as he filled a couple of cups.

'Feeling left out of things?' she said, looking pointedly at his all-too-obvious erection.

'My chance will come,' he grinned. 'Those women look awfully greedy and I'll be one of the few able to provide them with seconds! Anyway, how're you doing? Who's your friend?'

'I've no idea, although now you mention it, he does seem rather familiar. I wonder where I've seen him before.'

The man in question watched Pooki chatting to the slave. It had been ridiculously easy to gain entrance to the feast. He had had the villa under observation for some time. When he noticed the slave carrying the invitations, it had been the work of moments to engage him in conversation and find out what and when they were for.

Then he had followed the slave until he had delivered an invitation to a villa where the resident had been out. Using the first excuse that came to mind he had called on the villa, been admitted by a slave and waited for an opportunity to steal the scroll bearing the invitation.

When Pooki returned with the drinks, he made her put them down on a table while he kissed her. He very nearly forgot why he was there, as being kissed by Pooki was a highly erotic experience.

It wasn't just the way her tongue seemed to send sparks of electricity shooting round his mouth, it was her total commitment to the act. Her body seemed to glue itself to his and he was as aware as never before of the pressure of a pair of breasts against his chest and a firm little mound rubbing against his erection.

When he finally came up for air he reached for the drinks. He definitely felt in need of one. It was with a trembling hand that he managed to drop the tablet into hers. Before he had a chance to do anything more she managed to distract him totally once again.

The touch of the hand that had burrowed its way into the folds of his toga brought the instant realisation that, however much he needed it, his drink could wait.

Once again he lost himself to her kiss. This time he could feel her nipples, hard against him, whilst the feel of her cool, slender fingers teasing his already stiff flesh into undreamt-of rigidity was fast convincing him that the most sensible course of action was to leave the Duke of Krantz's employment forever.

Only with a supreme effort of will was he able to break away from her embrace. He looked at her with a respect bordering on awe and resolutely ignored the voice of his conscience telling him to abandon his mission.

Handing Pooki her cup he took a deep draught of his own. Her eyes sparkled at him over the rim of hers as she sipped delicately. She even managed to make the simple act of drinking highly suggestive, he thought. He finished his drink and waited for her to catch up. About five minutes, he thought, before she begins to become drowsy.

No one would think twice if they lurched out together, apparently heading for somewhere more private. Once out of the villa, it would be fairly straightforward to spirit her off the planet. He had prepared thoroughly, well aware that this would be his last chance. She would be carefully stowed in a large, specially designed trunk and flown out in a hired cruiser.

The only trouble was, he thought to himself, that all this running around arranging things had worn him out. What he really needed was a good night's sleep. Maybe he would delay his flight until the next day. He lapsed into unconsciousness just as he decided it would be sensible to grab a few hours' sleep.

Pooki looked at the inert body in some surprise. A few

227

minutes ago the man had been raring to go. Now he had fallen asleep. She felt slightly insulted and was gently slapping his face in an effort to revive him when Sonus appeared at her side.

'Help me move him,' he whispered urgently.

'Why? What's the matter?' Pooki said, confused.

'I was watching him. Just before he passed you your drink, he slipped something into it. While you were messing about, I switched the cups round.' He looked at the unconscious body. 'Just as well that I did.'

Pooki was aware of the debauchery going on all around them. All she had wanted to do was join in. Now she had an unknown man trying to drug her. Suddenly she realised where she had seen him before. He had been the gambler on the riverboat. He had tried to drug her there as well. Not only that, her memory told her, suddenly dredging up all manner of information, he had sold her some drugs in California and handed her a horse in Victorian England.

Each time he appeared something funny happened. She remembered the robot in the South Seas. Maybe he had been behind that. Then she recalled that nothing had happened in California. But he had given her some tablets which she hadn't taken. Probably they were the same sort of stuff as he had just been trying to give her this time.

'Come on then,' she said. 'Let's take him out. Only I'd like to talk to him when he wakes up. I think he's been after me for some time.'

Now it was Sonus's turn to look confused. 'What do you mean?'

'I'll tell you later. You hold his arm round your shoulders and we'll try to give the impression we're going somewhere more private.'

'We're leaving an orgy in search of privacy?'

'Can you think of a better way of managing things?' she replied.

'Why not pretend he's so drunk we're taking him for some fresh air?'

'OK. I can't see the difference myself but however we do it, let's just get him out.'

As it happened, no one gave them a second glance. They were all too busy with their own affairs. It took them no more than five minutes to take the man to Pooki's room, tear a sheet into strips and tie him securely into a neat bundle which they rolled under her bed.

'We'll deal with him later,' Pooki stated and then they returned to the feast.

The guests had stopped eating food by this time and were concentrating on eating each other. There was very little clothing actually being worn now, although there were plenty of discarded items lying about.

The room was a sea of flesh. Thighs, buttocks and breasts were visible everywhere. There were not too many pricks visible – most of those had found a niche of one sort or another.

The only slave not involved in any of these activities was going round lighting the torches. As the flickering flames shed their golden glow on the piles of flesh, Pooki and Sonus made their way rather gingerly into the midst.

Sonus gave a startled yelp as a pair of hands first grabbed and then dragged him into a threesome. There was a cry of 'Fresh meat!' as his loincloth was ripped off and he was engulfed by naked bodies.

Pooki was not left on her own for long. A man beckoned her over to his couch. His desires were obvious. Pooki was about to take him in her mouth but he pulled her over him and as they kissed she felt him slide into her.

Having been more than ready not too long ago Pooki relished the feel of him inside her. As he thrust up into her she ground herself down on him.

When another prick appeared in front of her it was the work of an instant to grab it and begin to suck. After a few moments the owner pulled it away, much to Pooki's disappointment. She had felt she was close to making it spurt and she wanted to taste it.

Instead, she felt herself being pushed forwards and the cheeks of her bottom parted. The feeling of this second prick making its entrance, almost next to the first, was amazing. She felt as though she was being stretched beyond the bounds of possibility and yet she could feel it sliding in, apparently with ease.

There was nothing she could do now as she was impaled upon two separate poles of flesh. As one withdrew, so the other plunged, time after time with almost clockwork precision. She realised she was letting out a long low wail of pleasure as the men continued their steady pillage of her body.

How many times her climaxes wracked her body she had no idea, and gradually became aware that they had stopped their onslaught only after they too, finally spent themselves.

The men disentangled themselves and reached for cups of wine. As they drank thirstily Pooki looked round.

Gala and another girl were busy between each other's legs. As they teased and titillated each other, their bottoms had obviously waggled invitingly, for both of them were being fucked from behind at the same time.

Sonus, Pooki noted, was standing between the outspread thighs of two women. One was lying face down on top of the other kissing her deeply. Sonus was dividing his attentions between them both, plunging first into one and then the other. It seemed to be an arrangement satisfactory to all three parties, judging from the cries and moans emanating from them.

Eventually, even the greediest of the guests was ready

for a rest. Marcus quickly gave orders for the room to be tidied and then led everyone else to the baths.

Piles of large soft towels were waiting at the water's edge for the bathers as they emerged after much splashing and grabbing. Pooki was one of many who found themselves the target of revitalised lust. When the guests, still draped in towels, returned to the dining room, it had been cleaned and tidied. Fresh bowls of fruit and jugs of wine had been placed on the tables and heaps of cushions had been left around the walls.

Pooki wondered how many robots had been used whilst they had been bathing. Certainly the few slaves left behind could not have accomplished the work on their own.

The pattern of things was much as before although the pace had slowed somewhat. Pooki found she was having to work much harder to coax life back into the cock she had in her hands. Fortunately, there was not the same sense of urgency as before and she could take her time.

When she finally straddled the now stiff piece of flesh she was struck by the sight of Gala, covered in grapes, being nibbled and licked clean. As the man beneath Pooki bucked his appreciation of her efforts into her she had an idea.

Once disentangled, she peeled a banana and inserted it into herself. Her intention was to offer some fruit to every man in the room. As it was, she never made it past the first two. They were so taken with the idea that nothing would do but they had to eat several bananas each from Pooki's rather novel fruit-holder. Having done that, they decided that she should drink some wine. This could only be done, they insisted, by them dipping their members in their goblets and she licking them dry.

After only a very few licks they were unable to dip their pricks in the goblets, as they were too stiff. They didn't have far to look for something they could dip them into.

231

Neither man was willing to let the other go first and so once again she found herself entertaining two men simultaneously. Once again the outcome was more than satisfactory to them all.

When the orgy eventually ended, some hours later, Pooki had never felt so battered. Every available inch of her had been the object of someone's lust at one time or another. She had lost count, much earlier, of the number of times she had been penetrated. Her mouth, cunt and anus all felt they had been stretched beyond the point of no return. Yet when she examined herself in the polished metal mirror before she finally collapsed into her bed, she could detect no difference in her reflection except a certain amount of redness in certain places and a rather wicked, self-satisfied twinkle in her eye.

She fell into exhausted sleep wondering what she was going to do with the still unconscious body under her bed.

Chapter 10

Listening to Credo talking softly into his video console, Ami stretched her long legs into a more comfortable position and regarded her toes critically. A little more polish was needed, she decided. Credo ended his conversation and turned his attention back to his wife.

'Sorry about that, my love, but there's still no sign of Olga. Apparently she was last seen near to the palace and our people are worried she might try something. I'm sure she'll be picked up soon. As long as she doesn't do anything stupid there'll be no reason to hold her. From all accounts she was completely unaware of what Krantz was up to. Anyway, what were we talking about?'

'You were telling me about your conversation with Krantz,' she reminded him.

'Oh yes. Well, after we had that call from Pooki, I contacted Security on Paradise and they agreed to ship the man back to us post haste. Once he realised where he was and who he was dealing with, he confessed very quickly. As a result, I have told Krantz he has one week in which to leave Rontar before he will be arrested and brought to trial, charged with treason.'

'I don't suppose he was too pleased with that,' said Ami.

'No he wasn't,' agreed Credo. 'But what choice does he have? At least he's allowed to leave, which is more than anyone else would be allowed.'

'You're right, darling,' said Ami, already slightly bored with the whole subject.

When Pooki had called, telling them what had happened and how the man had been after her almost from the moment she had set foot on Paradise, Ami had been alarmed and worried. Once she had reassured herself that Pooki was no longer in any danger, her worry changed to anger, directed at whoever had instigated this threat to her daughter's wellbeing.

Now that the whole business was virtually finished, she wanted to forget it all, welcome her daughter home and start making plans for the wedding. Once the happy couple had been dispatched on their honeymoon, their elders could set about the serious matter of celebrating the union.

Such celebrations usually lasted for a good week or so and offered ample opportunity to renew old acquaintances, strike up new ones and generally indulge in a good old-fashioned binge. She could feel the familiar stirring in her loins at the thought of it.

'All his lands and properties here on Rontar will revert to the Crown until such time as we see fit to dispose of them,' continued Credo. 'And you know what that means?'

Ami brightened at his words. 'It means all sorts of people will come flocking round trying to grab a piece of his estate.'

'That's right,' Credo grinned, only too aware of where Ami's thoughts were taking her. 'We shall be invited to all sorts of entertainments in the hope of gaining our favour.'

'I suppose every cloud has its silver lining,' Ami conceded. 'But what about Olga? Will she be entitled to anything?'

'Oh, I expect something will be arranged,' Credo replied airily.

'Admit it, Credo,' Ami challenged him, 'you've a soft spot for that woman!'

'Not so much of a soft spot . . .'

'. . . As a hard prick!' she finished for him, crossing the room to curl up on his lap. 'It's a good job I know you love me, or else I might become rather jealous. And speaking of a hard prick, what's this I can feel, poking against my ass?'

'Why don't you find out for yourself?' he suggested.

Ami needed no second invitation and within a very short time she had Credo just where she wanted him, which just happened to be where he wanted to be too.

'Credo,' she murmured, undulating gently beneath him.

He raised his head from where it had been nuzzling one of her breasts.

'Mmn?'

'Do you have any engagements tonight?'

He thought for a moment before turning his attention to her other breast. It seemed to him that the nipple could just be teased a fraction stiffer.

'I don't think so,' he mumbled.

'Good. Then why don't you come to my sitting room round about nine o'clock?'

Credo knew his wife well enough to realise it would do him no good to ask her why. He also knew that it was well worth responding to such invitations.

'Very well, my dear, nine o'clock it shall be. Now will you be good enough to stop talking and concentrate on what I'm doing to you. I am the King you know!'

'Very well, Your Majesty . . .' her words tailed off as actions began to speak louder.

* * *

A few million miles away Pooki, Sonus, Gala and all the others whose time on Paradise had reached its end were having their final briefing.

They were being informed of the transport arrangements for their return trips, being issued with their fees for the work they had done and, perhaps most importantly, were being given their references.

For some, a good reference from Paradise was the key to many doors throughout the galaxy. It could, for example, mean the difference between being able to open a successful house of pleasure on a planet or a mediocre one. There was nothing like a glowing testimonial, prominently displayed, to bring the customers flocking in.

To others it might make a good marriage to a wealthy man or woman a probability where before it was only a possibility.

Once the briefing was completed, the employees were free to occupy their time in any way they saw fit until their flights were called. Most people returned to their rooms to read their references. Pooki was no exception.

It was with relief and pride that she read she had been awarded a distinction, Paradise's top award. She knew that Paradise had inspectors pretending to be visitors in all the zones, but like everyone else, she had no idea who they were or how many had tested her.

Gala bounced in, proudly displaying her own distinction. When she read Pooki's she grinned.

'Well done, Pooks! I knew you had it in you.'

'You're right, but I had to have several in me before I knew it too,' she laughed.

'By the way, what did Sonus get? Or should I call him Janus now?'

'Call him either. I think I'll stick to Sonus. Anyway I don't know. I haven't seen him yet.'

'Well, give him my regards when you do. Oh yeah, and have a good wedding.'

'What do you mean? You sound as though you won't be coming to it,' Pooki said, confused.

'That's right, kiddo. I've just been told that there are some rather interesting sub-sectors on this planet where you can find some real action. You would have been invited too, but Central knows that you have to go back and marry and become Queen and all that boring stuff. I think I'm going to stay.'

'But what will I do for a bridesmaid?'

Gala hooted with laughter.

'Me, a bridesmaid? Everyone on Rontar knows the only thing a maid and I have in common is we're both female. I'd probably spend the entire wedding trying to lay the best man. And then I'd have to lay everyone else just to see if he really was the best man.'

Pooki was forced to admit Gala had a point. 'But when will you come back? I'll miss you.'

'You won't have time to miss me. You're going to be so busy for the next few years you won't miss anybody. Then, just when you think you have it all worked out, Sonus will decide it's time a little prince or princess appeared. No, I think I'll be better off here. Who knows? I might even end up running the place.'

'You probably will at that. You'll stay in touch though?'

'Of course. Now, go and find out what Sonus was awarded. Then tell him you don't believe it and demand he proves it to you.'

Pooki decided that sounded like a good idea but before she could even leave her room, her flight was called. She gave Gala a last hug and headed for the departure area.

Sonus was there when she arrived. His flight was due to leave before hers and they had only a few moments before he left.

'Well, I guess I'll see you at the wedding,' Pooki said, disappointed that they were not travelling together as far as Rontar.

'I guess so. I was kind of hoping we could share a cabin on the way back, but there's a ship going past Morex on its way to the Qu'reg sector so they put me on that.'

'Never mind, there's always the honeymoon. By the way, what grade did you score?'

Sonus grinned at her. 'I'll tell you if you tell me.'

'No way! That's something you're going to have to find out for yourelf.' Pooki grinned back. 'A girl's got to have some secrets.'

'Fair enough, but it'd better be a good grade or I'll send you back.'

'Listen, you Morexian peasant, when I get you alone on our honeymoon I'm going to fuck your brains out.'

'Tch! What sort of language is that for a future Queen to use? And anyway, if you're going to spend all your time denigrating two hundred years of royal lineage, I'm not sure I want you as my Queen. However, if you promise you'll talk dirty to me on our honeymoon I may reconsider.'

'I promise I'll do anything you want me to,' she replied.

They barely had time for a final hug before he had to board his shuttle. Two hours later Pooki was on board her own ship, settling into her cabin for the flight back to Rontar.

In the royal palace it was nearly nine o'clock and Credo was on his way to Ami's private sitting room. Each of them had their own private suite consisting of sitting room, bedroom and bathroom, which allowed them to entertain simultaneously when necessary. In fact, their rooms were interconnected by cunningly concealed doors, but Credo knew he was expected to arrive in the conventional way.

He knocked on the door and as he waited he wondered, as he had been doing all day, what lay in store for him. He knew full well that Ami would be aware of his state of anticipation. That was part of the game and he had to admit she played it to perfection.

She opened the door to him, immaculately dressed in a long sheath of white silk. The front of the dress was buttoned up to her throat and its hem reached almost to the floor. Despite being completely covered, every curve and contour of her matchless figure was emphasised by the clinging material.

Credo smiled in appreciation and bestowed a light kiss on the cheek she offered him.

'Why Credo, what a surprise!' she lied. 'Never mind, perhaps it's all for the best. I believe you two know each other,' she finished as he stepped past her and saw her companion.

Credo was not quite as surprised as he should have been to see Olga Gresheck, Duchess of Krantz. He had had his suspicions from one or two things his wife had said earlier. He made a mental note to continue the pretence of having called on his wife unexpectedly as he bowed formally to her while she rose to make her curtsey.

'Your Majesty,' she said, allowing him to kiss her hand.

'Duchess,' he replied, equally gravely.

Despite her dubious circumstances, Olga was also dressed in the height of fashion. Trust Ami to see to that, Credo told himself. She was wearing a formal one-piece that left little to the imagination. Credo had no idea how Ami was going to manage things but he knew her well enough to know that she would have the situation completely under her control and that before the little episode ended a good time would have been had by all.

'Now Credo,' Ami began, 'it's fortunate that you dropped by this evening as Olga has been telling me her problems and I think that maybe you will be able to help.'

'Indeed,' he remarked. 'In what way?'

'Well, since the Duke has been banished and his estates confiscated, it leaves poor Olga in a somewhat precarious position.'

Credo nodded agreement, still not sure what he was expected to say.

'Now I know that until certain legal issues are resolved it is impossible to say what, if anything, will be left for Olga. I also know that it would not be proper for either of us to give or even lend her some money, but the poor child is virtually destitute and came to me as a last resort.'

'Beyond offering the Duchess my deepest sympathy,' Credo replied, 'I cannot think how else we can be of assistance.'

'Ah, well, that's where we women have come up with a plan,' Ami said. 'One that should take care of everything.'

'I can't wait to hear it,' Credo replied.

'I thought as much. However, before we tell you about it why don't you make yourself comfortable? Olga, be an angel and fetch Credo a glass of wine.'

They both studied Olga's neat little bottom as it swayed to the table where the wine was cooling. They grinned at each other as the one-piece was stretched tightly across her cheeks when she bent to pour the wine.

Ami waited until they were all sitting comfortably before outlining her plan.

'It seems to me that the only way that Olga can come by some money legitimately would be for her to win it in a game of some sort.'

'I don't suppose she could work for it?' Credo suggested apologetically.

'Work!' Ami was shocked. 'What could she possibly do, in a short space of time, that would earn her sufficient funds to make ends meet?'

Credo looked at the brunette sitting demurely opposite him. He already knew of the charms underneath her tight suit and of her ability to use them. He could think of several of his friends who might be tempted to advance her a few credits for the exclusive right to avail themselves of them, especially as the news of her husband's downfall was spreading like wildfire across the planet.

There would be no shortage of 'helpers' if, after having thoroughly tested her skills, they could brag afterwards how they had screwed Krantz's wife.

Ami, of course, was well aware of the train of Credo's thoughts.

'What we don't want,' she said firmly, 'is for Olga to have to lower herself to make ends meet. I think that as a medium-term measure she could become one of my ladies-in-waiting, but in the short term she will still need some credits.'

'And in the long term?'

'In the long term, she can wait to see if there is anything for her from Krantz's estates and she can take her time and see what else may be available. She could even remarry if the courts decided Krantz's actions have provided sufficient grounds for divorce.'

'I shouldn't think there's any doubt about that,' Credo remarked. 'So that brings us back to the short term.'

'Quite so. What I propose is that you and I embark on a little game of chance with the Duchess and see if she can't manage to win a few credits from us.'

Credo thought he could see where things were leading and opened the way for Ami to continue.

'That sounds quite feasible but, and I hate to be the one to cast a wet blanket over your little scheme, what happens

241

if the Duchess should happen to lose? Interesting though it would be to see her leave without the shirt on her delectable back, so to speak, she would then be in an even worse position than before.'

'Naturally we cannot allow the Duchess to leave in an even more impoverished state,' Ami continued smoothly, 'so, in the event of an unfortunate run of cards, Olga must agree to pay some sort of forfeit in lieu of credits. In fact,' Ami decided, apparently as an afterthought, 'we must all agree to pay forfeits to keep everything above board.'

'Very well then.' Credo pretended to be convinced. 'How do we go about it?'

'Do you remember that game you once played on Morex? I thought we might try that.'

'That would certainly do,' Credo agreed. 'Are you sure you want to do this?' he asked Olga.

She had been sitting very primly in her chair, delicately sipping her wine from time to time and watching them both through her large dark eyes. She presented the very picture of innocence. In fact, the picture was such a convincing image of naivety, a young girl, helplessly adrift in a wicked world, forced by circumstances beyond her control to rely on the help of her older and wiser friends, that Credo found it hard to believe this was the same girl who had performed so uninhibitedly for him a few months ago. Only the lushness of her body and the promise of many subtle and varied delights, lurking deep in her eyes, gave the lie to her girlish appearance.

'If you think it will work,' she said. 'I don't wish to cause you any trouble.'

'Of course it's no trouble,' Ami remarked firmly. 'Go on Credo, bring the counters.'

Obediently, Credo fetched the little box that held the smooth white counters, carved carefully from the horns of the Predallian swamp-horse.

242

Ami quickly gave them each twelve, explaining the rules as she did so.

'As long as you have some counters you're all right,' she said. 'At the end of the game you may cash them in for credits. If you lose them, then you have to pay the forfeits until you can win some back again.' She looked at Credo again. 'I think we will have to rearrange our seating. If Olga sits next to me on the sofa and you pull up that little table and a chair we may begin.'

Once the seating had been changed to Ami's satisfaction, she dealt the cards.

The game was very simple. Each player was dealt two cards and they bet on the probability of their combined total being closer to fifteen than those of their opponents. The cards were counted at their face value with all royal cards being valued at ten. If you were dealt cards that added up to more than fifteen you were allowed to change one. You were also allowed one extra card if your total was low, and you were allowed to discard one in order to stay under fifteen.

Before the cards were turned, each player bet on their own chances of being closer to fifteen than anyone else. To do so they deposited a number of counters in the bank. The player closest to fifteen was paid twice his stake, the bank providing any extra counters should they prove necessary. In the event of a tie, the bank paid the joint winners.

As he watched Olga puzzle over her first two cards Credo was struck by her slim fingers. The memory of those fingers and what they could do came unbidden into his mind. He was looking forward to enjoying the experience again, as well as seeing what they could do to his wife.

Credo had played this game before with Ami and knew what was expected of him. By claiming to have lost, he was not obliged to reveal his hand and thus it was easy for him to fritter away his little pile of counters. With Ami dealing, using the little tricks she had picked up somewhere, it was a simple matter for her to arrange the winners and losers.

Thus after twenty minutes or so, Credo had to confess he was out of counters and asked what his forfeit was to be.

Olga had played eagerly, giving little squeals of delight if she won and making moues of disappointment when she lost. Now, she looked at Ami with interest as she pretended to give the matter some thought.

'I know,' she said at length, 'you shall give Olga a kiss!'

Credo pretended to hesitate. 'Are you sure?' he asked. 'Do you think that in the circumstances it would be appropriate?'

'You have agreed to pay a forfeit,' Ami said sharply, 'and I, as the winner, have the right to decide what it should be.'

'I know, and nothing would give me greater pleasure,' Credo lied, hoping for much greater pleasure later on, 'but is this fair?'

'Stop wasting time,' Ami replied, 'and fulfil your obligations.'

'Very well then, if you insist.'

Credo half rose from his chair and, leaning over the table, kissed Olga lightly on the cheek.

'Pooh! That wasn't much of a kiss. Still, no matter, whose turn is it to deal?'

With Ami's sleight of hand and Credo's subtle distractions they continued to manage who was to win and lose. It was Ami's turn to lose next and Credo's to win. He demanded a kiss from her and received a rather more thorough one than he had given Olga.

244

The next hand saw Credo losing to Olga and he waited for his forfeit with interest. Flushing slightly, she announced she wanted another kiss, but this time along the lines of Ami's.

Still pretending a little reticence, Credo kissed Olga again, this time on the lips. He felt her mouth open slightly but decided against prolonging the contact and returned to his seat after only a few seconds.

For a few hands the pattern was repeated, to the satisfaction of all concerned. The kisses Credo was both giving and receiving were becoming longer and deeper. A little tap on his foot, from Ami, signalled she wanted things to move a little further.

'This time, my dear,' he smiled at his wife as he won and she lost, 'you shall give Olga a kiss.'

It was Ami's turn to pretend to hesitate before leaning over to give Olga a peck on the cheek.

'No, no, that will never do. Give her a proper kiss,' Credo insisted.

Assuming a quite uncharacteristic reluctance, Ami kissed Olga squarely on the lips. Watching closely, Credo noticed Olga's initial stiffness soften as Ami gently stroked her face at the same time. Once again, Olga seemed a little flushed and Credo noted with interest that her nipples were now clearly visible through the material of her suit.

After another drink and several more kisses Ami decided to move to the next stage of the game. Once again Credo was the loser.

'Something different this time I think,' she decided, pretending to give the matter much thought. 'What do you suggest, Olga? Oh, I know! Let's make him take something off! Credo, please remove your shoes and socks. I hope he remembered to wash his feet,' she remarked as Credo, with much grumbling and muttering, removed the articles in question and tossed them into a corner.

Credo thought he detected a tiny smile of understanding on Olga's face as they bent over their next hand. This was confirmed when he lost the hand to her.

She grinned at Ami.

'Can I make him take something off too?' she asked.

'I don't see why not. He's always trying to take my clothes off.'

'Very well then.' Olga looked at Credo. 'Remove your jacket if you please.'

With muttered complaints about the run of luck he was having, Credo did as he was told, while Ami chortled at the thought of him having to play in his underclothes.

'I know for a fact they're rather skimpy,' she confided to Olga.

However, fortune seemed to favour Credo on the next two hands and he managed to compel Ami to kick off her shoes and Olga to part from her soft suede boots.

It was now blatantly obvious where things were leading, but they continued to play with every semblance of seriousness. Soon Ami was forced to wriggle herself out of her dress and reveal the most wispy chemise and G-string Credo had ever seen. He knew it was only because she had been anticipating playing this game that she had bothered to wear any at all, but for all the concealing they did she may as well not have bothered.

The chemise was so transparent you could have read a book through it. Her breasts were plainly visible, each topped with a dark red nipple. They appeared to be crying out for attention and Credo found himself becoming impatient for the game to end so he could do them justice.

Ami's G-string was just that – a string. The strip of silk that passed between her legs was not wide enough to cover her lips and instead, nestled damply between them, emphasising rather than concealing.

When Olga next lost and was ordered by Ami to remove her suit, she seemed a trifle reluctant. When the one-piece finally came off the reason became plain. Just as Ami normally did, Olga wore no underclothes at all and Credo was able to remind himself again of the perfection of her body.

Two hands later all three were totally naked. Credo was conscious of two pairs of greedy eyes riveted to the sight of his manhood.

'Well,' he announced, sitting down again after pulling off his last items of clothing, 'do we continue with the game or stop now that we have no more items left to forfeit?'

'We can't stop yet,' Ami declared. 'Olga hasn't won herself any credits.'

'We're going to need some more forfeits then,' he remarked.

'I'm sure we'll be able to think of some, don't you Olga?'

Olga licked her lips and nodded.

'Very well.' Ami shuffled the cards and dealt slowly. Olga almost snatched hers up in her eagerness to continue. Credo poured out more wine before collecting his. Ami won and he lost. She considered for a moment.

'Credo, you must give Olga a long kiss but, at the same time, you must caress her breasts.'

Olga's eyes were sparkling as he moved next to her on the sofa. As their lips met and his hand slid over her stomach and upwards to cup one of her soft breasts, her tongue darted into his mouth. Beneath his palm he could feel the nipple harden as he teased the puckered flesh.

All too soon he felt Ami tap his shoulder.

'That's long enough, my dears. Credo, it's your deal.'

He knew that Ami would have rigged the deck to provide the next winner and loser whilst he was kissing Olga so he dispensed with shuffling and merely dealt. This time he won and Olga lost. She looked at him expectantly.

'Olga my dear, we can't have Ami feeling left out of things. This time, you must do to her what I have just done to you.'

'Mmmn, yes please,' sighed Ami, shivering in anticipation and leaning forwards towards her.

Credo noticed that Olga didn't content herself with simply caressing one of Ami's breasts. She contrived to press one of her own against Ami's other one.

When he judged that the embrace had lasted long enough, he tapped Olga on the knee and they broke apart, both obviously wanting more.

It was Olga's turn to deal and this time there seemed little point in tampering with the cards. Things were going well enough not to need any stage-managing. Credo lost to Ami and, without saying a word, she just lay back and opened her legs. No words were necessary. He simply slid to his knees and buried his face in her musky wetness.

Practice makes perfect and Credo had had many years of practice between Ami's thighs. It was the work of only a few minutes to make her writhe and moan as her orgasm overtook her.

The look Olga gave him when he emerged told him that he would be called upon to do the same for her at the first opportunity. Ami had apparently seen the look too for, as the winner of the next hand, she commanded Credo, the loser, to pay homage to Olga's eager slit.

'Just lie back and enjoy, darling,' she urged. 'Don't worry about Credo, he loves doing it.'

This was undeniably true and as Credo nibbled his way from mid-thigh to furry groin he delighted in the texture and taste of the soft folds of flesh. Her juices were slightly more pungent than Ami's and as he lapped and teased he wriggled his hands under her bottom to pull her more firmly against him.

Her hands were running through his hair as he worked. Dimly he heard her moans and then her thighs locked around his head as she shuddered in release.

As she relaxed and he gently disentangled himself he was all for abandoning the game and burying his prick wherever he could. The women however, had different ideas. He knew that Ami, whilst enjoying sudden and brief encounters if the circumstances seemed appropriate, delighted in prolonging her sexual experiences and Olga seemed quite content to explore the possibilities of forfeits a little longer.

Another hand was dealt and although Credo felt sure there had been no rigging of the cards, he found himself the loser yet again. Ami, the winner, took pity on him.

'Credo, you may put it in me. But only for a little while!' She winked at Olga. 'We don't want to have to stop now, do we?'

Olga watched in fascination as Ami lay back once more and offered herself. Reaching over her to support himself on the back of the sofa, Credo slid smoothly into her hot tunnel. Thrusting slowly, he had the satisfaction of feeling her responses building quickly. Just as he judged she was approaching another climax he withdrew, claiming apologetically (and untruthfully) that any further movement would have precipitated his own climax.

The rueful look she gave him acknowledged both the skill of his teasing and his lie.

At last he won a hand. Olga was in his debt and he wasted no time in indicating her forfeit. As her eager mouth began its work, carefully licking off Ami's juices from his throbbing prick, he glanced over at his wife.

She was busily trying to finish what he had started and the sight of her, in all her naked glory, flushed with lust, legs wide apart, blatantly gratifying herself whilst at the same time another, equally gorgeous woman, was sucking expertly on his prick was too much for him. With a groan Credo surrendered himself to sensation and allowed Olga to milk what she could from his pulsating loins.

When she raised her head again she looked adorable. Her hair was delightfully dishevelled, her eyes were sparkling with enjoyment and smeared over her cheek was a mute testimony to the success of her recent activities.

She watched with interest as Ami skilfully manipulated herself and then suddenly reached over and began to help. Ami opened her eyes at this and smiled her appreciation. With her free hand she pulled Olga's head to hers and began to lick off the traces of his emission.

'He tastes quite nice, doesn't he?' she asked Olga.

'Yes, and so do you,' she replied, sliding down to try at first hand what she had previously only tried at second.

Credo watched with enjoyment as the two of them intertwined on the sofa. Ami was not slow to give as good as she was getting and soon the three of them were resting with fresh glasses of wine.

'Why don't we find somewhere more comfortable?' Ami suggested after a few minutes when their breathing had returned more or less to normal. She stood up and walked gracefully into her bedroom.

Credo offered his arm to Olga and they followed.

'Is this where I have a chance to enjoy that properly?' she murmured, glancing down at his still deflated prick.

'I sincerely hope so,' he replied as he handed her into Ami's queen-size bed.

For a moment or two they lay there, savouring the warmth and comfort, and then Olga, lying snugly in the middle, allowed her hand to creep down between Credo's

250

legs to feel if anything was stirring. Ami was quick to realise what was going on and disappeared under the covers. A few seconds later, Olga's hand was displaced by a pair of familiar lips. Judging from the way that Olga began to writhe, Credo guessed that Ami wasn't confining her attentions to him alone.

As soon as she had encouraged life back into him she surfaced triumphantly and Credo leaned over Olga to kiss her. His hand met Ami's between Olga's thighs and together they played with what they found, whilst Olga used both her hands to equally good effect.

Slowly, Credo and Ami subsided on to Olga and their mouths met in a greedy, wet triangle. Above the sheet, tongues flashed from mouth to mouth, below it, fingers darted into slippery openings, or massaged rigid flesh.

Credo bent his head to begin nibbling at one of Olga's nipples, aware of Ami working on the other.

Beneath them, Olga was in ecstasy, moaning and gasping as they moved down over her smooth belly and into the wet fur below. Their tongues met again as they competed for space on the little button or licked along the silky slit. Credo gave way to his wife and licked his way further round, across the tight ridge of skin separating one entrance from another.

Olga raised her hips, encouraging his efforts, and as Credo and Ami continued to work on the nearly frantic girl she wailed and thrashed her way to a shuddering orgasm.

'I think she's ready for you now,' Ami decided.

'Oh yes please,' Olga gasped.

'Just a minute then.'

Ami rolled Olga on top of her so that she could continue between her legs. Credo, finding Olga's cunt already occupied, parted her cheeks and thrust into her anus. Olga wailed again but pushed back against him, helping to complete his entrance. Her head was rolling from side to side on the pillows as she responded to the double assault.

With his balls nudging his wife's face as she sucked and licked below him, Credo began ramming into the tight little opening. He barely had time to make more than a few strokes before Olga, her breath rasping in short gasps, suddenly arched her back and screamed her release.

As she collapsed, barely conscious, on to her stomach, Ami wriggled out from underneath.

'My turn now,' she said firmly, pulling Credo between her outspread thighs. Within a few minutes she began to wail herself and with a final howl of satisfaction she reached her own climax. Credo was a mere two strokes behind and gratefully flooded into her.

They looked at Olga, now curled into a ball next to them.

'I can see why you like her,' Ami admitted. 'She is rather cute.'

'Yes, she is,' he replied. 'But not as cute as you.'

She smiled and kissed him gently.

'I'll tell you what,' she suggested. 'Why don't you have her as your mistress for a while? She can be one of my ladies-in-waiting until everything is sorted out.'

'That's a fine idea,' Credo agreed.

'But you must let me share her,' Ami warned. 'I rather like her myself and I've a feeling she could turn into quite a little asset when we have our symposiums.'

'She has got rather a nice little asset, hasn't she?'

'Filthy beast! Now, come and have a bath with me.' She looked again at the sleeping figure. 'Olga might keep until morning, but I won't.'

So saying, she took a firm but gentle hold on the royal sceptre and led him into her bathroom.